KATE HALENA

Somewhere Between LIES

KH 1987

First published in 2026 by KH 1987.
Brisbane, QLD, Australia.

A catalogue record for this book is available from the National Library of Australia

Halena, Kate.
Somewhere Between Lies.

ISBN: 978-1-7642828-0-2 (eBook)
ISBN: 978-1-7642828-1-9 (pbk)

Line Editor: Cassie Robertson (Joy Editing)
Proofreader: Lynne Hardman; Devon Burke (Joy Editing)

Cover Design: Kate Halena Designs

For you, whoever you are, wherever you are—thank you for reading.

Even in the darkest days, there is hope—
and within that hope, the courage to rewrite your life.

Somewhere Between LIES

1

"You've got to be joking."

Hands on my hips, I stared at the hole in my low-profile tyre and the mark gouged into the rim. Moments earlier, I'd swerved to miss a pothole and driven straight into an even bigger one that could have stuffed the suspension in my white BMW, but thankfully didn't.

"Seriously!"

I wasn't sure whether I wanted to laugh, cry, or have a full-blown nervous breakdown. Though honestly, I wasn't far off the last one. The past few months had been a nightmare I wanted to escape—and this? This was the cherry on top.

I sighed. "Just what I needed."

Flies swarmed me, drawn to the perspiration clinging to

my skin and clothes in the brutal midday heat. I stood there on the side of the road, middle of nowhere. Dry grass, spinifex, a few sad-looking bushes, orange dirt stretching out forever… and one random kangaroo with a front-row seat to my breakdown.

My first real taste of the Australian outback. Lucky me. I'd never driven this far out of the city—usually I flew. In, out, done. None of this middle-of-nowhere situation.

I looked up the road, then back the other way. There wasn't a single car in sight. No movement, no sound except for the cicadas, screaming as if they had a personal vendetta against silence.

I was utterly alone… well, almost. The kangaroo was still there, staring at me as though I'd rolled in for its personal amusement.

"What are you looking at? Reckon this is funny, do you?" I pointed at it. "I know this is your fault. You were probably hoping for some entertainment to fill your day."

Wasn't this how every horror movie started? Stranded in the middle of nowhere. No one knows where you are. Then some psycho rocks up and—well. It ends badly.

Yeah. I wasn't going to let that happen. I'd listened to enough true crime podcasts about the Australian outback to not let myself fall victim even though I was stranded.

Since my car didn't have a spare tyre, only one of those useless repair kits meant for tiny punctures, not a full-blown tear,

I needed a tow truck to save the day.

I yanked open the passenger door, dug my phone out of my handbag, and switched it on. I'd turned it off before I left. It was my way of shutting everything out for a few days, putting some distance between me and everything I'd left behind.

It was almost three o'clock in the afternoon.

No signal.

I swallowed.

Yep. This was definitely the start of a horror movie.

In this day and age, no signal? You'd think one of the network providers could have managed something out here.

Maybe if I walked a bit farther…

I locked the car with the fob and headed down the road, holding my phone up as if that was somehow going to help. I waved it side to side, squinting at the screen.

Nothing. Not even a flicker.

I glanced back at my car. Still close enough. No way was I letting it out of my sight—not that I could get lost along this stretch of highway.

As I kept walking, I heard a car approaching, so I looked over my shoulder. A woman in a four-wheel drive, music blaring, singing along as if she didn't have a care in the world. She looked at me, then she just… kept going. She didn't slow down. She didn't even pretend to consider stopping.

"Wow. Cheers for that," I muttered. Though to be fair, she

probably listened to the same podcasts.

I lifted my phone again like an idiot.

Still nothing.

Ping!

I froze.

Then I looked at my phone. A notification.

"Yes!" I jumped like a complete lunatic.

One bar. One glorious, pathetic little bar.

Without even checking the notification, I went online, searching for tow truck companies near me before the service dropped. The page crawled, taking forever to load, and I held my breath as I waited.

The results finally loaded. Most of the companies were based in Broken Hill as it was the closest town under an hour away.

I tapped the first one from the top and hit Call.

It rang.

And rang.

And rang—

Then finally, a man answered.

"Oh my God," I said, relief hitting all at once. "I'm stuck on the side of the road with a flat tyre about forty-five minutes out from Broken Hill and need a tow truck."

"Umm…" he hesitated. "All my drivers are out on jobs. They won't be available—" the line crackled, cutting in and out

"—for at least two… maybe three hours."

My stomach dropped.

Three hours?

Out here?

Alone?

The sun would have set by then.

My heart raced. The longer I stayed out here, the more my brain would fill in the gaps, and none of them ended well.

Trying to keep my voice steady, I said, "I'm a woman. I'm alone. In the middle of nowhere. I really don't want to end up as some headline or podcast episode." I paused, then added, "I don't care what it costs. Can you please get someone out here sooner?"

"The towing call-out fee is $360," he said, his voice warping through the weak signal.

"That's fine. I'm happy to pay."

"I didn't catch your name."

"Jessie…"

"All right, Jessie. I'll text through what I need."

Seconds later—*ping!*

I checked the message.

Full name:

Pickup location:

Drop-off address:

Make and model:

Rego:

Standard stuff.

"If you can send those details back, I'll book the job and get an invoice out to you, then I'll shuffle one of the jobs around and send someone out," he added. "Still looking at about an hour."

An hour.

"Yeah… okay," I said, scanning the area again, just in case someone had magically appeared while I wasn't looking. If it came down to it, I'd drive on the flat. Rim be damned.

"Great."

The line dropped.

I typed out the details and hit Send, then I stood there like a statue, staring at my phone. No way was I moving—not when I had reception.

A few minutes later, the invoice came through and I paid it straight away as if handing over the money would make them drive faster.

And just like that, I had nothing left to do. It was a waiting game, so I slowly headed back to the car, cursing and kicking a few rocks along the way.

It felt unreal—me, Jessie Florence, stranded on the side of some nowhere road, hours from anything familiar.

I'd never pictured myself leaving Sydney. I'd wrestled with the idea for weeks, if not months, until it reached the point where staying felt worse than leaving. As if I might actually suffocate if I didn't go.

Why?

I had everything money could buy. Everything people say you're supposed to want, including the one thing I had until it was gone: love.

And yet, there I was. Middle of nowhere. Flat tyre. One judgemental kangaroo standing off to the side as though I was part of some reality show.

But this little setback? Not exactly enough to send me running back home in tears. I'd come too far to turn around. My parents had always drilled it into me—*when you make a decision, you stick to it*. No backing out. No second-guessing. They had a piece of wisdom for everything, whether I'd asked for it or not.

So if the universe thought it could stop me from starting over… it was going to have to try a hell of a lot harder.

An hour later, a tow truck appeared, pulling up in front of me. The driver hopped out. Mid-forties, wearing high-vis, the kind of guy who looked as though he'd seen it all. "Jessie? I'm Gary."

"That's me."

He glanced at my car, then let out a low whistle. "7 Series BMW. Fancy. Not exactly an outback car… or one you usually see out here. Definitely not one you'd want to take too far beyond the city."

We both stood there, staring at it.

The car had been a gift from my parents for my twenty-first birthday over a year ago. It was perfect in every way until I'd driven over the pot hole.

I folded my arms. "It's not like I was off-roading. It's an asphalt road."

He laughed. "Yeah… fair call." Then he nodded towards the side of the road. "At least it wasn't a roo. They've got a habit of jumping out in front of you."

He got to work, loading the car onto the tow truck using chains and a winch. Once it was secured, he climbed back into the cab, and we headed off towards Broken Hill.

After a minute or so, he glanced at me. "So… where are you heading? Don't see many young ladies like you out here."

"Adelaide." I wasn't in the mood for small talk. Hadn't been for months. Zack Baltimore's death hadn't just hurt—it had wrecked everything. It had shattered the balance in my world and left a void that consumed me.

That's what happens when someone you love dies.

He raised a brow. "Holiday road trip?"

"No."

"Work?"

I shook my head.

He glanced back at the road. "Relocating?"

A pause.

"Maybe."

*　*　*

My move was impromptu. I hadn't bought a place, hadn't rented or booked accommodation like my parents did before travelling. They were organised and their moves were calculated—they were business-minded to the core. But me? I'd thrown some clothes in a suitcase, tossed a bag of essentials in the backseat, and pointed my car towards Adelaide. I hadn't even surfed the internet to get better acquainted with the town. Just me, the open road, and a vague, slightly delusional hope that I'd figure it out when I got there.

That plan had already hit a pothole—literally.

After the breakdown, getting towed into Broken Hill, replacing a tyre, and spending the night in the only motel that had a vacancy—which smelt like stale air and bad decisions—I hit the road again early the next morning.

Fuelled by servo coffee, a bad night's sleep, and some reckless kind of hope, or maybe even desperation, I finally arrived in Adelaide. I spent several hours cruising around with no real direction, unsure where to go or what part of town I wanted to live in. Having driven down Anzac Highway, I ended up in a beachside suburb called Glenelg.

I turned left onto Colley Terrace—a street lined with pine trees—and parked opposite the beachfront apartments, taking it all in. I'd lived in a big city for most of my life. In comparison, Adelaide seemed like a country town. Different. It was a welcome change. Something about Adelaide whispered that I might be able to find peace here.

"All right, time to explore," I said to myself as I climbed out of my car into a chilly breeze. "Or maybe not."

For a sunny day, the temperature was deceptive. I grabbed a jumper from my suitcase in the boot and put it on, then slipped back into the sanctuary of my car. I turned on the engine and cranked up the heating, letting the warmth seep into my bones. It was too cold to leave my car, but the idea of spending the night in my car? Yeah, that wasn't happening. I was exhausted after three days of driving. My stomach was grumbling, as I hadn't eaten all day, and the thought of a hot shower was too tempting to ignore.

I'd passed a few hotels and motels on the way, but I wanted one closer to the beach, somewhere at the heart of this new place I wanted to explore. As I scanned the area, I spotted a hotel not far down the street, facing the ocean. It looked... promising.

I pulled out of the parking bay and drove up to the front of the hotel. Unprepared, with no reservation in my name, I held onto the hope that they had a room available and preferably one with no lingering sense of regret baked into the walls. I was looking for more than just a place to crash for the night—I needed a landing spot, somewhere I could figure out what "home" might look like in this new city.

Leaving my luggage locked in the car, I walked up to the hotel's entrance. The building, standing tall against the coastal backdrop, didn't stop the salty breeze from almost pushing me over.

The lobby was modern, spacious, and best of all, warm. I felt my shoulders relax as I approached the front desk. A woman in her mid-twenties with long, burgundy hair sleeked back in a ponytail looked up from her computer and greeted me. Her name badge read "Lindsey."

"Hi there," I said, "I'm new in town and looking for a place to stay. Do you have any rooms available?"

Lindsey's fingers flew across the keyboard as she checked. I held my breath, suddenly aware of how much I needed this—a decent bed, a proper shower, and a place that didn't feel as though it came with a side of regret. Even if it was only for a night or two.

"Of course." She glanced up. "How long do you plan on staying with us?"

"It's hard to say. Maybe a week or two," I said. "Until I find something more permanent."

"No problem at all," she said with a reassuring smile. "Let me see what we have." She scanned the monitor for availability. "Actually, you're in luck. A suite has become available due to a last-minute cancellation. It's yours for two weeks if you would like it. The rate is $238 per night."

Without hesitation, I said, "I'll take it."

"Perfect. If I could just get you to fill out this form?" Lindsey said, sliding it and a pen across the counter towards me.

I picked up the pen, quickly filled in my details, and handed it back to her with my bank card.

As she typed my information into the system, she casually asked, "Do you have a particular area in mind for your permanent place?"

It took me a second to catch on to what she was asking. "Honestly, I haven't thought that far ahead," I admitted. "But Glenelg seems like a great place to start."

I wouldn't usually open up to someone I'd just met, yet something about this place, or perhaps the situation itself, made it easier to share.

She looked up. "Well, if you're looking for help finding a place, let me know. I used to work for a real estate agency a few streets away. I can introduce you to an agent who knows the area well and can get you a great deal."

"Really?" I was taken aback by her kindness. "I might take you up on that offer."

Being in Adelaide, a city unfamiliar to me, the offer seemed invaluable. I didn't know the suburbs—what was good and what wasn't or where to begin my search for a new home.

"It's no trouble at all." She handed back my bank card and gave me my room key—a small plastic card with the room number printed on it. "You're on the fifth floor. Elevators are down the corridor to your right. Let us know if you need anything."

"Thank you," I said.

My suite, unlike a standard hotel room, had a separate bedroom, dining area with a kitchenette, and living room that opened onto a balcony facing the beach—modern but nothing over the top. It was better than I expected for the price I'd paid and, thankfully, nothing like Broken Hill.

It didn't take long for me to settle in. After indulging in a hot shower, I put on fresh clothes and went downstairs to the hotel restaurant. Over dinner, I felt a comforting sense of normalcy creeping in.

When I finally returned to my room, I climbed into bed and reached for my phone on the bedside table. It had been switched off and buried in the bottom of my bag for most of the drive before I'd placed it on the charger. I'd needed that time alone, disconnected from everything and everyone. As I powered it on, the screen lit up with two notifications:

7 Missed Calls

1 Message

All from my sister, Alesha. I opened the message.

Hi Jessie! Where are you?

Are you okay?

So, I may not have told anyone I was leaving Sydney, not even my family members. I'd just packed a suitcase, thrown it into the boot of my car, and driven away. My parents weren't home anyway. They'd taken off on a journey of their own—a year-long road trip around Australia. Every few weeks, they messaged my sister and me photos from various places, all with the same caption: GUESS WHERE WE ARE? Who knew where they were now? I wasn't going to call them and ruin their adventure with depressing news about Zack. They'd find out upon returning to Sydney.

As for my sister, she had been at uni when I left. We'd never been particularly close, not in that sisterly way people always assume siblings are, even though she was only two years older than me. Being blood related didn't necessitate a sisterly relationship, and despite growing up together, we were more like acquaintances than anything else. She'd seen me struggling mentally over the past few months, I knew that much, but she'd kept her distance—maybe because she didn't know what to say. Or maybe because she couldn't bear to see me like that. Either way, it was why I hadn't reached out to her in my darkest hour. I guess that didn't stop her from worrying about where I was or if something had happened to me.

I responded to her message with a thumbs-up emoji, then wrote:

I HAD TO GET OUT OF SYDNEY.

She messaged back—one word.

OKAY.

That was it. A single word. She didn't ask where I was or why I'd left or when I'd be back. Just "Okay," as though she understood or maybe just accepted it. It was the closest thing to understanding we'd had in a long time.

15

2

My phone went off, jolting me from the depths of sleep. Groggily, I fumbled for it on the nightstand and squinted at the screen. It was 7:15 a.m.—half an hour behind Sydney. Still, too early for anyone I knew to be reaching out. Yet there was one message from an unknown number. *Who could it possibly be at this hour?*

I hesitated, my thumb hovering over the notification. Part of me didn't want to know who it was, but curiosity won. I tapped it open.

JESSIE. WE NEED TO TALK. PLEASE CALL ME. CON.

"Con" was short for Conrad Baltimore—Zack's older brother.

He'd never reached out to me in the past. Not once. Not even after Zack's funeral. It was why I'd never saved his number in my phone. So, why now? What could he possibly have to say? The reason eluded me. What I did know was that I wasn't ready to face him or whatever conversation he sought. Not yet. Maybe not ever.

I deleted his message and dropped the phone beside me on the bed, then sighed. It was time to get up, get dressed, and go out for breakfast. A part of me wanted to burrow back under the covers and hide from the world, but I'd promised myself that this was a fresh start. I couldn't let one message—or one person—pull me back under.

The first few days, I explored Glenelg and ventured into different parts of Adelaide—my attempt at familiarising myself with the town. Adelaide had its own style and culture. It was nothing like Sydney. Here, I could blend into the backdrop, just another stranger in a city, and that was exactly what I needed.

Breaking my usual routine, I stopped over at Cibo Espresso on Moseley Square and ordered a coffee and a chocolate muffin. The previous mornings, I'd skipped breakfast altogether.

Sugar—a great start to the day.

As I waited, I looked towards the beach. The Ferris wheel wasn't moving yet, the jetty empty, but the pale sky and the palm trees made it beautiful. It was the sort of scene my old self would've photographed. I couldn't walk past anything like it without taking a photo—I loved photography. But now I watch.

My phone went off in my pocket. I took it out and there it

was—Conrad's number flashing on the screen. My heart clenched. What did he want? Maybe the call was his way of making sure I didn't ignore his text. My finger hovered over the screen, but I restrained myself from answering the call. *I don't care what you want,* I repeated in my mind until the phone stopped ringing.

The barista called out my order. I grabbed my coffee and muffin and headed off, almost colliding into a woman crossing my path. I recognised her instantly. It was the girl from the hotel reception.

"Lindsey?"

She perched her sunglasses on top of her head, and it seemed to take her a few seconds to recollect my name. "Jessie? How's the house hunting going?"

"I haven't started yet—" I began, but the sound of my phone buzzing cut me off mid-sentence. I glanced at the screen— it was *Conrad*. Again. "Excuse me a second."

I held up the phone in a silent apology to Lindsey as I stepped away. My heart pounded. I was caught between two worlds—one I was trying so hard to leave behind, the other a future I hadn't fully stepped into yet.

As Lindsey joined the queue to place an order, I stared at the screen. Part of me wanted to press *Ignore*. But the other part of me—one I wasn't proud of—was curious because this was the second time he was calling me. Before I could talk myself out of it, I swiped to answer.

"What do you want!?" The words came out harsher than I intended. It was unlike me, but his persistence had pushed me to the edge.

"Jeez… That's no way to answer your call," he said.

"Why are you calling me again? If I wanted to talk, I would've called you after I received your message."

"Well, you answered this call and you haven't hung up yet," he said, sounding unfazed. "That's a good sign, isn't it?"

"You have a minute before I do."

There was a pause, just long enough for me to consider hanging up anyway. Then he said, "I have something for you."

"What is it?"

"It's a letter… from Zack."

The words hit me like a punch to the gut, knocking the air right out of me. I froze, unable to speak, barely able to breathe. Memories of Zack surfaced, sharper and clearer than they had been in months—the love that had been everything to me and the loss that had left me shattered. I'd come here to escape that pain, to find some way to live without the constant ache of missing him. But hearing his name—and the thought that he'd left a message for me, something I hadn't known existed—made all those walls I'd built around my heart start to crumble.

"You still there?"

Without a word, I disconnected the call.

I forced myself to focus my attention back on the here and now. Lindsey was standing next to me with her coffee in hand, having somehow been served faster than the others who were still waiting.

"Do you need help house hunting?" Lindsey offered. "I have some free time this morning."

"Are you sure?" I was surprised she was willing to help me—a near stranger. For all she knew, I could have been some kind of psycho. But then again, she could have been one too. Shoving that thought aside, I wasn't going to turn down her offer or her friendship.

"Definitely," she said. "I have time to kill, and real estate used to be my game. Plus, I'm interested to see what's out on the market these days."

After I finished my sugary breakfast, we set off, making our way to the real estate agency she used to work for, which was a few streets away.

As we walked, curiosity got the better of me, and I wanted to get better acquainted with my new friend. "If you don't mind me asking, how come you don't work in real estate anymore?"

She laughed a little wryly. "Too much pressure and stress. Gaining clients, building their trust, convincing them I could sell their property at top dollar. Working long hours. It wore me down. It's harder work than people think and not what I expected when I first entered the industry."

"I get that," I said. "A lot of jobs seem glamorous until you're on the inside."

"Exactly." She sighed. "I couldn't see myself doing that type of work for the rest of my life. Wish I'd known that sooner—it would've saved me a lot of time and energy."

In a few minutes, we were at the real estate agency, SA Real Estate. For a small office, it was spacious with its minimalistic interior design. Property listings were displayed in clear frames along the wall on the left side and in the front window. Flyers and business cards decorated the unattended reception desk.

Lindsey approached the counter and hit the bell.

I scanned the listings while we waited—apartments and houses varying in style, age, and price. Most were within my budget. It would be a challenge to find a place that felt like home before my time was up at the hotel though.

"Lindsey, fancy seeing you here again."

I looked over to see a woman in her forties emerge from an office to the right, gliding across the floor as though she was on a runway. Everything from her black pencil skirt and buttoned-up blouse to her high heels seemed polished. Her face was doll-like—an advertisement for Botox, fillers, and plastic surgery—but somehow completed her look.

"Never thought I would see you back here after you handed in your resignation," she said with a smirk.

"Neither did I. Is Shane around?"

"Shane is at an open house with Mitch. They won't be back for a few hours. Anything I can help you with?" The woman's eyes flicked over to me, assessing me in a practiced way that made me feel as if I was already being appraised as a potential client—or maybe just as a curiosity.

"No, that's all right," Lindsey replied, grabbing a property listing flyer off the counter. "Just let him know we'll drop by later this arvo."

The woman nodded, her eyes still lingering on me for a second longer than necessary, then she slipped back into her office without another word.

As soon as we stepped outside, Lindsey exhaled sharply, rolling her eyes. "I never liked that woman. She's like a shark when it comes to sales. She sold thirty properties in a year."

Disregarding her comment, I said, "I thought you were busy later on."

"I have an appointment at the hair salon, but I'm free after that. You should come along with me. I mean, unless you're busy…"

A few hours later, I found myself sitting next to Lindsey in a small salon. She was getting her burgundy hair colour recone—the bold red tones were faded, and her natural blond was showing. And somehow, she'd convinced me to lighten my own hair, going several shades lighter than I'd ever dared.

I'd never changed my hair colour. It had always been dark brown—a signature look I'd thought I would never change. But now, as the stylist carefully placed foils throughout my hair, I caught a glimpse of myself in the mirror and couldn't help but muse. *New life. New look.* I could work with that.

Lindsey browsed through the flyer. "So, what's your budget for a house?"

The question made my stomach tighten. Not every unemployed twenty-two-year-old had access to nearly a five-million-dollar budget courtesy of their parents. It wasn't exactly something I wanted to broadcast. I'd always been uneasy about the way people's perceptions changed when they found out I came from money. Better to keep it vague, at least for now.

"Uh… it depends," I mumbled, hoping that would be enough.

She stared at me. "You're really not prepared, are you?"

I snatched the flyer from her hand and looked over it. The vibrant images of houses and apartments filled the pages, each promising a new life within its walls.

"See anything you like?" she asked.

Flipping through the pages, I stopped at an elegant apartment that caught my eye. It was a three-bedroom penthouse with a view of the marina. "This one looks awesome." I showed her.

"Wow, that's a stunning place. But you saw the price,

right?" She pointed at the bottom of the page, where *$2 million* was printed in bold. "That's an 'amazing' price tag."

Oh no! I should have looked at that before I pointed it out.

"So… what do you do for a living?" she asked.

My mind went blank, and I felt my cheeks burn. This was exactly the kind of conversation I hadn't anticipated—I'd never bought a house before. I hesitated a beat too long, and the silence only made it worse.

Lindsey waited for my response before continuing, "You must be raking in the big bucks."

"Actually…" I took a deep breath, hoping to come across as casual. "I don't have a job—"

"Wait. What?" She stared at me. "Then… how on earth are you planning to pay for this place, or any place, if you don't have a job? How are you even going to get a loan?"

I swallowed, knowing I'd trapped myself and there was no dodging this. "Who said anything about a loan?" I knew the truth would eventually come out, as much as I hated that thought. "I… I have money."

Her eyes widened. "You have *money*. Like, enough to casually throw down two million dollars?"

"It's not as dramatic as it sounds," I said, trying to downplay it. "My parents set up an interest account for me when I was young. They made regular deposits."

It wasn't exactly a lie. They had done it for my sister too.

It was a substantial allowance, which we could spend or save. They wanted us to understand the value—and power—of money. My father would lecture us on spending it wisely. He even taught us about investing, shares, and the stock market, hoping one of us would become a banker. Alesha hadn't gone down that path. And me? I hadn't figured out what I wanted to do yet. So, at this point, neither of us was living up to that dream.

Lindsey seemed to digest this information. "Wow! Two million dollars. That's incredible. I wish my parents had done something like that. I would've been thrilled if they'd saved enough money so I could buy a new car. But a whole property fund? They must be smart."

"I guess so."

"What do they do for a living?" she asked.

I hesitated, then sighed. "They're property developers."

I'd always been careful not to advertise my family's success in real estate, aware of how it cast a shadow I couldn't escape. People tended to look at me differently when they found out, as if I were just another spoiled kid riding on someone else's accomplishments. I didn't want that here. Not in Adelaide, where I was supposed to be starting over.

"Can we keep this between us?" I asked. The fewer people who knew about my family, the better. "I'd rather not have people know."

Over an hour later, we stepped out of the hair salon, both

of us sporting fresh, professionally styled looks. My reflection in the window stopped me in my tracks—I barely recognised the girl staring back. My hair was several shades lighter, catching the light in a way that made me look almost… carefree. I wondered why I hadn't done it sooner. Better late than never, I supposed.

We headed back to the real estate agency. It was much busier than when we'd first dropped in. The receptionist was on the phone, and a couple was waiting at the counter. Lindsey and I hung back, and I took the opportunity to scan the listings displayed along the window and wall again. A single-storey, four-bedroom beachfront house caught my eye, followed by a fancy two-storey one and a few modern apartments. I could already tell the next few days would be packed with viewings.

"Hi, Shane," Lindsey said, distracting me from the listings.

I glanced at them. The guy she was talking to looked familiar. He was tall, with dark brown hair that appeared effortlessly styled. His business-casual attire was polished, and his movements betrayed a confidence that made it seem as if he owned the room. But behind the refined, professional exterior, he reminded me of Shane Westenberg, a friend from high school in Sydney, someone I hadn't seen in over six years. But this wasn't the Shane I remembered—this was a polished, grown-up version, as if someone had taken the unruly kid from high school and upgraded him.

"So, what brings you back here?" he asked Lindsey.

"I'm helping a friend find a place." She gestured towards me. "Jessie, this is Shane. Shane, this is Jessie."

Our eyes met.

My heart skipped a beat.

Without doubt, it was Shane Westenberg. The idea that it could be him hadn't even crossed my mind when Lindsey had first mentioned his name. After all, Shane was a common enough name, and we were in Adelaide—far from Sydney, where I'd last seen him. The likelihood of us crossing paths seemed improbable. Yet here he was, not just in the same city but standing right in front of me, embodying a transformation so profound it bordered on the unbelievable.

I opened my mouth to say hi, but the word didn't come out.

Was this really Shane, or was I dreaming?

He was no longer a drunken mess. Gone was the image of the dishevelled, intoxicated individual I'd known—the guy who was always leaning too heavily against the nearest wall, a can of pre-mixed bourbon in his hand, eyes glazed over. Back then, he had been lost to the world, in a haze of alcohol consumed at whatever party offered him refuge. His reputation was rooted in excess—his limit only found when he could no longer consume another drink, let alone stand. But the man in front of me was sober. Everything from his clothes to his hair and the way he carried himself was different. And he had a job, which was the last thing anyone who knew him had expected.

We stared at each other.

Did he not recognise me?

I extended my hand to shake his, feeling somewhat awkward.

"Jessie Florence?" His smile broadened. "I didn't recognise you for a moment. Did you change your hair colour?" He skipped right past the handshake and went in for a hug.

"Yeah... You look... different." The words felt clumsy, but they were all I could manage.

Before Shane said anything else, Lindsey's eyes darted between us. "Wait. You two know each other?"

"Yes, from back in Sydney," I replied, beating Shane to the explanation.

"We truly live in a small world," she mused. "In that case, I'm sure Shane will get you an amazing deal."

Shane's curiosity sparked again. "And how do you two know each other?"

The story of my newly found friendship seemed mundane in the wake of our unexpected reunion. "We met a few days ago."

He raised his brow. "Righteo... Interesting..." His gaze lingered, as if trying to piece together how I'd ended up here, far from the city we both knew. "So"—he shifted back into professional mode—"any listings catch your eye? Anything you want to take a closer look at?"

I showed him all the properties I was interested in, which were either on the flyer or in the displays.

He noted them down and said, "All right, we can check out the marina penthouse and the beachfront house today. The other properties are currently occupied, so I'll need to contact the owners and tenants to arrange suitable inspection times."

Collecting the necessary keys, he led us to a reserved area behind the agency where a row of luxury cars glistened under the sun. He walked over to a black AMG, unlocked it, and gestured for us to get in. I couldn't help but admire the car and the unmistakable allure of Mercedes before sliding into the passenger seat.

As we eased out of the lot and merged into traffic, Shane outlined our plan. "First stop is the double-storey beachfront house in Somerton Park. It's about a five-minute drive from here. The house sits on a generous plot with amazing oceans views. It's been on the market for a while, and the sellers are eager to find a buyer, so we've got some room to negotiate on the price."

"Why are they selling?" I asked.

"They relocated interstate for work," he explained as we pulled up in the driveway.

The house was on the corner, directly across the street from the beach. Perched on an elevated plot, it had uninterrupted views. A modest stone fence framed the property, offering a touch of privacy without obstructing the scenery.

I climbed out of the car and took it all in. The house had a rendered white exterior, and the side facing the beach was almost entirely made up of tinted floor-to-ceiling windows. Clearly, it had been designed to capture the view while keeping the inside private.

Shane walked up beside me. "Great view, right? Wait until you see inside."

He led us to the entrance, unlocking the door and pushing it open to reveal a spacious interior. Black and white dominated the decor, giving the space a modern, luxe appearance that felt warm. The open-plan living area had high ceilings and polished hardwood floors that flowed seamlessly towards the massive windows overlooking the beach. Sunlight poured in, reflecting off the walls and filling every corner with a soft glow.

"Wow!" Lindsey stopped in the doorway. "How much are they asking for this place?"

"Three and a half million," Shane replied. "But I believe we can negotiate down by a couple hundred thousand. This is a great opportunity."

We wandered through the house, with Shane pointing out features as we went—a gourmet kitchen with state-of-the-art appliances, a butler's pantry, a second-floor master bedroom with a private balcony, a backyard designed for entertaining. It was beautiful, no question. But my gaze kept drifting back to those windows, to the endless blue across the road. I could almost imagine myself here, curled up with a coffee, watching the waves roll in each morning.

Lindsey nudged me. "Is this within your budget?"

I hesitated, feeling the weight of the number settle over me. The figure hovered at the edge of what I was prepared to invest. Even with my resources, the absence of a steady income and my determination to be financially independent made me cautious. I didn't want to rely on my parents forever, and buying something this extravagant felt… risky.

"It's at the top end," I admitted, already calculating the long-term responsibilities. "I'll think about it."

"Ready to check out the marina apartment next?" Shane asked.

"Definitely. Let's go."

We drove over to the three-bedroom penthouse on the marina in Glenelg, listed for two million dollars. Situated on the top floor of the five-storey complex, the apartment had high-end security systems that made it feel like a fortress—something I couldn't help but appreciate. Guests couldn't just walk in; they had to be buzzed through the glass doors, which also activated the lift to their destination. Residents, on the other hand, used access cards—both to enter the building and to reach their floors.

The place was spacious, luxurious in all the right ways, with sweeping views of either the marina or the surrounding parkland from every window. Each bedroom was its own private retreat, complete with a balcony, walk-in wardrobe, and an ensuite. The living area and kitchen had sleek wooden floors, but the bedrooms were carpeted in a slightly outdated beige that felt out of place against the rest of the apartment's modern interior. It was a small flaw, but one I couldn't ignore.

"This apartment has incredible views." Lindsey joined us. "That little photo on the flyer doesn't do it justice."

Shane turned to me. "So, what do you think?"

"It's in a great location." It was close to cafés, restaurants, shops, and even a short walk from the hotel I was temporarily calling home. I could imagine settling in here, making it my own. "If the owners are open to updating the flooring, replacing the carpet with wood to match the rest of the apartment, I'd be interested in making an offer."

"I think I can make that happen."

3

I exchanged phone numbers with Shane and Lindsey at the front of the building. Lindsey, who lived only a few streets away, bid us farewell and headed home while Shane and I strolled towards my hotel, which was across the road.

"How come you left Sydney?" he asked.

"I wanted to start a new life." It was the best way I could sum it up without going into details.

He nodded. "I understand. Sometimes a fresh start is what we need. I remember in high school you were dating Zack. You two were inseparable… If you don't mind me asking, are you still with him?"

His question hit me in a way I didn't expect. The reality of Zack's absence was a truth not widely known, not even by those from our shared past in Sydney. Fighting against the surge of emotion his name invoked, I held back tears, maintaining my composure, and chose to keep my response simple. "He passed away."

Discussing Zack's death was a bridge I wasn't ready to cross. The wound was far too fresh.

"I'm so sorry for your loss," he said. "I feel bad for asking."

"It's okay. You didn't know." I brushed off the discomfort his question had inadvertently caused.

A brief silence fell between us.

"Are you sure you want to buy the apartment?"

"Why do you ask? Did someone die or get murdered in it?" As much as I loved scary movies, I didn't want a paranormal flatmate.

"Neither." He laughed. "Nothing like that. The owners bought a bigger place."

"Right. Then what's the catch? Why shouldn't I buy the apartment?"

"There were three other places you wanted to check out. I'm just making sure you aren't making a hasty decision you might regret."

"Ahh… the voice of reason. I appreciate that. But I really do love this apartment. The second I walked through the door, I could see myself living in it," I said as we approached the entrance of the hotel. "And the views! Don't get me started."

He smiled. "All right. The apartment it is, then."

"You know," I said, smirking a little, "I never imagined you'd become a real estate agent."

He raised an eyebrow. "Is that so?"

"Yeah, I mean, I didn't even know you went on to study anything."

"Come on. You thought my parents would let me lounge around without a plan? No way. With a doctor for a mum and a pharmacist for a dad, the pressure was on. They had high expectations. They made it very clear they expected me to follow a respectable career path. Believe me, the idea of their only son becoming a dropout or deadbeat was their worst nightmare. They would have died of humiliation. They were on my case about choosing a career path since the tenth grade."

"I'm surprised they let you party as hard as you did."

He laughed. "Well, they weren't exactly around to keep tabs on me all the time. Some nights, the freedom was too tempting."

"And you managed to keep your grades up with all that going on?" My curiosity was piqued.

He shrugged. "My grades were decent. Nothing spectacular, but enough to scrape by and dive into real estate. It wasn't the future they had mapped out for me, but in the end, I think they were relieved I didn't completely veer off course or become a failure."

* * *

The sellers accepted my offer, agreeing to the terms Shane skilfully negotiated on my behalf. Within three weeks, I'd moved into the apartment and purchased the essentials of a new life—comfortable beds, a dining room set, a couch, a coffee table, a TV, and an outdoor table and chairs for the balcony. Despite filling it with furniture, the place still looked empty. It was heaps of space for one person, and that was what I loved about it—it wasn't the size of a shoe box, like other apartments.

I invited Lindsey and Shane over for a housewarming party. In the short time I'd been in Adelaide, they'd become more than acquaintances—they were my friends. My only friends here actually. I hadn't attempted to meet new people. The friendly faces at the local supermarket, though familiar, didn't count.

We cracked open a bottle of champagne, filling our glasses before stepping out onto the balcony. The cool evening air brushed against my face as we looked over the marina. The sky was streaked with shades of pink and orange, the last light of day fading into night.

"To new beginnings!" Lindsey said, raising her glass.

"To Adelaide," Shane added, clinking his glass against mine.

"And to friends," I finished.

We sipped our champagne, and I let myself soak in the moment—I'd taken a leap coming to Adelaide and purchasing my first property.

"So," Lindsey said, "now that you've made this big purchase and settled in, what's next for you?"

The question caught me off guard. "Honestly, I haven't planned much beyond this," I admitted, the vastness of my future sprawling out before me like the cityscape below the balcony.

"You know, you could get a job or study—or both," she suggested. "You know what? My university has an open day coming up in August. Why don't you come along? Just to check it out, see if you're interested in any of the courses they offer. I'll even tag along with you."

Her suggestion opened a new avenue of thought. It had never occurred to me that Lindsey was studying since her real estate career hadn't worked out the way she'd wanted and her qualifications had gone to waste.

"Wait. You went back to study?" I asked, curious what field she had chosen on her own path to reinvention.

"Yep. I'm doing a degree in business with a focus on tourism and event management. It's why I'm working at the hotel." Her voice was filled with excitement. "One day, I want to own a hotel."

Shane and I exchanged a look.

"Really? Why a hotelier?" I asked. I'd never heard anyone say it with so much passion.

Her eyes lit up. "The idea of running a hotel, making all the decisions, building a place that feels like a home away from home—it's thrilling to me. I admit, when I first started working at the hotel, I was sceptical about the whole industry. I didn't think it was for me. But you know what? It grew on me. I love seeing people come and go, hearing their stories. It made me want to create my own space, something that reflects my vision. Right now, I'm focused on working my way up into a management role to get experience, but eventually… I want to open my own hotel."

Her words hung in the air, inspiring, as though she'd cast a vision for a life I hadn't even considered. I admired her focus, her sense of purpose. She'd reinvented herself, and it was clear she'd found a path that excited her.

"So, what do you think?" she asked. "Do you think you would be interested in going to the open day? It will be fun."

"I don't know." My gaze shifted to Shane, wondering what he thought of the idea.

He shrugged. "You never know, you might find a degree you like. It wouldn't hurt to look."

4

After four weeks of nagging, Lindsey convinced me to attend the open day. The truth was, I couldn't keep dodging the inevitable decision about my career path. This was an opportunity to see if there was a degree that sparked a genuine interest within me. The feeling of not knowing what I wanted to do with my life had been hanging over me since high school. The prospect of being labelled the family's underachiever wasn't something I was willing to entertain. The last thing I wanted was to become the failure in my family, the one who didn't quite measure up. That reason alone was enough to motivate me to go.

I drove into the city early in the morning. I was fortunate to find a spot in a multistorey carpark just off Hindley Street. Incredibly, it was across the road from the university, and it wasn't brimming with cars. Perfect!

Lindsey was waiting for me at the front entrance, near a "Welcome to Uni" booth. She looked ready to face the cold. Wrapped up in a thick jacket and pants, she was warding off the biting winter breeze, while I shivered in my sweater and jeans, regretting my lack of layers and hoping for the sun's mercy as the day progressed.

"Let's get coffee," I suggested, craving a hot drink and caffeine kick to start our day.

"Sure, but let's grab a welcome pack first. It will guide us through today's events." She approached the booth. "I checked out their website last night—there's a whole lineup of presentations we can attend. I'm sure you'll find something that catches your interest."

The booth was manned by three students bundled up in university hoodies, radiating enthusiasm despite the morning chill. They handed each of us a welcome pack filled with brochures outlining the day's schedule and details about the university. We skimmed through the contents, then made our way to the café.

As soon as we stepped inside, the rich aroma of freshly brewed coffee washed over us, a cosy escape from the crisp air outside. Judging by the crowd gathered around the counter, plenty of others had had the same idea. It was going to be a bit of a wait.

We placed our orders and found an empty table, spreading

the brochures across the surface. Lindsey pulled out the schedule, her eyes scanning it intently, then looked up.

"See anything you like in the first session?" She pulled a pen from her pocket, ready to mark down options.

I picked up my copy of the schedule. My gaze drifted across the list of programs, pausing when I saw "Construction Management." It reminded me of my parents. Years ago, I'd contemplated the idea of following in their footsteps but concluded my own aspirations lay elsewhere. "Nope."

Over fifteen minutes later, the barista called our order number. I collected the drinks and returned to our table, finding Lindsay marking potential sessions on the brochure.

"How about the 'Careers in Law' presentation?" she mused, her pen hovering over the option. "If I wasn't studying hospitality, law was my next pick."

"'Careers in Law' it is," I agreed, taking the pen from her to underscore our mutual selection.

We mapped out our day—selecting presentations and info sessions that covered a range of fields. The plan was to dive into as many areas as possible, hoping something might resonate. It was a strategic approach to broaden my horizons and fine-tune my interests.

Between the presentations, we spoke with students and teachers, some of whom recognised Lindsey from their classes, and made new friends. Lindsey struck up a conversation with a guy called John who was volunteering at an info booth. They'd been on the same campus for months but somehow had never crossed paths. That was, until now. By the end of their chat, they'd exchanged numbers, and I could tell Lindsey's interest went beyond academics.

Just before three o'clock in the afternoon, we called it a day and headed back to our cars, which were parked in the same carpark but on different levels.

As we stepped into the elevator, I said, "Thanks for talking me into coming to the open day."

"Anytime," she replied. As the doors opened on her floor, she turned back. "Make sure you apply, okay?"

I laughed.

After we parted, I made a couple of stops on the way home. Firstly, I bought a laptop—something I would need for my studies and in general, as I'd left my old one in Sydney. Then I swung by the Telstra store and signed a contract to have the internet connected at my apartment since I hadn't done so earlier on. There was a wait time for installation, so I picked up a USB modem as a temporary fix to get me started.

Back home, I set up the new laptop on the dining room table, then ordered pizza for dinner and made myself a cup of tea. While the laptop went through its setup routine, I reached for a cigarette from the pack I had stashed in my handbag. I smoked now and then and usually kept a few packs around—just in case.

I'd taken up the habit after Zack passed away and would have one whenever anxiety had me on edge.

I stepped out onto the balcony, lit up, and leaned against the railing, gazing at the marina. The sun had set, and the lights from the apartments on the other side cast a glow over the water. The cigarette offered a strange comfort that was euphoric. Its sharp taste grounded me in the moment, a brief escape from the swirl of thoughts about uni and the unknown path ahead.

When I was alone, Zack's memory often quietly surfaced. He'd always been the one pushing me, nudging me to think about my future, prodding me about my career aspirations. The thought of him brought bittersweet comfort—I knew he would have been my biggest supporter in this new venture. I could almost hear him saying, "Go for it, Jess. You've got this."

I exhaled the smoke, whispering, "You'd be proud," and imagined him standing beside me, sharing this moment of quiet reflection.

The door buzzer jolted me out of my thoughts—my pizza had arrived. I took one final drag of my cigarette before stubbing it out in the ashtray on the balcony table and went to grab my food—not the healthiest choice, but the easiest option.

My laptop was ready to use when I returned. I brought up the browser and navigated to the university's website. As I scrolled through the degrees on offer, I took a bite of pizza.

Medicine. Once upon a time, I'd thought about becoming

a doctor, but my enthusiasm towards it had fizzled out quicker than I'd expected. I also couldn't see myself as a lawyer, architect, or engineer, despite having the grades to secure a spot in any of those types of degrees. As I sifted through the choices, never had I felt the need to get my life together more than I did now.

My father had a master's in business administration and a degree in finance. My mother was an architect with a background in construction management. Alesha had finished a journalism degree and was now studying marketing, her life seemingly plotted on a stable course with a steady relationship. Even Shane had managed to clean up his act and was on the right path. And Lindsey—she was already working towards her dream of managing, maybe even owning, a hotel one day.

They were older, sure, but that didn't matter. I was supposed to be figuring things out too. Everyone seemed to know where they were going. Everyone except me.

As my eyes skimmed the list of degrees on the university's website, I stopped on "Bachelor of Finance." A smirk crept onto my face. The idea of me, Jessie Florence, diving into the world of banking—my parents would be thrilled. For a moment, I entertained the vision of myself poring over ledgers and financial forecasts before continuing down the list. Nothing stood out, and I found myself staring at the degree in finance again. The thought of becoming a banker was oddly tempting. Something about the order, the structure, the way numbers made sense—it felt… right.

And honestly, I had nothing to lose by applying.

Before I could second-guess myself, I filled in and submitted my application. Just as I hit submit, my phone buzzed. Conrad's number flashed on the screen. I made a mental note to save his number in my phone.

"I thought you'd given up," I answered the phone. It had been two months since his last call.

"Do I ever give up?" His voice, a familiar yet unexpected presence in my day. "I figured you could use some space after... everything with Zack."

"How thoughtful of you." My words came out harsh, but I appreciated him giving me space.

There was a pause on his end. "That letter I mentioned on our last call... I'm going to drop it off to you shortly. Zack left it to you. It was a part of his will."

I hadn't told him where I was, and the assumption that I was still in Sydney underscored the distance that had crept between us. "I'm not in Sydney."

"Oh, where are you?"

"I've moved to another city. I needed to get away and start over," I explained with as little detail I could. "So, why didn't you tell me about this letter right after his death? Why now?"

"You were upset. Really upset. You hung up on my parents twice when they called and told you what happened. And you didn't come to the funeral. Can you imagine us giving you the letter back then?"

"I'm sorry." It was all I could say in response to my behaviour as I reflected on that day.

I'd never forget the call from Zack's parents. The moment their words sank in, it felt as if the ground had vanished beneath me. I hung up before they could say more. When they called again, I answered—then hung up after a couple of minutes. Each disconnection was less about anger and more about denial. A desperate attempt to block out reality. It was as if hanging up could undo their words.

I'd seen Zack earlier that day. The idea that he was gone, forever out of reach, was a reality I couldn't reconcile. My mind refused to accept it, as though I was in some alternate universe where the rules of existence no longer made sense. And as I had paced the living room with the phone in my hand, searing pain consumed me. It felt as though all four chambers of my heart had ruptured at once. Nausea swept through my body as the room spun. I wanted fresh air.

I'd tried to step outside for air, but instead, the floor seemed to be moving in my direction—or maybe it was the other way around... I don't know. I'd collapsed onto the floor, shock rendering my body numb. My sister had run to my aid, panicking, having no idea what was happening.

"You don't need to apologise," he said. "We understand. It was as painful to you as it was to us. We know how much you and Zack meant to each other. We wanted to give you space. It seemed like the right thing to do at the time."

Their empathy touched me in ways I struggled to express.

"My parents are hosting a special lunch this Saturday," he continued. "They've invited friends over and wanted you to be there too. But I'll let them know you're out of town and can't make it. I can mail the letter to you, if that's easier."

The Baltimores had been like a second family to me, long before Zack and I became a couple. Our families' ties ran deep, anchored in years of friendship and business partnership in property development. I'd spent countless hours at their home, sharing meals, stories, and feeling as though I belonged there. I'd known them ever since I could remember. Declining their invitation felt wrong, like turning my back on a part of myself.

After a pause, I mustered the words I had been searching for. "Don't send it. I'll come to Sydney and get the letter in person. Tell your parents I look forward to seeing them on Saturday."

5

I booked a round-trip flight to Sydney and a two-night stay at the Park Hyatt. I'd always wanted to stay at the hotel, but it never felt necessary when I lived in the city.

Heading to Sydney the evening before the lunch, I packed a few essentials and outfits for the occasion, alongside the keys to my parents' house. I hadn't planned to stay there, but I wanted to stop by and see how things were since I'd left. However, as I zipped up my suitcase, I couldn't shake my unease about the trip. Part of me had never expected to go back to Sydney, even though I knew that wasn't realistic—my family was there, and no matter how much I wanted to escape the memories, I couldn't just cut them or Sydney out of my life.

After a two-hour flight, I was happy to step into the hotel

room. Drawn to the window, I was greeted by the sight of the Sydney Opera House, its sails lit up in an array of colours. Sydney. For so long, I couldn't imagine living anywhere else. This was the city where I was born, where I grew up, where I'd thought I'd spend the rest of my life. It was the place that held my loved ones and my memories.

And yet, standing here now, gazing at the familiar skyline, I realised that time had a way of reshaping perspectives. That was exactly what had happened to me. My life had taken an unexpected turn, and the city that had once defined me no longer felt like home.

The next morning, sunlight filtered through the hotel window as I got ready for lunch with the Baltimore family. I took my time, fussing over every detail of my makeup, wanting to look my best. I hadn't seen them in months, and today felt like a moment that deserved extra care. I slipped into a short floral dress and matched it with white heels, checking myself in the mirror one last time before I left.

I caught a taxi to their place earlier than planned. From the street, their house appeared to be double-storeyed, but the reality was far more impressive. The other side, which faced the river, revealed its true scale—a colossal four-storey mansion. It was a display of their architectural finesse and considerable wealth. The grandeur of their house couldn't be missed. It was an embodiment of their achievements and the legacy they had cultivated over time, just like my parents.

I pressed the buzzer at the front gate, and a familiar figure emerged, walking towards me—Conrad. My breath caught for a moment. I'd forgotten how much he looked like Zack. Everything from his blond hair to his facial features reminded me of him, except Conrad was much older.

"Jessie," he said.

"Conrad," I managed to say.

He opened the gate, stepping aside to let me in. "Thanks for coming. For a second there, I almost didn't recognise you. Did you change your hair colour?"

"I sure did," I replied warily. "I wanted to try something new."

I followed him through the front entrance into the foyer, past a majestic spiral staircase, to the elevator. White walls, marble floors, recessed LED lighting, and gold fixtures—classy and expensive. The place was a modern-day palace.

Descending to the ground floor, we got out of the elevator and Conrad led me through to the large entertainment area. A bar lined one side of the room, and floor-to-ceiling glass doors opened out onto a yard that stretched all the way to the river. Outside, a long table had been set up under the shade of a canopy. It was ideal weather for an outdoor lunch.

I was the first guest to arrive, but I didn't ask who else

would be joining us. I'd find out soon enough.

"Jessie! How lovely to see you." Conrad's mother, Esmeralda, appeared from inside to greet us. Adorned in a dress from one of the latest designer collections, she was ready for the occasion. Her hair, a cascade of platinum-blond waves, framed her face, and her makeup was perfectly understated, giving her a natural look.

"Esmeralda." I closed the distance between us. "Thank you for inviting me."

"You look stunning, Jessie. It's been far too long." She hugged me and led us back inside. "We're so glad you could make it. Conrad mentioned you've taken quite the step, moving away from Sydney."

"I have," I replied.

"I know Zack's passing wasn't easy on you. It wasn't easy on us either." Mentioning his death opened a depth of agony I could hear in her voice. She went over to the bar, where an envelope lay, and picked it up, bringing it back to me. "He left you a letter." She held it out. "It was a part of his will."

My gaze dropped to the envelope in her hands. My name was scrawled across it in Zack's unmistakably messy handwriting. Growing up with money, our parents taught us to be practical—nothing was ever simple and everything was documented. I took it slowly, as if the paper might dissolve under my touch. The envelope itself felt sacred as the reality of holding a piece of him sank in. It was as though time itself had paused, the world narrowing down to just me and the envelope.

"And thirty million dollars," a voice said from behind me.

The words jolted me, and I turned to see Lloyd, Zack's father, striding into the room. His entrance was calm but authoritative, and his casual attire didn't soften the intensity he brought with him. Tall, with greying hair and reading glasses perched atop his head, Lloyd radiated the poise of someone who had spent his life in the business world.

"I'm sorry, what?" The question slipped from me before I could catch it.

Lloyd gave a single, deliberate nod. "Yes, thirty million. Zack left you his money because he wanted to make sure you were looked after—that was just who he was when it came to you."

I sat on the couch, the letter clutched tightly in my hand as my mind spun. Thirty million dollars. The last thing I'd wanted or expected was Zack's money. I stared at the envelope. What could he have written? The guy I loved had left me this unimaginable gift, as if money could somehow fill the void he'd left behind. A wave of nausea twisted in my stomach, and I had to close my eyes, breathing slowly to steady myself.

I didn't want the money. Every fibre of my being ached with a longing for Zack. I would have traded every last dollar—every cent, every ounce of financial security—for one more moment with him, one more chance to hear his voice and see him.

No amount of money could ever replace what I had lost.

I wasn't sure whether to tear open the letter and read it right away or save it for later. I debated for a few seconds before I felt compelled by a need to connect with Zack's final words to me. How could I not?

I carefully opened the letter, as if opening a door to a room filled with his essence. His handwriting, familiar and uniquely his, brought an immediate rush of tears.

Dear Jessie,

If you're reading this, then it means I'm no longer there to tell you in person how much you mean to me. It breaks my heart that these words have to reach you this way. More than anything, please know this first: I love you. I've always loved you—more than words could ever express. You've been the sunshine in my life, a source of joy and endless inspiration. And even though I'm no longer by your side, my love for you will never fade.

Jessie, promise me you'll keep living: chase every dream, take every chance. Don't let the memory of us stop you from moving on. I want you to find happiness again, to open your heart to new adventures and people, because life is meant to be lived, even after loss.

Thank you, Jessie, for being the person who's been part of my life for as long as I can remember—for growing up beside me, believing in me, and loving me through it all. You touched my heart and soul in ways no one else ever could. You are, and always will be, my love, my partner, my inspiration. That's why I've left what I could—not because you need it, but because I know you'll use it to create something lasting, something that's yours and in the life you're meant to build.

Love,

Zack

I folded the letter and held it, unsure what to think of it. His words brought me a level of comfort, but at the same time, despair—despair that he wasn't here to say these things to me himself, that this letter was all I had left of him.

Esmeralda sat next to me. "It breaks my heart that my youngest son isn't here."

I knew no parent should ever have to experience the agony of outliving their child.

Her words hung between us. We were both grieving Zack in our own ways—me as someone who loved him deeply, and her as a mother who had lost a piece of herself.

* * *

Guests arrived one after the other. We took seats at the elegantly set table under the shade. The table was a masterpiece of understated luxury—crystal glasses gleamed in the sunlight, and intricate floral arrangements spilled across its length. Esmeralda and Lloyd sat to my left with Conrad on my right—occupying the seat that had once been Zack's. The sight unsettled me more than I wanted to admit. But sitting between them, I felt as if I were a part of the Baltimore family once again.

Amidst the chatter and clinking of glasses, my gaze kept drifting towards the empty chair beside Conrad. Its vacancy felt like an unresolved question hanging over the gathering. Who was running late? Or had someone not shown up at all?

It wasn't long before the answer materialised in the form of Olivia Konstanzo.

Her presence instantly shifted the energy at the table. Olivia wasn't just anyone; her life had been intertwined with my family's and the Baltimores' in ways that carried weight. Once a figure in the world of fashion, she had partly left it behind when she married Mark Konstanzo, a key partner in my parents' property development empire. Their union was a blending of two distinct worlds—glamour and business. But that chapter had ended abruptly with Mark's tragic death a few months before Zack's, leaving Olivia to navigate a world she'd barely understood.

She'd gone from being a semi-retired model at twenty-eight, whose experience was in runways and photoshoots, to navigating the world of property development and construction by herself. It wasn't a natural transition, and everyone knew that. For her to level up to Mark's experience and understanding, the road ahead would be long and unforgiving. But Olivia was still here, facing it.

Her arrival cast a poignant shadow. Even before she spoke, I could feel the grief she carried, a weight that seemed to settle in the space around her. Her dark brown hair was down, and she wore a black cocktail dress paired with high heels. It wasn't her usual style; Olivia was known for wearing lighter shades. Today, she stood out—no one else wore black. It was a gloomy look for a warm, sunny afternoon and spoke volumes without a single word.

Taking her place beside Conrad, she shot a fleeting glance in my direction and whispered something to him. Whatever she said, it made him nod subtly.

I couldn't help watching her. My curiosity twisted into something I couldn't quite name—sympathy, maybe, or fascination. Olivia had always been a larger-than-life figure, someone who seemed untouchable in her beauty and confidence. She'd been the woman in the glossy magazines. But here, in the Baltimore family's backyard, she was just Olivia. No runway, no spotlight, no air of perfection—only a grieving widow trying to hold herself together.

As lunch unfolded, everyone was absorbed in conversations around the table, including Olivia. I excused myself to use the bathroom. On my way back, I felt a cold, bony hand clasp my arm, stopping me in my tracks. I was pulled aside, finding myself face to face with Olivia.

"Did you think a change in hair colour would make you unrecognisable?" she asked through gritted teeth.

"Excuse me?" I pulled my arm out of her grip and stepped back.

"I know Zack was blackmailing my husband!" Her words sliced through the air. Restrained anger burned in her eyes as if she were daring me to deny it.

"What are you talking about?" I stared at her. "Zack… blackmailing? Are you serious?"

Zack would never have stooped to something so manipulative. The very notion was out of character. And yet, the accusation made me wonder what Mark could have done to invite blackmail. He had always struck me as professional—careful. Whatever Olivia thought she knew felt less like truth and more like grief creating a story, searching for someone to blame.

"Don't play dumb!" Olivia's voice cracked. "I know he had something to do with my husband's death." She burst into tears.

As the weight of her words settled, I gathered my thoughts and said, "I understand you're trying to make sense of Mark's death, but what you're saying isn't true. Your husband died in a car accident. It was all over the news. Zack was with me the night it happened… Blaming him won't bring Mark back, and it won't bring you peace." I placed my hand on her shoulder. I could see that she was hurting. "You need to get help, Olivia."

I thought she might lash out again, but instead, she simply stood there, tears streaking her cheeks.

When she didn't seem interested in my comfort, I returned to the table. She followed shortly after, her composure restored.

My encounter with Olivia had shaken me. I hadn't expected such a confrontation, but I understood why she'd targeted me—I'd been in a relationship with Zack, which made me the villain in the narrative her grief had constructed.

Throughout lunch, she put on an act, smiling as if nothing had happened between us. She was so well spoken that no one would have suspected she'd had a mental breakdown.

6

"I'll make the arrangements for Zack's money to be transferred to you," Conrad said as I was leaving. "I'll call you in a week or two."

With a final wave, I left the Baltimore residence. The events of the lunch had reignited the pain of losing Zack. I couldn't shake the darkness that clung to me as I made way to my parents' place, which was several properties down. I was only stopping in briefly before heading back to the hotel.

The winter sun was beginning its slow descent, casting a golden glow across the sky. As I reached the front gate, I pulled out the remote from my handbag and opened the gate. In seconds, I was at the entrance, unlocking the door and walking into the foyer. The eerie silence was deafening. Beneath the surface of familiarity was an undeniable sense of emptiness and misery, further adding to my pain.

I went upstairs to my room. Everything was exactly the way I had left it—a snapshot of my life frozen in time, much like the photographs I'd once taken with such fervour.

I went to my walk-in wardrobe; the sight of it was overwhelming. Rows of designer clothes hung neatly, shoes arranged in perfect order, handbags displayed on shelves as though they were pieces of art. Shopping had always been my weakness, and I'd buy something new at every opportunity, convincing myself each purchase was justified. Most of it had never been worn. I grabbed a few things but knew I would need to return and pack up all my stuff to take to Adelaide.

Lingering in my room, my gaze landed on the dust-covered camera on my bedside table, its lens pointing accusingly at the space I'd abandoned. Photography used to be my escape, an outlet for my creativity and a way to document moments and capture beautiful views. Zack was the one who'd introduced me to it, gifting me the camera for my birthday. After he died though, I couldn't bring myself to pick it up again. The passion towards it disappeared, and the camera became a constant reminder of him and our time together.

Even as I stood there, a memory of us at his favourite music festival came rushing back. It was peak summer and it was hot. I was dressed for the chaos: denim shorts, crop top, sunglasses that slipped down my nose, and white designer sneakers. I had glitter streaked across my arms and face.

Zack and I were there with friends, taking random photos of each other posing with drinks, pulling faces, singing, and dancing. As he took a photo of me dancing with our friends, he said, "You make the world beautiful."

"You're such an idiot!" I'd yelled back, but I was smiling too hard to mean it.

Those photos were still on the SD card in that camera—left untouched since that day.

Something within me stirred—a whisper of the person I used to be, urging me to take the camera with me. I picked it up and tucked it into my handbag along with the charger.

Downstairs in the kitchen, I spotted a pile of letters scattered on the counter—the housekeeper must've brought them in before she left for the day. I flicked through them, pulling out the ones addressed to me.

"Who are you, and what are you doing here?" challenged a voice, breaking the silence.

"Geez!" I flinched, dropping the letters. "You scared the living daylights out of me."

I placed my hand against my chest and took a deep breath. I thought my soul had left my body for a moment.

Alesha was the last person I'd expected to see because she usually spent weekends at her boyfriend's place. She was a few metres away, her dark brown hair pulled back in a messy ponytail, her grey trackies and crop top giving her a casual, unbothered look—except for the baseball bat gripped tightly in her hands. She was ready to swing.

"Jessie? Is that you? Did—did you dye your hair?" She lowered the bat and moved closer.

"Of course it's me!" I collected the letters off the floor and shoved them into my handbag. "And what the hell, Alesha? Were you planning to knock me out or something?"

"I didn't know who was in the house," she said defensively, setting the bat on the kitchen counter.

"Scared much?" I nodded towards the bat. It seemed unusual for her have a weapon.

"Being alone in this huge house can get scary," she confessed. "Especially with all the break-ins I've been hearing about on the news. What's with the new hair colour?"

"Just felt like a change," I replied, brushing off her question.

"So, where did you run off to?" she pressed.

"Somewhere." I adjusted the strap of my handbag.

"Well, I'm glad you're back." She smiled.

The sincerity of her words tugged at me, but I knew my stay was temporary. "I'm actually leaving shortly," I admitted. "I only came by to check in and grab a few things."

"What do you mean, 'leaving'?"

"I've bought my own place," I said. "In another state. It was time I moved out and moved on with my life. Staying here wasn't helping me. I think sticking around and being miserable was just making everything worse."

As the words left my mouth, I realised how true they were. Leaving Sydney had been hard, but it had also been necessary.

"Have you told Mum and Dad?" she asked.

"Nah. I'll tell them everything when they come back at the end of the year."

"Are you okay?"

Considering the enormity of everything that had led me to this point—I was doing better than expected. "Yep. Never been better."

* * *

The next morning, on the way to the airport, I asked the taxi driver to make two stops. The first was to buy flowers—something to take to Zack. My next stop was the cemetery where he was buried. I hadn't been to his grave before, and I regretted skipping his funeral, not standing beside his family and friends as they said their goodbyes. It had remained a subtle ache within me and a reminder of the unspoken goodbyes. I'd avoided it then because I couldn't bear to let go. For me, Zack's death was a nightmare I couldn't wake from. However, I wanted to pay him respect and face the reality I wished I could ignore—he wasn't coming back.

Clutching the flowers tightly, I asked the driver to wait and climbed out of the taxi. The directions Conrad had given me at lunch played over in my head as I hurried into the cemetery. It stretched before me, a serene expanse marked by rows of headstones. The place held the stories and silences of countless lives.

For ten long minutes—minutes that felt like hours—I searched. My heart thudded as my eyes scanned the gravestones, row after row, until finally, I found it.

In that moment, amidst the quiet rustle of leaves and the distant songs of birds, I found myself at a crossroads of emotions as I read his gravestone.

FOREVER IN OUR HEARTS
ZACK BALTIMORE

The finality of his absence etched in stone and earth. There was no more pretending, no more clinging to illusions that he was just… away—that somehow, someday, he might walk back into my life. Zack was gone. Truly gone.

My knees buckled, and I knelt next to his grave, placing the flowers at the base of the headstone. I stared at his name for what felt like forever as emotions raged inside me: regret, love, loss, anger… and an overwhelming, suffocating sadness. For so long, I'd avoided this moment, but now it was as if the silence was waiting for me to speak, to finally say all the things I'd been carrying in my mind since the day he left.

"I'm sorry," I whispered. "I'm so sorry I didn't come to your funeral." The words spilled out as if they had been trapped, locked behind a dam for months. "I couldn't do it, Zack. I couldn't face it. I couldn't stand there and watch them bury you, knowing it was real, knowing I'd never see you again." My voice cracked. "Even now, I don't know how to do this. I don't know how to live in a world without you in it. It feels as though a piece of me was ripped away that day, and the hole you left… It's unbearable." Tears streaked down my cheeks, but I didn't wipe them away. "I keep trying to move forward, but I feel as if I'm dragging this weight, as if I'm constantly looking back over my shoulder, hoping for you—hoping for something I know will never come."

The quiet seemed to lean in, as though it were listening. The only sounds were the gentle rustling of leaves and the distant traffic.

"You were my light," I said. "You made everything seem brighter, more alive. And now… everything just feels dim. Hollow. I know you'd want me to be stronger. You'd want me to live. But God, Zack, it's so hard. I miss *us*."

Speaking to Zack—or perhaps to the wind and the whispering leaves—was cathartic. I let the words linger in the air, hoping he could hear them, hoping he'd know how much he meant to me.

"I hope you're at peace, Zack. I love you. I always will."

I stayed there a few minutes longer. Then finally, I rose to my feet, brushing the dirt and grass from my knees.

The crunch of gravel beneath my shoes broke the stillness of the cemetery as I headed back to the taxi. But before I could make it to the car, something caught my eye—a figure in the distance, between the rows of headstones.

It wasn't a ghost.

It was Olivia.

Even from afar, she was unmistakable. She was dressed in black again, though this time more casually—her colour of choice since her husband's death, like a religious tradition she was upholding.

There she stood, holding a bouquet of flowers. Our eyes met, unwavering, as though she had been watching me the entire time.

My steps faltered. The question came unbidden: *Did she followed me?* It was an unwelcome suspicion that flickered through my mind. The confrontation we'd had played on a loop in my head: her anger, her accusations, the raw pain in her voice. Was this some sort of calculated move?

Shaking off that thought, I assumed it was a coincidence. The cemetery was the final resting place for many, including her late husband. Perhaps after our candid exchange the day before, she had chosen the path of healing, which started with Mark.

I didn't stop to exchange words with Olivia. Instead, I glanced back briefly as I climbed into the taxi. She hadn't moved, still standing amidst the gravestones, her silhouette framed by the late-morning light. For all her sharp words and accusations, I found myself wishing she'd find peace, just as I was trying to.

Two hours later, I was at the terminal of the bustling airport. Announcements blared over the loudspeakers—delayed flights, gate changes, and final boarding calls clashing with the murmur of countless conversations around me.

Exhausted, I slumped into one of the plastic chairs near my boarding gate, trying to tune it all out.

Ping!

The notification startled me. I pulled out my phone and glanced at the screen. It was a message from Shane.

It had been weeks since I'd last seen or heard from him, which was strange considering we lived in the same city and had rekindled our friendship. But he'd mentioned how demanding his job was, and I'd chalked up the silence to that.

HI JESSIE. DO YOU WANT TO GO OUT TO DINNER TONIGHT?

The message sparked a smile, cutting through the fatigue that had settled into my bones. I shot back a playful condition with my reply, half joking, half hoping he'd take me up on it.

Only if you pick me up from the airport in three hours.

He messaged back.

See you at 4 p.m.

True to his word, Shane was waiting when I stepped out of the terminal in Adelaide. Wearing a black, long-sleeved button-up shirt and dark jeans, he was ready for dinner, unlike me. My attire and appearance were a far cry from the polished version of myself. I needed a shower and a change of clothes before we went out.

When he spotted me, he grinned and opened his arms for a hug. "Where did you travel to?"

"Sydney."

"Visiting your parents?" he asked as he reached for my suitcase and guided it smoothly through the crowd towards the carpark.

"No, they're travelling Australia," I clarified.

"Righteo." He smiled as we headed to his car. "I'll take you home first, then we'll go to dinner."

Fifteen minutes later, we were at my place. Shane made himself at home, grabbing a beer from the fridge before heading onto the balcony. Meanwhile, I rushed to take a shower and get ready.

Refreshed, I slipped into a black-and-white long-sleeved dress that was short but classy, paired with black high heels and a matching handbag. After applying some makeup and spritzing on a hint of perfume, I finally felt more like myself.

Peeking out onto the balcony, I found Shane seated at the outdoor table, phone in hand, watching an NRL game.

"Hey, I'm ready," I called as I stepped outside. "Let's go."

He looked up. "Finally," he teased. He drained the last of his beer in one quick gulp before rising to his feet and slipping the phone into his pocket. His eyes swept over me. "You look amazing."

The restaurants on the marina were a short stroll from my place. As we walked towards them, a chilly breeze hit us as if the Ice Age was making a comeback.

"You're not too cold, are you?" Shane asked.

"I should've grabbed a jacket," I admitted. "But I'll survive. The restaurant is close by."

Speeding up our pace, we reached the Italian restaurant that Shane loved before I transformed into a human ice block. As soon as we stepped inside, the aromas of garlic, tomato sauce, and freshly baked bread filled the air.

The hostess greeted us and led us to our table, tucked into a cosy corner by the window, away from the occasional draught by the door. The restaurant was busy. It was lucky Shane had thought to reserve a table—it was the kind of night that left walk-ins waiting.

As I settled into my seat, I perused the menu, trying to

decide what to order while Shane hadn't even glanced at it.

"You're not even going to look?" I asked.

"I know what I want. I always get the ragu here—it's the best. No need to waste time."

"Of course you do," I teased.

A waiter approached and took our drink orders first—glass of white wine for me and a beer for Shane. By the time the drinks were brought to our table, I'd finally made up my mind and went with the carbonara while Shane ordered his meal.

As the waiter left with our orders, Shane leaned forward slightly, resting his arms on the table. "So, how was Sydney?"

I swirled the wine in my glass. "It was good. I don't think the city ever changes." I took a sip. "I dropped in at my parents' place while I was there, and I made a decision—I'm moving all of my stuff out."

His brows lifted slightly. "You're not planning to ever return there, are you?"

"No," I said. "Adelaide is my home now."

Shane raised his beer in salute. "Cheers to living in Adelaide."

I raised my wine glass. "Cheers."

We clinked glasses.

"Are you busy next week? Or the week after?" I asked.

"Maybe," he hesitated. "What's on your mind?"

I paused, contemplating the best way to phrase it. "I could

use some help packing my stuff in Sydney, bringing it all back here to Adelaide."

He smirked, his beer poised mid-air. "So, basically, you need free labour?"

"Pretty much," I said.

He took a swig of his beer. "How long do you think it will take?"

"No idea. I've never moved before," I admitted.

"Are you hiring a removalist?"

"Nah. I'd rather take my time and do it myself because I'm leaving the furniture behind—only taking my clothes, accessories, and the smaller stuff. Whatever can fit in my car. I'm also looking forward to the drive…" I trailed off, my thoughts drifting to Sydney.

"Well, I guess I could visit and stay with my parents while I'm there—it's been ages since I've seen them."

"Great." I smiled.

"I'll check with my boss tomorrow about getting some time off, and I'll let you know," he said.

Our meals were served—always more on the plate than I could consume regardless of my appetite. It looked so delicious that I immediately started eating. Shane's ragu looked equally tempting, but he barely acknowledged it before attacking it like a man on a mission. I sneaked a bit off his plate and he laughed.

After dinner and a few more drinks, Shane paid the bill and

we left the restaurant.

The marina was quieter now, the buzz of earlier diners replaced by calm. Dim lampposts cast a warm glow across the paved walkway and the water's surface. Our footsteps echoed, blending with the occasional clink and creak of yachts shifting gently at their berths.

The cold hit me immediately, sharper than before. The breeze cut through my dress, leaving me shivering. Wrapping my arms around myself, I mentally cursed my decision to leave the house without a jacket. My tipsiness wasn't helping either—my steps were unsteady, and every wobble felt like a betrayal by my high heels, which were wedging themselves into the backs of my feet. I clung onto Shane's arm for support, and he adjusted his pace to match mine.

"Thank you for coming to dinner," Shane said as we approached the front of my apartment complex.

"No, thank *you* for inviting me." I reluctantly released my grip on his arm. The cold air heightened my awareness of the farewell that awaited.

"Good night," he murmured, closing the distance with an unexpected kiss.

For a second, time froze. My thoughts scattered in every direction, leaving me unsure of how to react. The warmth of the kiss lingered even after he pulled back, my cheeks heating as if they'd been set on fire.

Did Shane just kiss me?

I stared at him, utterly speechless. *What just happened?* Were we still friends, or had we crossed some invisible line into something else?

I liked Shane—this Shane more so than the wild, chaotic version of him I'd known in Sydney. That Shane had been unpredictable and self-destructive, but this Shane? He was completely different.

Watching him walk to his Merc in the visitors' parking lot, I wondered what the kiss meant for our friendship and whether it marked the beginning of something new.

A part of me wanted to leave it there, to let him go and figure things out on my own. But another part of me—one I couldn't ignore—longed to speak up, to clarify what that kiss meant. Gathering my thoughts, I finally shouted to him, "Does this mean we're dating?"

He turned back. "Depends on what you want."

I'd never thought Shane felt that way about me—or was I oblivious? How long had he been harbouring these feelings towards me? And more importantly, was I ready for something more with him?

Silence hung between us.

It was unchartered territory, which had me fearing it would jeopardise our friendship if things didn't work out. But could it work? Who was to say things wouldn't work out? Things had already shifted between us the moment he kissed me.

"I'll take that as a yes," I shouted.

He retraced his steps and kissed me again—this time more intensely and passionately, leaving no room for doubt. It was a declaration, sealing the silent agreement we had stumbled upon.

"I'll call you tomorrow." He dashed to his car.

I headed to the entrance of the complex. In a daze and somewhat excited for the first time in ages, I mentally zoned out in the elevator and ended up in my apartment without remembering how I got there.

7

The idea of Shane and I together—as strange as it seemed, it was growing on me. The more I thought about us being together, the more I believed a relationship would work out. Shane had changed, and so had I. It could also help me move on from Zack and might make me feel less empty. I didn't know if I liked Shane as more than a friend, but I was interested in exploring a relationship to find out if I could feel more for him.

My phone rang, interrupting my thoughts. Shane's name appeared on the screen as if summoned by my thoughts. "Hi, stranger," I answered the phone.

"Hey," he said. "I've spoken to my boss, and he's given me the green light to go to Sydney on short notice—two weeks' notice. I didn't want to push my luck with a week as I'd leave clients hanging."

"That's great!" With his help, I could tackle the mountain of packing much faster.

"It'll be nice to get away for a bit and see my parents. It's been so busy recently because of the demand in properties." He paused. "Oh… and about last night—I meant what I said. I was serious about us being together."

A smile tugged at the corners of my lips, one I couldn't hold back. "I gathered that."

"Good. Just wanted to make sure we're on the same page."

* * *

The two weeks flew by faster than I'd expected. I filled my days catching up with Lindsey and her friends—long brunches, late lunches, and a trip to the hair salon for a touch-up. Before I knew it, Shane and I were loading our bags into the boot of my car, ready to hit the road. I'd packed light, opting for a compact travel bag while Shane brought along a small suitcase.

Sliding into the driver's seat, I adjusted the mirrors and turned on the car while Shane settled into the passenger seat.

"Ready?" I asked.

"Let's do it." He fastened his seatbelt.

Within thirty minutes, we were on the outskirts of Adelaide, winding through the picturesque landscapes as we headed towards the Victorian border. We stopped a few times for snacks and bathroom breaks, stepping out at roadside rest areas where the occasional kookaburra called from the treetops. When we reached the New South Wales border, we needed to refuel the car.

We pulled into the first servo we saw, which looked as though it had been plucked straight out of a travel documentary about the middle of nowhere. The small building stood isolated, surrounded by bushland and endless vegetation. There wasn't a single house in sight, just the chirping of cicadas and the occasional rustle of wind through the dry grass.

Shane hopped out to refuel while I climbed out to stretch my legs. I arched my back and glanced around, taking in the vastness of the bushland. The quiet was tranquil, almost meditative.

I was about to get back into the car when movement caught my eye. High above, a bird was soaring gracefully through the sky, its wide wings slicing through the air. It swooped down into the tall grass, then rose again, before repeating the motion with precision. Intrigued, I watched it before realising it wasn't just any bird—it was an eagle.

"What's it doing?" I murmured, my gaze fixed on its sharp, deliberate movements. Was it hunting?

Leaving the car door ajar, I wandered towards the edge of the bushland, drawn by the bird's dance. I strained my eyes, trying to see what had captured its attention.

Then, out of nowhere, a small black silhouette darted from the dry grass onto the gravel driveway of the servo. It moved so fast it took me a second to realise what it was—a kitten, its tiny frame no match for the predator stalking it.

In an instant, the eagle seized its chance. With a sharp cry, it plunged downwards, talons outstretched, aiming for its prey.

"No!" I shouted instinctively.

The kitten was faster than it looked, dodging the eagle's attack with a frantic burst of energy. It zigzagged across the gravel, a tiny blur of determination and fear. The eagle rose again, circling overhead, its shadow flickering across the ground like a dark omen.

"Shane!" I called, panic rising in my chest as I watched the helpless kitten fight for its life.

He glanced up from the pump, startled, and followed my gaze. "What the hell?"

Without thinking, I charged towards the kitten, adrenaline driving my every step. Waving my arms wildly to scare off the eagle, I yelled, "Shoo! Go away!"

The eagle hesitated mid-dive, thrown off by my sudden intrusion. For a moment, I wasn't sure if it would back off or if I was about to find myself in a very different kind of predicament. My heart pounded as the bird, momentarily thwarted, retreated into the sky.

The kitten didn't waste a second. It made a beeline for my car, skittering across the gravel and diving straight through the open driver's side door.

So much for the peaceful charm of the outback. The encounter reminded me of nature's brutal cycle—predator and prey locked in a duel that only one would survive. I didn't need to say which one.

"What the hell just jumped into the car?" Shane asked as he finished refuelling.

"A kitten," I said breathlessly as I walked back towards the car.

His eyebrows shot up. "You're kidding. Out here? What are the odds?"

"No joke. It's in the car."

"So… what's the plan? Are we getting it out, or are we adopting a feral hitchhiker?" he asked.

"I'll try to get him out," I said, not entirely sure what I was doing.

As Shane headed into the servo to pay, I crouched by the open car door, peering inside. There, under the driver's seat, I spotted it—a tiny black shape huddled deep in the shadows. The kitten's green eyes glowed faintly in the gloom, wide with fear. Its little body trembled, and as I reached out a hand, it let out a low warning growl.

"*Great*," I muttered. "A spicy kitten." Keeping my

movements slow, I extended my hand again. "Hey, it's okay," I said softly. "I'm not going to hurt you, promise."

The kitten didn't budge, its growls deepening into a low, pitiful rumble. It was clearly terrified, its tiny claws digging into the car mat as it pressed itself into the corner.

"Come on, kitty," I tried again, inching my hand closer.

This time, I managed to curl my fingers around its small, fragile body. It let out a startled hiss and squirmed in my grip, its claws sinking into my skin. I winced but held on, carefully pulling it from its hiding spot.

Once out in the open, I held the kitten to my chest, feeling the rapid flutter of its heartbeat. Its tiny body was tense, trembling with residual fear, but it didn't try to escape.

Inspecting it closely, I noticed the marks of the eagle's assault—scratches and minor shallow puncture wounds marred its back and sides, red marks where talons had made contact. None of the injuries seemed life-threatening, but they were tender and swollen, and I knew the little thing needed to see a vet. It had been incredibly lucky to escape with its life.

Settling into the driver's seat with the kitten in my lap, I glanced around. "Where did you come from, huh? Who do you belong to?" I asked, though I knew there wouldn't be an answer.

The kitten tilted its head up at me. Its tiny mouth opened, releasing a plaintive meow as if attempting to communicate its story.

"That doesn't help."

It didn't have a collar, no tag, no sign of belonging to anyone. Out here, in the middle of nowhere, it seemed unlikely that it had an owner. But still, I wondered—could it have wandered from the petrol station? Maybe the people who ran the servo knew something.

Shane opened the passenger door and slid into his seat, his gaze settling on the tiny ball of fluff in my lap. "You found it."

"Yeah," I replied, brushing a bit of dirt off the kitten's fur. "But I have no idea who it belongs to. Do you think it might belong to the servo owners? Maybe it wandered off?"

"There's only one way to find out." He nodded towards the building. "Let's go in and ask."

Cradling the kitten close to my chest, I followed Shane into the servo. The space was small and smelled faintly of greasy fast food, the kind sitting under the heat of a bain-marie. Behind the counter stood a middle-aged woman with short brown hair and a face that carried a kindness that came with years of living simply.

"Excuse me," I said as we approached her so she could see the kitten nestled in my arms. Its head poked out, its wide eyes scanning the room nervously. "We found this kitten outside. Do you know if it belongs to anyone around here? It jumped into my car out of nowhere."

Her eyes lit up when she saw the kitten, and a smile tugged at her lips. "Oh, what a darling little thing," she said, her tone warm and motherly. "But no, that's not mine. Actually, no one around here keeps cats—it's all dogs in these parts."

I frowned. "Really? No one owns a cat around here?"

She shook her head. "Not that I've ever seen, and I've been here close to ten years. We do get feral cats passing through every now and then, but they don't stick around long. And certainly none that look as friendly as this one."

"Feral cats?" Shane asked.

"They're usually pretty wild," she explained. "Keep their distance from humans. You can tell pretty quick when one's feral—they won't let you near 'em, let alone pick 'em up. This little one doesn't seem like that at all."

I glanced down at the kitten nestled against me. This didn't feel like a feral cat—it felt like a kitten that had once belonged to someone.

"Thank you," I said to the woman.

"Good luck with the little guy," she said, waving as we walked out.

Back at the car, I held up the kitten, studying it closely. Its green eyes blinked at me, its tiny whiskers twitching.

"Do you think it's feral?" I asked Shane.

"Not a chance. You heard the lady. Feral cats wouldn't come near you, let alone let you hold them without losing a finger. It would take you ages to tame it. If anything, I'd guess someone abandoned it. Or maybe..." He paused, glancing towards the open expanse of bushland. "Maybe the eagle carried it off from somewhere else. You never know out here."

"What should we do with it?" I asked.

Shane leaned against the car. "Well, that depends on what *you* want to do."

I looked at the kitten again. Its wide green eyes blinked up at me, and I felt the faintest purr vibrating against my chest. Whatever its story was—wherever it had come from—one thing was clear: I couldn't just leave it out here.

"Well," I said finally, "I guess we've got a new passenger."

Shane grinned. "Looks like it."

Sliding back into the car, I carefully handed the kitten to Shane. "We should definitely have a vet look at it once we're in Sydney, check if it's microchipped." The words felt logical, practical, but as they left my mouth, I hoped the kitten wouldn't be claimed.

The thought surprised me.

In the brief time we'd spent together, I'd already felt a bond forming—this small, vulnerable creature had sparked something unexpected within me. The idea of handing it back to someone else, of severing this fragile connection, felt… wrong.

I couldn't help but think about my childhood, the notable absence of pets in our family. We'd never had a dog bounding through the backyard or a cat curled up on the couch. For some reason, it had never been part of the picture, and I realised I'd never questioned why. Was it because we were too busy, our lives too structured and focused on practicality? Or had my parents simply not wanted the responsibility?

8

At the clinic, I gently handed the kitten to the veterinarian. She confirmed his sex and guessed his age—an eight-week-old male—and carefully checked him over, her gloved hands running over his fragile frame.

"He's lucky," she said. "Aside from a few superficial wounds from the eagle's talons, he's in good health. Just a little bruised and shaken. A simple course of antibiotics will prevent any infection, and he should heal up just fine."

Relief flooded through me as I exhaled a breath I hadn't realised I'd been holding. "Thank you."

The vet scanned him for a microchip, but the absence of one deepened the mystery of his origins. She shook her head. "He's either a stray or someone didn't bother to chip him."

For me, this was good news. No microchip meant no immediate need to search for an owner. No looming possibility of having to give him back. This small, vulnerable creature could truly be mine.

"Good news," Shane said. "Looks like you've got yourself a cat."

"Yeah. I think I do."

The vet continued her work, giving him the necessary vaccinations and prescribing antibiotics.

"He'll need a follow-up visit for boosters in a few weeks," she explained, gently handing him back to me.

After paying for the appointment and vaccines, Shane and I left the clinic and headed to Shane's parents' place in Bondi.

"Just pull up into that driveway," he instructed as we turned onto his street.

I'd been here several times before—late nights or, rather, early mornings—after Zack and I had found Shane too drunk to make it home alone. We'd bring him back, help him up the stairs to his room, and leave. Back then, Zack always drove, so I never paid much attention to where we were or what the place looked like.

Seeing it in daylight felt different. His parents' house was a restored double-storey dark brick home. White window frames stood out against the aged brickwork, and the hedges along the path were trimmed with meticulous care. It wasn't grand—at least not to me. I'd grown up surrounded by designer mansions and high-end architecture, so homes like this felt modest, though they certainly didn't come cheap.

Shane unbuckled his seatbelt and glanced at the house. "I'll just go let them know I'm here," he said, climbing out of the car.

He didn't take his suitcase from the boot yet, probably figuring he'd bring it in once he'd said hello. I rolled the window down and watched as he walked around to the right side of the house, where the front door was, and rang the doorbell.

A few moments later, the door opened, and a woman—his mother—appeared. She was dressed in an orange-and-white knee-length dress. Her expression shifted from surprise to delight the moment she saw him.

"Shane!" she exclaimed, pulling him into a hug. "It's been so long—I can't believe it's really you."

"Yeah… it's been a while." He rubbed the back of his neck as she stepped back to look at him properly.

Then her gaze drifted past him—towards the car. I felt her eyes on me before she even spoke.

"And who's that?"

Shane followed her gaze. "That's Jessie."

"Jessie?" she repeated.

"We went to the same school."

Realisation dawned in her expression. "*Her*?"

Even from the car, I heard the tone—unmistakable, laced with disapproval. *Her?* What was that supposed to mean?

"Mum," Shane said, "that was years ago. And she wasn't doing anything wrong—she and Zack were helping me. I was the idiot who drank too much. She had nothing to do with it. So just drop it, okay?"

"So you keep saying," she replied. "But it's hard to believe she had no part in it if she was at the same place you were..." She leaned in then, lowering her voice—too quiet for me to hear from the car.

"A girl like that?" he shot back. "What's that supposed to mean?"

"I thought you'd have better judgement by now. Is she your girlfriend?"

"Mum." He exhaled. "I'm a grown man. You don't get to decide who I spend time with."

"I'm your mother," she retorted. "I'm allowed to be concerned."

"Concerned or judgmental? Because it sounds like the latter." He paused. "I came here to spend time with you and Dad, but it seems like things with you never change. You're still judgmental. You were a control freak then, and you're still one now."

Her mouth opened, but no words came out.

He shook his head, stepping back towards the car. "I'm

your only son, and yet I feel like you still hate me. You never helped me. You never even once called me in three years."

"Shane…" she called after him, her voice trembling.

But he didn't stop. He didn't glance back or say goodbye. He headed straight for the car.

Opening the car door, he slid into the passenger seat and said, "Please drive."

I started the engine, glancing sideways at him. What happened on that doorstep had shaken him in a way I wasn't used to seeing.

Unsure what to say, I reversed out of the driveway and headed off.

Silence filled the car for a while as he stared out the window.

"I know you heard that. I'm so sorry… You don't deserve to be spoken about like that. Especially after everything you've done for me. You could've left me at those parties. Most people would've. But you didn't. You and Zack always made sure I got home. You cared enough to help me even when I didn't deserve it. And she acts like you're the problem."

"It's okay." I reached across the console and rested my hand on his—not only to comfort him, but because I *wanted* to show him he wasn't alone.

"You know, I feel like my mother's always hated me." His gaze stayed fixed ahead. "She'd always criticise everything I did.

She was so judgemental and pushy. Nothing I did was ever good enough. She'd start arguments over nothing and then ignore me for days."

He gave a short, bitter laugh. "That's why I partied and drank so much. It wasn't just for fun. I couldn't stand being at home. Couldn't stand her. It's why I moved to Adelaide four years ago. I was working as a real estate agent here, but I needed to get away. I thought maybe… after a few years, things would be different. You know, that distance might fix something, but I was kidding myself."

I didn't know what to say. I'd never heard him talk about his family before—never like this. I'd always assumed he'd been the kind of person who liked to have fun, not someone running from something.

"I can't imagine that," I said quietly. "My parents and I— we're close."

"Yeah," he muttered. "You're lucky."

I hesitated. "What about your dad?"

"He's no better. He never said much, but that was the problem. He just stood there and watched. Never defended me."

"I'm sorry."

"Yeah," he said. "Me too."

On our way to my parents' house in Point Piper, we made a quick stop at the chemist to pick up the antibiotics prescribed for the kitten. When I turned into the driveway of my childhood home, my sister's white Audi was parked in front of the garage—she was home. I pulled up next to her car and we got out. The kitten leapt out behind me. After gently scooping him up, I opened the boot of the car to retrieve my travel bag while Shane grabbed his suitcase.

"This place is incredible," he murmured. "What do your parents do exactly?" He didn't wait for my response. "They're builders, right? This is… beyond impressive."

Although Shane and I knew each other from high school, he had never visited my home.

Deflecting, I offered him a playful smile. "Let's just say they've been successful in their ventures."

"Fair enough," he said.

Holding the kitten in one arm, I rummaged through my bag for the house keys. Shane was soaking in every detail of the home's exterior while he waited for me to unlock the door. His interest in the architecture and design of the place was probably intensified by his passion for real estate—and perhaps wealth.

When we went inside, almost immediately, my sister was there to greet us. This time, thankfully, she wasn't armed with a baseball bat, though I suspected it wasn't too far out of reach. Alesha was dressed in her signature casual comfort—grey trackies and an oversized jumper that hung off one shoulder.

"What are you two doing here?" she asked, her gaze flicking between Shane and me. Recognition sparked in her eyes when she saw him. Shane didn't need an introduction. They had been in the same grade, though back then he'd been a much different version of himself. "Shane… long time. You're looking very different these days."

"We're here to pack up the rest of my stuff," I explained, knowing I hadn't given her any heads-up about my plans—or my arrival. I'd simply shown up. Classic me.

Her eyes widened. "I didn't think I would see you back so soon."

"Well, surprise!" I laughed to ease the tension.

Alesha's eyes narrowed. "Right… so, what's going on between you two? Are you two together?"

I opened my mouth to respond, but Shane beat me to it. "Yeah."

"Jessie and Shane. Who would've thought?" Her voice echoed through the foyer.

Hearing our names in that manner stirred something deep inside me—something I hadn't expected. A flicker of guilt pressed down on me, whispering that maybe I was betraying something sacred even though Zack wanted me to find happiness again.

"You look much happier than I've seen you in a while," Alesha said. Her gaze shifted to the kitten cradled in my arms. "And who is this? Oh my… It's so adorable. Can I hold it?" She reached out, and I let her take him from me.

"Temporary passenger," I said. "We're figuring it out as we go."

"Where did you get it from?"

"The middle of nowhere…" I said, then recounted the story of how the kitten had come barrelling into our lives—the eagle, the vet, and everything in between.

"Crazy," she said. "So, the Cat Distribution System is real."

I blinked at her. "The what?"

"You know, the internet thing," she said. "Cats find people, not the other way around. Like, the universe just… delivers them." She looked at the kitten and cooed, "And you, little guy, seem to have hit the jackpot."

The next morning, after breakfast, I stood in my walk-in wardrobe overwhelmed. Racks upon racks of clothes and shelves adorned with accessories and more clothes greeted my eyes. It looked more like a boutique than a personal wardrobe—a fashion haven I wasn't sure would fit into my car. I knew there'd be tough decisions to make on what to keep and what to donate to charity.

Where would I even start?

"You could open a shop with this collection," Shane teased me.

I couldn't blame him for doing so. The sheer volume of clothes I owned was daunting. I'd been accumulating clothes for years, too lazy to clear them out sooner. Many still had the tags on them, never worn, and some I had forgotten I owned.

I stretched to reach the top shelf, my fingers just grasping the handle of one of the suitcases stashed up there. Tugging it down, I caught it before it could smack me in the face. "Got it!"

I pulled down two more suitcases, both medium sized, and placed them on the floor beside me.

Shane glanced at the suitcases, then at the racks bursting with clothes. "You know those aren't going to cut it, right?"

"I know. I'm going to have to improvise. I'll use large black garbage bags for the rest."

"Very classy," he said.

Shane helped me pack. We started with the items hanging on the racks, packing them with the wooden clothes hangers into a black bag—I would need the hangers in Adelaide.

"What about this one? Keeper or no?" he asked, holding up a black dress for inspection.

I glanced over, barely registering the dress in his hands. "No—"

My phone buzzed loudly from where I'd left it on the floor, cutting me off. The sound startled us both. I grabbed it.

Conrad's name lit up on the screen.

Without hesitation, I answered, trying to mask the surprise in my voice. "Hello?"

"Hi, Jessie, how long are you in Sydney for?" Conrad asked.

I frowned. "How did you know I was in Sydney?"

"I saw your car in the driveway yesterday," he said.

"Are you stalking me now?" I teased him.

"No, Jessie." He laughed. "We're neighbours. I happened to see your car when I was driving past. So, how long are you staying?"

My eyes veered in Shane's direction. He was holding up another dress for my approval, clearly confused by my sudden shift in attention. He mouthed, "Who is it?"

I gestured for him to wait and stay quiet. "A few days. Why do you ask?"

Shane was still staring at me, waiting for an answer.

I hit the mute button on my phone. "It's Conrad."

"Conrad? As in Zack's older brother?" Shane asked.

"Yeah," I replied, hoping to satisfy his curiosity.

"What does he want?" he pressed.

I shrugged, placing a finger to my lips, signalling for him to be quiet, and unmuted the phone. "Sorry, the call cut out for a few seconds. What were you saying?" I lied, having not listened to what he'd said.

Leaving the walk-in wardrobe, I stepped out onto the balcony, ensuring I was out of earshot. I needed space to think—and to talk—without Shane's questions hovering over me. It was time to find out what Conrad wanted without interruption.

"I was just saying," Conrad continued, "the reason I was asking how long you're in Sydney is because my family is hosting a dinner party on Saturday. My parents wanted me to invite you. And your sister too, if she's interested."

The invitation, unexpected yet not unwelcome, sparked a flicker of interest. The thought of stepping into Zack's world again after everything… It felt heavy, yet oddly tempting.

"Sounds great," I said after a beat. "I'm sure my sister would love to come along. What time should we be there?"

"Six P.M." There was a pause before he added, "Oh… and before I forget, Zack's money has been released and should get deposited into your account soon."

"Thank you." Grateful and conflicted didn't begin to cover it—Zack's final gift sent a piercing pain through my chest.

"Anyway," Conrad said, "we'll see you on Saturday."

"See you then." I ended the call in a daze.

When I returned to my room, Shane was leaning casually against the doorway to my walk-in wardrobe, but the way his arms were crossed told me he wasn't as relaxed as he wanted to appear. "So, what did Conrad want?"

"He invited my sister and me to a family dinner on Saturday," I answered, omitting the part about my financial windfall. Money, after all, wasn't something I openly discussed, not even with Shane. It was about steering clear of unnecessary attention and avoiding the pitfalls of envy or resentment.

"Really? What's the occasion?" There was a subtle shift in his demeanour.

"They enjoy hosting dinner parties. It's their way of catching up and spending time with friends…"

* * *

Having finished packing on Friday evening, our Saturday was freed up. With many clothes and accessories bagged for donation, I set out for a charity store located a few suburbs away. Shane, on the other hand, had made his own plans—he was catching up with a few friends from high school. It sounded far less dramatic than the short visit to his parents', and honestly, I was glad for him.

When I got back, I was faced with the universally dreaded task of any pet owner: giving medication to a cat. And not just any cat—my cat, who, in his short time with me, had already proven himself an escape artist, a drama queen, and a master of evasion. The strategies that websites and forums swore by fell flat, leaving us locked in a battle of wits and agility. I wished the veterinarian had prescribed a liquid antibiotic.

My first strategy—hiding the tablet in a treat—was met with immediate suspicion. He sniffed it, then looked up at me as if I'd committed some unforgivable betrayal. Plan B, disguising it in wet food, was equally fruitless. He simply ate around it with the precision of a surgeon. By Plan C, I found myself in a full-blown wrestling match, like that of an intense gladiator duel, where each of us vied for victory. The room turned into a chaos of flying fur and the occasional frustrated growl—on both sides.

"Would you stop being so dramatic!" I exclaimed, exasperated as he twisted away yet again, his small body somehow defying the laws of physics.

Finally, with a mix of sheer willpower and a firm grip, I managed to get the tablet into his mouth and watched triumphantly as he swallowed it—victory, at last.

"Why must you make it so difficult?" I sighed, holding him up as if he'd bested me in a championship fight.

He squirmed out of my hands, landed gracefully on the floor, and promptly groomed himself with exaggerated movements, as if to erase any memory of the indignity he'd just endured.

Shaking my head, I made my way to the bathroom to cleanse the battle wounds on my hands and arms. My arms were a roadmap of scratches, faint red lines crisscrossing my skin as if I'd tangled with a thorn bush. After cleaning myself and slathering on some antiseptic, I wandered into the kitchen in search of lunch.

As I passed the floor-to-ceiling windows, something outside caught my eye. There, by the pool, was Alesha. She sat on the edge, her feet skimming the water's surface. The sun cast a warm, golden glow around her that made the scene feel almost cinematic. Beside her, a bottle of wine stood like a silent companion. In her hand, a glass of deep red shimmered as the sunlight danced through it.

I hadn't seen her at all earlier that day, so she must have just crawled out of bed. She was still in her pyjamas: an oversized shirt that seemed more fitting for a lazy Sunday morning, not the middle of the day. It struck me as odd. Alesha wasn't the type to lounge, let alone sit by the pool drinking alone. She only ever drank in social settings, and even then, it was all about cocktails and group selfies—not a solo glass of wine. The sight of her sitting there, dishevelled and detached, sent a ripple of concern through me.

She set her glass beside the wine bottle. Her movements were unhurried, almost calculated. Then, from a pack I hadn't noticed, she pulled out a cigarette. My eyebrows shot up. A cigarette? Since when did Alesha smoke? The flick of her lighter snapped me out of my thoughts. The small flame illuminated her face briefly before the tip of the cigarette burned to life. Smoke curled upward, wrapping around her like a veil. I stared, half in disbelief. This wasn't the sister I knew.

She picked up her phone and typed with an urgency that seemed out of place in the tranquil setting. It raised a silent alarm. What could have led her to seek comfort at the poolside with a bottle of wine and a pack of cigarettes? Had something happened? Was it the isolation of the last few months? Or something else entirely?

I slipped outside, the warmth of the sun clashing with the cool breeze as I approached the glass pool gate. "Hey, Alesha."

She didn't respond. Her focus remained tethered to her phone as though I didn't exist. Not until I walked over and sat down.

I reached for the wine bottle, turning it in my hands to inspect the label. "Château Palmer," I read out, recognising the name from our parents' wine cellar. Alesha had definitely raided the good stuff. "What's the occasion?"

My question seemed to drift past her as she didn't answer me. Instead, she dialled a number on her phone, then hung up once it reached voicemail. Undeterred, she redialled. Then again. And again.

I grabbed the phone out of her hand mid-dial. "What's going on?"

"Jessie, give it back!" she snapped.

"Not until you tell me what's going on," I said. "You're sitting out here alone, chain-calling someone, drinking Mum and Dad's best wine, and smoking, of all things. Talk to me. What's going on?"

"It's nothing," she muttered.

"Bullshit," I shot back. "This isn't nothing."

There was a moment of silence as she puffed on her smoke. It was clear she was debating whether to confide in me, but eventually, she caved in. "Liam broke up with me."

I was shocked. "What? Why?"

Their relationship had always seemed like one of those

perfect romances. What had started in her first year of uni had blossomed into something that everyone assumed would lead to marriage. Not once did I, or anyone, imagine things would end between them—it was unthinkable.

"Because he found someone else and was cheating on me."

My jaw dropped. "He *what*?"

With a swift motion, she drained the last of the wine from her glass and promptly refilled it. The bottle clinked against the edge of the glass, a subtle betrayal of the tremor in her hands. Watching her, I realised she wasn't taking the breakup lightly. She was resorting to an alcohol-fuelled self-destruction path that seemed out of character for someone who had appeared to have life figured out.

"That's horrible." The words tumbled out of me.

She tilted her head as if my reaction were amusing in some twisted way. "Is it horrible? Like, seriously, is it truly horrible?" She took another drag of her cigarette, her gaze distant.

I frowned. "Of course it's horrible—"

But she cut me off. "Horrible that he didn't love me enough to stay faithful? Horrible that he may not have loved me at all?" She shook her head, letting out a mirthless laugh. "What if love itself is the horrible part? What if it's all just… a lie? Some big, shiny illusion we've all bought into. We chase it, we build our lives around it, but what if there's no such thing as 'the one'? What if we're just gaslighting ourselves into believing it exists? We ignore the red flags, the cracks, the things that don't feel right—all because, somewhere between the lies, we're so desperate to hold onto the idea of love."

I didn't know what to say. She wasn't just questioning Liam or their relationship—she was questioning everything, the entire framework of love and what it meant. It was a dark, cynical spiral, and it scared me.

"Alesha…" I was unsure where to even begin.

"I gave him everything," she continued. "I trusted him. I believed in us. And he just… threw it all away. Like I was nothing." Her fingers tightened around the stem of her wine glass. "How do you come back from that? How do you trust anyone again when the person you thought you'd spend your life with betrays you like that?"

"You don't come back from it all at once," I said. "You do it in pieces. Little by little."

She let out a bitter laugh, one that barely sounded like her. "Little by little?" She shook her head. "What if I don't have any pieces left? What if I'm just… broken?"

Her words left me at a loss. As she plunged deeper into her rant, her thoughts became more tangled, and I was beginning to question her sanity. Clearly, she was drunk.

"How much have you had to drink?" I asked.

"Enough," she answered.

In an uncharacteristic move—maybe in solidarity—I

reached for the open pack of cigarettes on the pool deck and pulled out one. With a flick of her lighter, I lit it, the smoke swirling around us.

"Maybe you should cut yourself off after this glass. Getting drunk this early in the day isn't great," I suggested between puffs, trying to mask my concern.

A gust of wind whipped my hair across my face in a wild frenzy. Alesha didn't seem to notice. She took another long sip of her wine, her eyes fixed on some distant point. Then, without warning, she dropped a bomb.

"I'm pregnant."

My eyes widened in disbelief, my mouth agape, words failed me.

Pregnant. Alesha was *pregnant*.

The gravity of her admission momentarily paralysed my thoughts, shifting my focus from her to the cigarette between her fingers.

"What?" I finally said. "You're pregnant?"

She nodded.

Acting on pure instinct, I plucked the cigarette from her hand, tossing it aside where it fizzled out in the water splashed by her earlier movements. "Are you crazy?" The words burst out before I could hold them back. "You shouldn't be smoking—or drinking—if you're pregnant."

"Oh, so now you're the expert on my life?" she snapped.

"I just found out, Jessie. And it's not like I planned for this to happen. Do you think I wanted any of this? The breakup? The baby?"

"No, I don't think that. But, Alesha, this changes everything. You have to start taking care of yourself—for the baby."

"Jessie, I don't even know if I want to keep it."

I didn't know what to say. There was no manual for this, no perfect response. So, I sat there, the cigarette I'd forgotten about between my fingers.

Alesha sighed. "You know, I've always done things by the book. Never smoked, never partied too hard, always stayed on the straight and narrow. And for what? The second I find out I'm pregnant, it's like my life flips upside down. Everything I thought I had figured out just… crumbled." She paused, a frown creasing her brow. "What will our parents think?"

I didn't sugarcoat it. "Well, first of all, they're going to be shocked. But, Alesha, remember—they're our parents. Initial reactions aside, they'll come around. Their love for you doesn't come with strings attached. They'll stand by you no matter what. I'm sure of it."

"I don't know if I can do this," she said.

I tried to understand the full extent of her dilemma as I stubbed out my cigarette on the stone tiles. "So, are you seriously considering not keeping the baby?"

"I don't want to," she admitted. "But the idea of having an abortion terrifies me just as much. I couldn't live with myself if I ended it. I'm stuck—I feel trapped."

Her honesty floored me. Alesha had always been the composed one, the sister who had her act together. Seeing her unravel like this left me reeling.

"What does Liam think?" I asked, hoping he might offer her some support.

"Liam," she spat, her voice dripping with disdain. Her eyes glistened with unshed tears. "He doesn't even know. I've been calling him, texting him, trying to tell him, but he's ignoring me. All I wanted was to tell him in person or at least over the phone. I wasn't going to leave some cold, detached voicemail or text, but it doesn't matter. He's ghosted me."

Before I could respond, she stood abruptly, grabbed her wine glass, and drained the rest in one swift gulp. Her sudden movements startled me.

"Alesha…"

She hurled the glass into the garden, where it shattered with a sharp crack.

I froze. "What the hell, Alesha!"

Without answering, she leapt into the pool.

I waited, expecting her to resurface. But as seconds ticked by, the surface remained undisturbed except for a few lazy ripples. My stomach knotted with unease.

"Alesha!" I called, standing. "Cut it out! Don't be stupid!"

Still, nothing.

Bubbles broke the surface, and my heart raced. Was she screaming underwater?

Panic surged through me. My hands trembled as a hundred horrifying scenarios played out in my mind. What if this wasn't just her being dramatic? What if this was something more— something darker? Alesha wasn't herself, and her erratic behaviour had reached a boiling point.

"Alesha!" I shouted. "This isn't funny! Come up right now!"

When she still didn't surface, I didn't wait. Adrenaline fuelled my movements as I kicked off my shoes and dived into the water. The cold water took my breath as I opened my eyes to the murky blur of chlorine and sunlight.

I spotted her—motionless at the bottom, her hair fanned out like a dark halo around her face. My chest tightened, a scream threatening to escape. My thoughts screamed louder than the silence around me. *No, no, no.* I propelled myself downwards, my arms reaching for her, my heart hammering.

Grabbing her arm, I yanked her upward with all the strength I could muster, breaking the surface with a gasp. Brushing the wet hair from my face, I confronted her. "What were you thinking?! Are you out of your mind?"

She coughed and spluttered as she leaned against the pool

edge, gasping for air. "I wasn't trying to…" Her voice was barely audible over her ragged breaths. "I just wanted to feel something. Anything."

"Alesha, you scared the hell out of me," I yelled. "I thought—" I swallowed hard, unable to finish the thought. The idea of losing her, of pulling her out too late, was too much to bear. "I thought you were trying to—"

"I feel so embarrassed. I thought he was the one. How wrong was I? He fooled me."

The rawness in her voice wasn't only heartbreak. It was the kind of despair that could pull a person under if they weren't careful. The cold water around us seemed insignificant compared to the storm raging within her.

"He's not answering my calls or responding to my texts," she sobbed, wiping her tears with the back of her hand.

The truth needed to be said, no matter how harsh it sounded. "He probably thinks you're obsessed about the breakup. Or worse, a psycho. I doubt he's going to answer any of your calls or texts… like, ever." I paused. "You need to stop reaching out. No more calls. No more texts. No more chasing him. And whatever you do, don't tell him you're pregnant."

"Why not?" she asked.

"Because he's already made his choice. He's chosen to remove himself from your life. If he had an ounce of decency, he wouldn't be ignoring you like this. It's his loss, not yours." I locked eyes with her, willing her to believe me. "This only shows his true character. He doesn't deserve to know. Don't give him the satisfaction or the power."

Her sobs grew heavier. "I don't think I'm cut out to be a single mother," she choked out between cries.

"Why not?" I asked.

"How will I manage?"

"Things will work out. I promise they will. The key is to stay positive and believe in yourself. You're so much stronger than you think. I know you'll be an amazing mother."

"How do you know?" she asked.

"Because I know you. You've always been stronger than you realise. Besides, you won't be doing this alone. Mum and Dad will be here to support you every step of the way."

"What are people going to say when they find out?" She shook her head, tears still falling.

"Who cares what anyone says? Own it."

"I just wish things had turned out differently. I wish he hadn't cheated and left."

"You deserve better than him," I said.

She shrugged. "Maybe I do, maybe I don't." The cryptic response was drenched in her self-doubt.

"You know what?" I said, determined to lift her spirit, even for a little while. "I just remembered—Conrad invited us to his parents' place for a dinner party tonight."

Her eyebrows rose slightly, a flicker of interest lighting up her otherwise despondent expression. "He invited us?"

"Yep," I replied. "It'll be good for you. It'll be good for both of us. We need to get ready if we want to make it on time."

She smiled, and it gave me a sliver of hope. She might not have been ready to let go of her heartbreak, but the prospect of something—anything—other than pain seemed to stir within her. "Okay."

We climbed out of the pool, the immediate chill of the air prickling my arms and sending goosebumps across my skin. Our wet clothes clung to us as water dripped, pooling on the ground. After I grabbed my shoes, we headed for the warmth of the house.

I hurried to my ensuite. The prospect of a hot shower to thaw my chilled skin was an oasis of comfort. The icy tiles under my bare feet made me wince as I fiddled with the lever on the shower, willing the water to heat up faster. Steam curled faintly into the air, but the cold was unbearable. Impatience got the better of me. Unable to wait another second, I stepped in fully clothed, the first blast of warm water hitting me.

Piece by piece, I peeled off the drenched layers, wringing water from them before hanging them over the glass door. The warm water cascaded over me. I simply stood there, letting the heat seep into me, but my thoughts wandered. They always did, drifting back to Zack.

I missed him. I missed the way his laugh could brighten

my worst days, the way his arms felt like the safest place in the world, the way he made me feel as though I was whole, as though nothing was missing. And how he made everything—good or bad—feel bearable. Zack had been so full of life, so spontaneous and playful. He'd once sneaked into the bathroom while I was showering, joining me fully clothed.

"What are you doing?" I'd exclaimed, half laughing, half exasperated, as he stood there under the spray, clothes and all, water dripping off his hair and nose.

"Making sure you're not having all the fun without me," he'd replied with a mischievous glint in his eye before pulling me into a kiss.

I'd barely had time to react before he grabbed the handheld shower hose and turned it on me, spraying water in every direction. Shampoo bottles flew everywhere, my protests drowned out by his laughter and my own as we turned the bathroom into a watery battleground.

That was Zack—always making moments bigger, brighter, and more chaotic in the best way possible. My heart ached as the memory faded, leaving only the echo of his laughter and the hollow space where he used to be. His smile, his voice, his touch—it all felt so vivid, so close, and yet impossibly far away.

Finally, I pulled myself back to the present. The once-soothing water had turned scalding. I reached for the lever, turning it off. Wrapped in a towel, I stepped out. The mirror was fogged up so I could barely see what was staring back at me—a ghost of who I used to be, a person I hardly recognised some days.

I padded into my room, water dripping from my hair and pooling lightly on the marble floor. My eyes scanned the space, noting how neatly everything was packed away. Suitcases lined the wall, stacked with all my essentials for the move to Adelaide. That was when it hit me—I hadn't left out an outfit for tonight's dinner party at the Baltimores.

I chuckled at my oversight, then crouched next to the luggage. "Of course," I muttered.

With no other choice, I rummaged through the packed suitcases and bags. One by one, I searched through carefully folded clothes, trying not to disrupt the Tetris-like precision I'd worked so hard to achieve. After some digging, I unearthed a colourful cocktail dress and black heels.

"Perfect," I murmured, laying them out on the bed. I slipped into the dress and stood in front of the mirror. It wasn't actually the perfect choice, but it would work.

With my hair still damp, I grabbed the blow dryer and set to work, styling it into loose waves. Once satisfied, I moved on to my makeup—nothing heavy, just enough to add a little glow and highlight my features. A swipe of mascara here, eyeliner there, a touch of blush there, and a hint of lip gloss to finish.

As I was putting away the last of my makeup, Alesha walked in. She had clearly gone all out for the evening. Her pink-

and-green floral cocktail dress wasn't too revealing but looked amazing. She'd paired it with pink heels, and her hair was styled in soft curls.

"Wow," I said, giving her a once-over. "You clean up nicely."

She grinned, twirling slightly to show off the dress. "Not bad, right? I figured if we're going to the Baltimores, I might as well look the part."

"You look great." I couldn't help but notice how heavily contoured her makeup was, as if it were armour masking her personal turmoil.

"And you," she said, motioning towards me. "Not bad yourself. I thought you'd packed away everything?"

"I did," I admitted. "Had to dig through half my stuff to find this. I didn't want to show up in trackies."

"Now that would've been a look," she teased.

9

Conrad met us at the entrance. "Right on time," he said, holding the gate open.

He escorted us through the house down to the backyard, which had been transformed into an enchanting setting for the dinner party. A long, elegant table stretched across the yard, adorned with sparkling glassware, gold-accented tableware, candles, lanterns, and fresh floral arrangements that looked as if they had been taken from a botanical garden. Delicate roses, peonies, and sprigs of greenery added a final touch to the table.

Above us, festoon lights were strung high, casting a warm glow over the yard. Strategically placed outdoor heaters radiated pockets of warmth, ensuring the cold evening air wouldn't send shivers through the guests and dampen the festivities.

The scents of mouthwatering dishes wafted through the air from the catering service stationed discreetly at the side of the yard. Judging by the aroma alone, this wasn't going to be a standard dinner—it was a curated culinary experience, no expense spared.

Guests arrived one by one, their finest attire rivalling the elegance of the setting. For once, Alesha and I didn't feel overdressed—or underdressed. It was a rare balance to strike, but somehow, we managed to blend into the crowd.

We took our seats at the table, positioned between Esmeralda and Conrad. I couldn't help but notice that there were a few extra seats compared to the lunch I'd attended a few weeks earlier.

Waiters moved along the table, pausing to pour champagne into the flutes set out before us. But as soon as they moved on, Alesha leaned closer to me. "Switch glasses with me when you finish yours," she whispered. "I don't want the Baltimores to suspect anything."

I glanced at her glass and understood her dilemma. Alesha couldn't exactly decline drinks without it raising questions she wasn't prepared to answer. This switcheroo was her way of deflecting attention while keeping up appearances. I gave her a slight nod of agreement, glad she was following my advice to avoid drinking.

With the exchange planned, we raised our glasses, joining

in the collective toast and clinking champagne flutes with the other guests.

And then Olivia arrived.

Her entrance, though not precisely punctual, didn't go unnoticed. She gracefully took her place beside Conrad. Wearing a sleek black dress and coat, it seemed she wasn't changing her style or colour anytime soon.

Alesha leaned towards me, her voice low. "Is Olivia seeing Conrad?"

I, too, couldn't help but wonder about the nature of Olivia's relationship with Conrad after Mark's death. The seating arrangement, similar to the lunch's, could have easily sparked speculation. Still, I reminded myself of the facts.

"No," I whispered. "She's taken over for Mark and sits closer. That's all it is."

As the evening wore on, plates of exquisitely crafted dishes were brought out to the table at pre-arranged intervals. My appetite wasn't great—as usual—so I picked at most things, taking small bites here and there.

Later, Alesha and I found ourselves immersed in conversation with other guests, some of whom were new to us. We chatted with Conrad's aunt and uncle, whose real estate holdings in Sydney were beyond comprehension. Cousins and their partners, as well as family friends—all successful individuals who had left their indelible mark on the business world—shared their stories and experiences with us.

In a smooth motion, I exchanged my sister's champagne glass for mine without anyone noticing.

After knocking back the drink, I excused myself and ventured to the bathroom. In a dimly lit hallway of the Baltimore home, I rounded a corner, stopping short. Déjà vu washed over me.

Olivia. Again.

She stood in the hallway. Her gaze locked onto mine with unnerving precision, the tension between us thick enough to choke on. My heart raced as I braced for whatever was coming.

"What are you even doing here again, Jessie?"

I sighed, already weary of this familiar song and dance. "No, not this again." I wasn't in the mood to rehash whatever grievances or suspicions she had.

She stared at me.

"I was invited. The Baltimores are like a second family. I have every right to be here."

"Not when I'm around," she snapped. "I know you knew what Zack was up to. He was scared the truth would come out—and then Mark died in that car accident." Her eyes narrowed. "Suspicious, don't you think?"

This wasn't just grief anymore—it was fixation. Maybe even a psychotic break. Her obsession with Mark's death had consumed her completely.

"Olivia, you need to get help. Grief—what you're going through—it can make you see things that aren't there. You've built this idea in your head, but it's not real," I urged in the calmest tone I could.

My words didn't land.

Her frustration boiled over, and before I could react, she shoved me. My body jerked backwards, and I stumbled, crashing into the bathroom door. Pain exploded through my back as the doorknob jabbed into my spine. A sharp gasp escaped my lips as the pain shot through me.

When I looked up, Olivia was already retreating down the hallway. She didn't look back—not even a glance. I clutched the doorframe for support, my vision swimming as I tried to process what had just happened. It was clear now—whatever darkness Olivia was battling, it was winning, and nothing I could say was going to pull her out of it.

Slumping down onto the cold bathroom tiles, I waited for the pain to subside. My mind raced, replaying her words, her actions. What was I supposed to do with this? Should I tell Conrad? Could I even trust anyone to take Olivia seriously when she was unravelling like this?

"Hey, what are you doing on the floor?" Alesha loomed over me, her figure silhouetted by the dim hallway lights, a glass of champagne in hand. "Please tell me you're not drunk."

"Of course I'm not." Grimacing, I began the awkward

process of sitting up. "Olivia pushed me."

Her eyebrows shot up. "She *pushed* you? Why?"

Settling against the wall, I reached for the glass in her hand and took it. The champagne was suddenly more appealing as a numbing agent than as a beverage.

"She's delusional," I muttered, taking a small sip. The champagne, far from the soothing elixir I had hoped for, left a harsh, bitter taste in my mouth. "She thinks Zack was blackmailing Mark."

"That's ridiculous. There is *no way* Zack would've done something like that," she said as she sat beside me.

Her words carried weight. Alesha had known Zack longer than I had. They were the same age, classmates through school, their lives intersecting often even if their social circles didn't always align. If anyone else could vouch for his character, it was her.

"I told her that," I said before taking another sip, "but she won't listen. It's as though she's made up her mind and nothing I say will change it."

"If she had a problem with Zack, then why is she attacking you?"

"She thinks I know more than I'm saying—and probably that I played a part in it because I was with Zack," I replied. "To her, that makes me guilty by association."

"That's ridiculous. Do you want me to talk to her? Because

I don't appreciate her accusing and attacking you—let alone dragging Zack's name through the mud. He's not even here to defend himself," she offered—a protective instinct I appreciated.

Shaking my head, I replied, "I don't think it'll make any difference. Olivia seems… She's lost. Lost in her grief, in her anger. It's like she needs someone to blame."

Alesha frowned. "That still doesn't give her the right to lash out at you."

"I know. But what can I do? She's clearly spiralling, and I don't think she's ready to hear reason. Every time I see her, it's as though she's further and further away from reality."

Alesha stared into the distance, her lips pressed into a thin line as if debating her next move. "Do you think she'll stop?"

"Who knows?" I sighed.

"If it happens again, you can't let her get away with it."

It wasn't like Alesha and I had ever been particularly close. In fact, I couldn't remember the last time we'd had a conversation that wasn't surface-level or polite. But today felt… different.

"You know…" I started, hesitating as I shifted the champagne glass in my hands, "it's strange. We've never really spent much time together like this." I veered into a topic that had always been on my mind. "I always thought you hated me. You avoided me so much when we were younger. Did you hate me?"

"What? No," she said. "I guess… I was just jealous of you."

I blinked. "Jealous? Of me? Why?"

"You seemed to have everything figured out, you know? You were excelling in school, surrounded by friends, and then there was Zack… You always seemed so happy. It felt like life fell into place for you, like everything was effortless. And I—well, I was just… me."

Jealousy.

That had been the silent wedge between us all these years. I'd always assumed she was distant, that our sisterly relationship was doomed because we were different. But now, hearing her admit this, I realised how much I'd misunderstood her.

"I had no idea you felt that way," I said. "I'm sorry if it seemed like my life was perfect. It wasn't—then or now. Sure, I did well in school, but I had no idea what I wanted to do with my life. I was completely lost. Being with Zack made me happy. I loved him so much, and he was the one thing in my life that felt certain. But after losing him…" I couldn't finish the sentence because his absence was impossible to articulate.

"I guess I was too caught up in my own insecurities to see that. I'm sorry, Jessie. It was stupid of me to feel jealous. I let it get in the way of us having a real relationship."

"It's okay." Her apology caught me off guard, but it wasn't unwelcome. "Honestly, I'm just glad we're talking about this now. Better late than never, right?"

She smiled. "Right."

For the first time in what felt like forever, I felt like I had an actual sister—someone I could talk to, someone who understood me in the same way I was beginning to understand her. We'd bridged the gap that had separated us for years. Silently, I prayed it wouldn't change and that this newfound understanding between us would only grow stronger, that we could finally be more than siblings—that we could be friends.

Rising to my feet, an unwelcome sensation gripped my back—a throbbing pain that seemed to worsen with movement. Wincing, I pressed my hand to the spot, fingers brushing against a tender area that felt swollen beneath the fabric of my dress.

"Is your back still hurting?" Alesha asked.

"Worse now," I admitted.

"Do you want me to have a look at it?" She offered as she stood.

Agreeing, I turned slightly, pulling my hair over one shoulder so she could unzip my dress just enough to inspect the area.

"It's swollen," she observed. "You're definitely going to have a nasty bruise. Do you think you should go to the hospital and get it checked out?"

The mere mention stirred unease in me. "No, I hate hospitals," I said quickly. The thought of sitting in a crowded waiting room, surrounded by sick people and recycled air, made my stomach sink. The last thing I wanted was to walk out with something worse than a bruise.

"What if it's something serious?" she asked.

"I don't know." I sighed, hoping the issue would resolve itself without the need for medical intervention. "If it gets worse, we'll go. But right now, I just want to get through this dinner and go home."

"It's your call. But don't wait too long if it doesn't improve."

She zipped the dress, and I adjusted the neckline of it. "We'll head home shortly."

As I stumbled down the corridor, staggering in my heels, Alesha's voice pierced my concentration. I turned to face her, wondering what she wanted.

"Jessie, this way." She waved to me.

I let out a soft laugh, shaking my head as I corrected my course. "Thanks for letting me wander aimlessly," I teased, heading back towards her.

But as I moved, something caught my eye—a sliver of warm light spilling through the gap of a set of double doors left slightly ajar. My steps slowed, curiosity pulling me closer like a magnet, though I already knew what lay beyond the doors:

Zack's music room.

I hesitated before easing one of the doors open, the soft creak of the hinges breaking the silence. The room was just as I remembered it: untouched, sacred, preserved, as if a piece of him still lingered there.

At the heart of the room stood Zack's grand piano. It beckoned me, drawing me closer as though it carried a whisper of him. My fingers traced the smooth, polished edge of the piano. Zack wasn't just a pianist; he had been a musical prodigy who started playing at the age of five after his mother signed him up for lessons.

But Zack hadn't been confined by the boundaries of classical music. He'd explored contemporary pieces and even composed his own works. Each piece he created was a part of him, a melody born from the deepest corners of his being. He'd had a deep love of music, an enduring passion that defined him. To Zack, music was more than a collection of notes and rhythms; it was a language, a means of connecting with the world around him on a level that words alone could never reach.

On the days when the pressures of university or his part-time job at the recording studio didn't claim him, Zack would escape here, to this very room. It was his sanctuary, a place where music flowed freely. Sometimes I'd linger quietly outside the door, listening to him play, until I finally gave in and interrupted his reverie.

"What masterpiece are you working on today?" I'd tease, stepping into the room with a playful grin.

Zack would pause mid-note, his fingers resting lightly on the keys as he looked at me with that warm, affectionate smile.

"None other than the next world hit."

I'd draw closer, finding my usual spot beside him on the bench. He'd always greet me with a kiss, his lips brushing mine as if sealing me into his world.

"You know how much I love you, right?" It wasn't just his words—it was the way he said them, like a promise, a truth so deep it didn't need embellishment.

When Zack was working on a composition, he kept a pencil and notepad perched on the edge of the piano. He would transcribe his musical notation so he wouldn't forget or lose that creative spark. His dedication and passion inspired everyone around him—especially me.

Lyric writing, though not his primary focus, was a different kind of magic. It brought a collaborative energy to his process, one that often drew me into his creative orbit. Zack had this unique way of drawing inspiration from the poetry books that cluttered his living space. Each verse he read seemed to ignite new ideas, fuelling his creative process.

When it came to testing these lyrics, I became his willing accomplice. He'd play and I'd sing, my voice breathing life into the words he'd crafted. And as we worked together, I found myself contributing more than just my voice. Emboldened by the atmosphere of creativity, I'd spontaneously add a verse or tweak a line here and there. Zack would gratefully capture the additions I made.

I loved singing, but I loved Zack's passion for music even more. Watching him pour his heart into every note, every lyric, was mesmerising. I wished I had a fraction of his talent, a skill that would reflect a part of my soul. But it wasn't jealousy. It was a privilege, really, to be part of his world, to share in his passion, even if I couldn't replicate it.

Taking a seat at the grand piano, I lifted the cover and softly ran my fingers across the smooth keys. I swallowed back the tears, closing my eyes, letting myself get lost in the stillness of the room.

I could almost feel him beside me. It was as if Zack were sitting here again, playing one of his compositions. The air seemed charged with his presence as his music filled my mind.

But the pain came swiftly after, like a crashing wave, shattering the illusion. He was gone. I would never hear him play again, never see him play again.

A single tear broke free, tracing a silent path down my cheek. Then another. I wasn't even sure how many tears I had left for Zack, but every time I thought I'd reached the end, more came.

"Jessie, are you okay?" Alesha's voice snapped me back to reality.

I lifted the glass of champagne to my lips and drained the last drops, trying to steady myself. "Yeah," I lied.

She sat next to me and asked, "How do you feel about Zack's passing?"

"Gutted," escaped my lips, barely capturing the enormity of what I felt. "I'm trying my best to move on, but…" I paused, struggling to find the words. "I wish we'd had more time. I wish he hadn't left the way he did. I miss him so much it physically hurts."

"Is everything okay?" Conrad's voice startled us both. He stood in the doorway.

Alesha nodded.

He strolled into the room and stood next to the piano. "You know, my parents refuse to sell the piano even though Zack's gone. None of us play, but they want it to stay here. I'm actually glad they haven't sold it. It feels like… like a piece of him is still here."

I ran my fingers lightly over the keys again, as though willing Zack's music to rise up from the silence. "I wish he was still here."

"Me too," Conrad replied. "I miss him every day." The moment hung between us until Conrad broke the silence, lightly touching my shoulder. "Come on. Dessert's being served."

We rejoined the party. Conrad grabbed us each another glass of champagne as waiters began placing decadent desserts in front of the guests—a tower of profiteroles drizzled with caramel, individual pavlovas topped with jewel-like fruit, and slices of rich chocolate torte.

As midnight drew near, Alesha and I headed home. The

champagne had done its job, leaving my steps unsteady and my thoughts pleasantly blurred. I was well past tipsy, teetering dangerously close to outright drunk.

When we opened the front door, Shane was there, the kitten perched in his arms like a regal prince surveying his kingdom. "Where did you two disappear to?"

The kitten, as if understanding Shane's question, stared up at us as if expecting a story.

"The Baltimores' dinner party," Alesha replied, removing her heels and padding towards the living room.

I, on the other hand, barely managed to haul myself upstairs. My limbs felt heavier than usual, and every step reminded me of how much champagne I'd consumed. By the time I reached my room, I was ready to collapse.

Shane followed with the kitten in his arms.

I flopped onto my bed, the room swaying gently around me. It was as if I were floating on a cloud of champagne-induced euphoria, where everything took on a dreamy quality. But even through the buzz, the ache in my back flared up, a not-so-subtle reminder of my earlier altercation with Olivia. I shifted, trying to find a comfortable position, but every move seemed to aggravate the soreness.

Shane lingered by the doorway, a silhouette against the dim light. "You okay?" He stepped inside and placed the kitten on the floor before switching on the light.

I sighed, rolling onto my side. "My back is killing me, but I'll survive."

"Why's your back hurting?"

Through the haze, I muddled out an explanation of the showdown with Olivia, recounting how she'd shoved me hard enough to send me colliding with the bathroom doorknob. My words slurred slightly.

"She pushed you?" Shane seemed surprised. His tone shifted, surprise giving way to concern. "Sounds like her husband's death really messed her up."

"That's the only thing that makes sense. But I still can't figure out why she's accusing Zack of blackmail and her husband's death. It's like she's clinging to this wild idea to make sense of everything." I tried to focus.

"Keep your distance from her. Olivia sounds like she's on the edge."

"I wish I could, but she keeps cornering me." I sighed. "You're in real estate—ever hear anything sketchy about a property developer named Mark? Could he have been involved in something dodgy? Anything someone might have used against him?"

Shane scratched his head. "Mark is a common name… Can't say the name rings any immediate bells, but let's be real— the property world is full of shady deals, backdoor negotiations, and money laundering. If someone wanted leverage on a developer, they wouldn't have to look far." He paused. "Are you saying Zack might've known something?"

"No!" I blurted. "Zack would never… I mean, I don't know. But blackmail? That's not who he was."

Shane raised his hands in mock surrender. "Okay, okay. Don't bite my head off. I'm just saying—Olivia might be making things up. Not that I know her."

I sat up. "You're probably right."

He leaned back against the wall. "Don't let her accusation get to you. She's clearly not thinking straight." Then he moved to sit beside me, wrapping an arm around my shoulders.

"You're right. I can't let her get to me." Rising from the bed, I crossed the room to the full-length mirror mounted on my wall. I tugged down the zipper of my dress, letting the fabric fall away from my shoulders as I tried to angle myself to see the damage. "Does it look bad?"

He came over and inspected it closely. "It's definitely swollen. Might just be a bruised muscle, but… it could be worse. Maybe a cracked vertebra."

"Thanks for the reassurance, Dr. Shane," I said.

"You should get it checked," he pressed, his voice low. "Better safe than sorry."

"I'll think about it," I replied, sitting back on the edge of the bed. The night had dredged up deep emotions I couldn't quite explain. "I just want the night to be over."

The kitten, who had been quietly watching, leapt onto the bed and padded over to me.

"Are you okay?" Shane asked, having picked up on my mood.

I couldn't bring myself to reveal the exact reason for my despair—Zack. Instead, I opted for a more digestible explanation for my mood. "I'll be okay. It's the whole Olivia thing. I don't want another run-in with her."

"We're heading back to Adelaide tomorrow. You won't have to see her again," he said.

10

Shane and I loaded the suitcases and bags into my car, transforming my once-cosy room into a barren space. It was a blank canvas I hadn't seen before because it was always filled with my belongings, bringing life into the room.

I took one last glance before I picked up my handbag and reached for the kitten, perched on the edge of the bed, and scooped him up. Heading downstairs, I found Shane and Alesha waiting by the car. Their conversation drifted towards me as I approached them, then their attention shifted to me.

"Ready to go?" Shane asked.

"Sure am." I smiled as I opened the back passenger door, then carefully placed the kitten into the pet carrier we'd bought for the trip back. My handbag, with all my essential items, I shoved behind my seat.

As I closed the door, my phone chimed in my pocket. Pulling it out, I unlocked the screen to find a text from my parents. It was a string of photos, accompanied by their signature caption: GUESS WHERE WE ARE? Their road trip across Australia had become an endless source of entertainment for us. Even from kilometres away, they found ways to pull us into their adventures, challenging us to decode the locations of their latest stops.

Alesha, standing a few feet away, was already looking at her phone. I knew she'd received the same message because her brows were furrowed. "I can't figure out where they are," she muttered, holding out the phone for Shane to see.

I glanced at the photos they sent, trying to decipher their location. One was of them in front of some dome-like rock formations while the other two were of a waterfall and gorge. These weren't just any landscapes—they were iconic, unmistakable, and I recognised them.

"They're in the Kimberleys," I said.

She studied the photos again and said, "It looks incredible. I wish I were with them."

"That makes two of us." I'd always wanted to visit the Kimberley region in Western Australia.

"Let's hit the road," I said to Shane.

As we said our goodbyes, I was consumed with sadness. Alesha and I shared a heartfelt hug. It was an unusual moment.

Growing up, we hadn't spent much time together—there'd always been this unspoken distance between us—but that had changed over the last few days. I hadn't thought that would ever be possible. I knew I was going to miss her.

"Keep in touch, okay?!" she called after us as we climbed into the car.

"I will!" I shouted back, waving one last time before pulling out of the driveway.

The drive back to Adelaide seemed faster than our trip to Sydney. Perhaps it was because I couldn't wait to return and be in my own space again—my new life.

"Home sweet home," I murmured as we walked through the door of my apartment. The place welcomed me like an old friend.

I set the pet carrier on the floor, noticing the kitten curiously looking around.

"Come on, let's get the rest of my things," I said to Shane, heading for the door.

One by one, we hauled each suitcase and bag from the car to the apartment. Each trip felt as if we were unpacking pieces of my old life, bringing them into my new one. We stowed my stuff in one of the spare rooms, transforming it into a temporary storage space. Once the last bag was inside, I released the kitten from the carrier, letting him explore his new surroundings.

"Thanks for helping me get all this back home," I said.

"Anytime." He smiled. "So, have you thought of a name for this little fella yet?"

I shrugged, watching the kitten prowl the living room, sniffing the floor and furniture, and cast nervous glances. "Nope."

"What about Lucky?" he suggested.

I laughed, crossing my arms. "Lucky? It sounds a bit feminine, don't you think?"

"Not necessarily," he countered. "And come on, think about it—he *is* lucky. He escaped that eagle, didn't he?"

"Well, true," I admitted. "But isn't calling a black cat 'Lucky' kind of ironic? I mean, aren't they supposed to be bad luck or something?"

"Only if you believe in superstitions," Shane said. "In some cultures, they're considered a lucky omen. They're thought to bring good fortune and protection. Besides, has he brought you any misfortunes so far?"

I stared at the little furball standing in a sunlit spot on the floor, looking anything but ominous. "Lucky, huh? I guess it suits him." The name grew on me and, given the circumstance of his miraculous survival, felt right. "Lucky it is, then."

"See? Told you it was a good name."

I smirked at him. "Don't get too full of yourself. You just got lucky with Lucky."

As Shane prepared to leave, he kissed me and said, "I'll

call you tomorrow."

"Drive safely," I said, walking him to the door.

* * *

Days had passed since my return from Sydney. My spare room, once cluttered with unopened suitcases and bags, had been returned to its usual state of order. With the last suitcase unpacked, it was time to indulge in a well-deserved rest. I kicked back on the couch, a glass of wine in hand, and Lucky cozied up beside me, purring.

The television played quietly as I sipped my wine. I'd found some peace over the past few days, even though the dull throb in my lower back told a different story. The bruise had bloomed into a smear of violet and sickly yellow, a fading but undeniable imprint of the confrontation I'd escaped.

As I aimlessly surfed through television channels, my phone vibrated against the coffee table, interrupting my quest for entertainment. Lindsey's name flashed on the screen. I hadn't spoken to her for a couple of weeks.

"Hey," I answered it, and she immediately launched into her exciting news.

"Jessie, my birthday is coming up this Saturday!" she exclaimed. "I'm planning a big night out. You have to come! It's going to be epic! Drinks, dancing, the whole vibe."

Her invitation took me by surprise.

"Like nightclubbing?" I asked. The concept felt foreign, not because I'd never been around crowds, but because I'd never liked being boxed in by them. Give me an open-air music festival any day. The sheer thought of squeezing into a dark, overcrowded club with flashing lights and no escape route made me nervous.

I'd only gone a few times when Zack had a DJ gig at a nightclub—and even then, I'd always preferred house parties, where he played to smaller crowds.

I could still picture him behind the DJ setup, his head bobbing to the beat, a small smile playing on his lips as he watched the crowd lose themselves in the music. It wasn't just entertainment; it was his passion, and it was magnetic.

"Jessie?" Lindsey broke my thoughts. "You there?"

"Yeah, I'm here," I said. "Sorry, I zoned out for a second."

"So, what do you think? Are you in?"

"I don't know, Lindsey…"

"Oh, come on! One night out. It'll be fun," she said.

Maybe… it was time to step outside of my comfort zone, try something different. "All right," I said finally. "I'm in. But just so you know, I'm counting on you to protect me from any cringe-worthy dance moves."

She squealed with delight. "You're the best! It's going to be amazing. I promise. I'll swing by your place Saturday afternoon, and we can get ready together."

* * *

On Saturday, just before four in the afternoon, my apartment buzzer went off. I hurried to answer it. It was Lindsey. Minutes later, she was at my door, all smiles and bubbling with joy about her birthday celebration. She wore a pair of jeans and a simple shirt—rather casual for someone about to embark on a grand night.

"Hey, Jessie!" She greeted me with a hug. "Ready to make this night unforgettable?"

I couldn't help but mirror her energy. "Absolutely. Happy birthday!"

"Thank you! I'm super excited," Lindsey said. From her oversized tote slung over her shoulder, she pulled out a bottle of champagne and held it up like a trophy. "Let's kick start this celebration."

I took the bottle from her with a laugh. "I like your style."

When we made our way into the kitchen, I grabbed a couple of champagne glasses from the cupboard while Lindsey set her bag on one of the dining chairs.

"So, here's the plan," Lindsey began. "I've booked a reservation for four at a restaurant by the marina—it's a short walk from here—then we hit the nightclubs in the city. A few more of my friends will be meeting us there."

"Great!" I said, popping open the bottle. I poured the champagne into the glasses, handing one to Lindsey.

"I've invited John—you remember him, right? The guy we met on campus?" she said before taking a sip of her champagne.

I nodded. "Yeah, I remember him. The cute one."

She grinned. "That's the one. He's coming tonight! We've been seeing each other for almost a month now. Can you believe it? After being single for ages, I was starting to think I'd never find the right guy. But John's different."

I opened my mouth to share my own news about Shane but held off. Our relationship was still so new, so delicate. Part of me wanted to savour it for a little longer. I didn't want to kill the thrill of a new relationship.

"And he's going to bring his friend along too," she continued. "His name's Sebastian. Super nice guy."

Lindsey placed her champagne glass on the counter and pulled items from her bag. Out came makeup, jewellery, and not one, not two, but *three* dresses, each one more glamorous than the last.

"Okay," she said, holding them up one by one. "Help me out here. Which one do you like the most?" It was clear she was determined to look her best.

I studied her options carefully. The first dress, a short metallic silver number, practically screamed, "Look at me!"—too flashy for my taste. The second was a colourful sequined piece that looked like a disco ball in fabric form. Then there was the third option—a short, black, sparkly dress. It had an understated elegance, the kind that made a statement without trying too hard. It was classy, and the way it would contrast against her burgundy hair made it the obvious winner.

"That one," I said, pointing at the black dress. "It's stunning, and it suits you perfectly."

Lindsey grinned, holding up the dress. "You think?"

"Absolutely," I replied.

"This one it is, then."

Then it was my turn.

We went to my walk-in wardrobe—much smaller than the one I'd had at my parents' place but still overflowing with an array of clothes and accessories.

Lindsey stepped inside, her jaw dropping as she took in the sight. "My goodness! I've never seen so many clothes anywhere other than a store."

"And yet, I still don't think I have enough." I sighed, knowing I could never satisfy my hunger for clothes and fashion. It was a guilty pleasure I indulged in every so often—and when I did, it was beyond the norm—though I hadn't in a long time.

Lindsey shook her head, laughing. "You have a problem, Jessie. But I love it."

Together, we scoured my collection, trying to find the perfect outfit for the night. After tossing aside countless dresses that were too casual, too formal, or just not *the one,* we settled on a short, colourful dress and paired it with black stilettos.

With our outfits chosen, we moved to hair and makeup. My usual makeup gave way to something more dramatic—winged eyeliner, shimmering eyeshadow, and a cherry lipstick. Lindsey opted for a sultry smoky eye that made her blue eyes pop.

Once we were ready, in high spirits, we grabbed our clutches and headed out the door.

As we approached the entrance of the restaurant, I spotted two guys waiting outside. John was one of them, and he looked as good as he had the day we met him, with his dark hair styled to perfection and a smile that drew you in. The guy next to him was, I assumed, his friend Sebastian. He was slightly taller, with light brown hair and an athletic build that suggested he was into sports. He was the definition of flawless in the looks department.

Lindsey led the way with the kind of confidence that lights up a path. "Hi, John. I'm not sure if you remember, but this is my friend Jessie."

John extended his hand towards me. "Of course, it's great to see you again."

"And this is Seb," she continued.

"Nice to meet you, Jessie." Seb gave a polite nod and a friendly wave. He was far more reserved than John, though no less friendly.

"Likewise," I replied.

We entered the restaurant and were guided to our table. Even though Lindsey had mentioned the reservation was for four, seeing the table set so neatly for us made it feel unexpectedly intimate.

Lindsey sat next to John, and Seb took the spot beside me. The moment he did, the whole setup clicked into place. This wasn't just dinner. It looked—and felt—exactly like a double date.

As the waiter handed us our menus, I realised Lindsey had planned it. She had no idea about Shane and me being together. I hadn't shared the news with her, nor was I going to bring it up now as it would only make things awkward and ruin the night.

"So, Jessie, are you ready for tonight's adventure?" Seb asked, breaking me away from my thoughts.

"Yes and no." I let out a half laugh, half sigh. "I've done the nightclub thing a few times, but it's really not my scene. I'm more of a house party and music festival person."

He grinned. "House parties and music festivals have their charm, but maybe tonight will surprise you."

I returned the smile. Seb's laidback demeanour was refreshing.

The waiter approached our table to take our orders. Drinks first, then dinner. It didn't take long before he returned, bearing a tray with our drinks, which he set down in front of us.

John was the first to raise his glass. "To Lindsey! Twenty-six and thriving."

We all lifted our glasses, clinking them together with a chorus of "Cheers!"

Seb leaned slightly in my direction. "So, Lindsey mentioned you've applied for uni."

"Yeah, I have. It was time for me to stop procrastinating," I confessed.

"I know exactly what you mean. When I finished high school, I had no idea what I wanted to do with my life, so I took a few years off to travel—Europe, South America. I figured I'd give myself time to figure it all out," he said.

"And a cultural experience to go with it. Did you travel solo or with friends?"

"I went solo. Jumped into it without much of a plan in mind. It was all about the journey, not the destination," he said before taking a sip of his beer.

"What was it like? Traveling alone, no set plans?"

He launched into a story about his time in South America, trekking through the Andes, sleeping in hostels, and bonding with strangers who became friends. "It was great."

As I listened to him recounting his adventures, I found myself reflecting on the nature of my own travels. My family's vacations, though plentiful and luxurious, were quite different from Seb's backpacking journey. We gravitated towards serenity above all else. Each year, my parents picked the destination, usually a beachside spot where they could unwind and forget about work.

Fiji, Vanuatu, Hawaii, the Maldives, and the islands of Greece were some of the places we had travelled to. Each was a paradise in its own right, with stunning beaches, clear waters, and an array of leisure activities.

We would swim, drink, eat, and enjoy being away from it all. It was never about the thrill of discovery, the kind that might lead one through the historic ruins of Italy or the vineyards of France. For my parents, that idea wasn't as appealing as just taking it easy. However, their trip around Australia marked a notable shift in their viewpoint. Perhaps with retirement nearing, they wanted to explore.

"I met so many different people who became my friends and experienced so many different ways of life," Seb said.

"That's amazing."

The idea of travelling to explore new places and cultures was a dream of mine, but I'd never taken it seriously—not like Seb had. I couldn't imagine heading into the world alone, armed with nothing other than curiosity. Too many what-ifs had always held me back—the dangers of certain countries, the fear of being vulnerable in unfamiliar surroundings. I could picture him wandering through ancient streets, soaking up the history and life of different cities, each with its own story to tell.

"My parents, on the other hand, thought it was a terrible idea," Seb said. "They hated that I was going to spend all the money I'd saved working weekends when I was in high school. They thought I should use it as a deposit on a house and focus on studying. Their whole plan was for me to settle down early, you know, get a head start on life."

"Sounds like they had a responsible and traditional route in mind," I mused, knowing I had gone down that path. "Do you think it was worth it?"

"Absolutely," he replied. "I was eighteen and had my whole life ahead of me to study, get a job, and buy a house—settle down. What was a few years out of my life before those types of responsibilities took over? I wanted to venture out into the world, but it wasn't just about seeing new places—it was about figuring out who I was, gaining perspective, and learning to stand on my own two feet. Honestly, it changed everything. It helped me figure out what I wanted to do, which led me to where I am now. And, surprisingly, it made me appreciate my studies."

"What are you studying?"

"Finance," he replied. "I'm also doing a paid internship at a bank in the city. Juggling the two can be a bit stressful, but I want to become an investment banker in the future."

The coincidence brought a smile to my face. "Really? I applied for the same degree."

"Seriously? That's great." Seb's interest seemed to have been piqued. "Have you heard back about your application?"

"I haven't checked my emails since applying," I admitted,

making a mental note to do so later.

"If you get in, I'll be a year ahead of you," he teased lightly.

He had a maturity about him that suggested he'd lived a little more than most guys his age. Then again, I wasn't entirely sure how old he actually was.

"How old are you?" I blurted, wine having given me courage to ask a question I normally wouldn't.

"Twenty-three," he replied.

I nodded—he was only a year older than me. The difference felt negligible, but his life experience made it feel like a wider gap.

Our meals were brought out, beautifully plated and smelling divine. One by one, the waiter set down our dishes, and the conversation shifted as we ate. By the time we finished our meals, we were ready for another round of drinks.

After dinner, the four of us strolled along the marina to a taxi rank nearby.

Seb fell into step beside me, keeping the conversation alive. "What do you enjoy doing in your free time?"

"Recently, not much," I admitted. "I used to go out and take photos… It was more of a hobby than anything…" My mind cast back to a time when I enjoyed taking photos.

"Photography, huh? What's your favourite thing to capture?"

"Social photos, selfies, sunsets, scenery shots—life, I guess. Things that I want to remember forever and the things I find eye-catching. There isn't anything specific."

"Why'd you stop?" he asked.

"I guess I lost that spark," I said, knowing misery had killed my motivation. "Life got complicated."

"Maybe you'll find your way back to it," he said. "Sometimes, the things we love have a way of circling back to us when we're ready for them again."

As we continued talking, I found myself drawn to Seb. Conversations with him felt natural, effortless, as though we'd known each other far longer than just one evening.

When we reached the taxi rank, we piled into a taxi and headed towards the city. Hindley Street, the main nightclub strip, was teeming with people. Some were sober while others were drunk and staggering around even though it wasn't even nine o'clock yet.

"Prepare yourself for a huge night," Lindsey announced as we got out of the taxi. With a spring in her step, she led the way like a mother duck guiding her ducklings, weaving through the throngs of club-goers.

Within minutes, we'd bypassed a long queue of eager patrons waiting at the entrance of a nightclub. Somehow, Lindsey had managed to arrange for us to skip the line, and the cover charge was waived.

As we went inside, it felt as though we'd entered another world. Strobes of neon lights flashed in time with the music, which pulsed through the dimly lit space, reverberating in my chest. The energy of the crowd was electric, bodies swaying and bouncing to the beat, and I tried to take it all in. It had been over a year since I'd set foot in a nightclub, and while I felt a little out of my depth, I couldn't deny the spark of excitement beneath my nerves.

Lindsey, John, and Seb seemed perfectly at home in the chaos. They eagerly guided me to a reserved area where a group of people, I assumed were Lindsey's friends, were already gathered. They erupted into cheers at our arrival.

Lindsey leaned in, shouting names over music as she introduced everyone. I nodded, even though I could barely hear a thing, let alone remember anything.

"Be right back!" Lindsey disappeared towards the bar with John close behind.

They returned a short while later, each carefully carrying some vodka mixes. They set them in the middle of the table, and Lindsey raised her glass high.

"Cheers to an awesome night!" she shouted, her voice barely cutting through the music.

We clinked glasses, sealing our entry into the night's escapades.

A few drinks later, we were on the dance floor. I let myself go, swaying and spinning to the rhythm. It was easy to forget everything here, to lose myself in the moment. My worries and doubts disappeared. I danced as though no one was watching, and for a while, I was free—free of the past, free of expectations, just free.

In the middle of it all, Seb moved closer. I didn't notice at first, too caught up in the song playing, but then his voice found me, cutting through the music. "Can I have your number?" he asked, his eyes locking onto mine.

I faltered, my movements stuttering as my mind scrambled for an answer. Around us, the dance floor continued to pulse with energy. Lindsey and John were in their own little world, as were the others. But for me, everything seemed to slow.

Seb's request was simple, but I hesitated. Maybe it was the way he said it, or maybe it was Shane slipping into my thoughts.

Shane, the unspoken secret.

I glanced towards Lindsey and John again. They were oblivious to my internal struggle. Saying yes shouldn't have felt like a big decision—it was just a number. Saying no felt rude and strangely defensive, as though I was assuming it meant something more than friendship. Guys and girls could be friends. The longer I dwelled on it, the more ridiculous my unease felt.

"Jessie?"

With a shrug and a sense of spontaneity I hadn't felt in ages, I decided to stop overthinking. "Sure, why not?"

Seb's grin lit up his face, and he pulled out his phone. We

exchanged numbers, and he said, "I'll text you."

Lindsey swooped in, her mood as vibrant as ever. "All right, people! Time to amp up the birthday vibes and hit the next club!"

We spilled out into the street, the air cool against our flushed faces. We roamed from one nightclub to another. Each venue was a remix of the last, with a new crowd, a different DJ blending similar beats, and the drinks, though served by new faces, tasted alike. Conversations became snippets, and the details of each place blurred in a haze of drinks and dancing we carried on through the night.

Slowly, I pried open one eye and blinked against the sunlight filtering through the curtains. My head felt like it was going to explode, and my mouth was as parched as a desert. It took a moment for my surroundings to register—my own room, my own bed. I was in my pyjamas. Relief washed over me. How I got there, though, was a mystery I wasn't eager to solve.

I propped myself up on the bed, hoping the headache would disappear, but it didn't. The aftermath of a night out, I presumed. Surprisingly, the nausea hadn't kicked in yet, a small mercy in the grand hangover scheme.

As I rubbed my temples, attempting to soothe the ache, something caught my eye: coloured stamps on my arm forming a haphazard pattern. They were a collection of nightclub insignias—

each one a token from the blurry escapades of the previous night. It was tangible proof that I'd danced my way through a series of venues unlike ever before.

With a sigh, I slumped back onto the pillows, the events of my adventure seeping back into my consciousness. I reached for my phone lying beside me on the bed. The time glared at me: 10:50 A.M. I'd managed to sleep in, which was a small victory considering the state I was in.

I looked at my notifications—I'd received two text messages.

The first one was from Lindsey.

SUCH AN AWESOME NIGHT! THANK YOU FOR COMING TO MY BIRTHDAY! X

I liked her text and went on to the next one, which was from Seb.

HI JESSIE, IT WAS LOVELY TO MEET YOU. HOW'D YOU PULL UP THIS MORNING? HOPEFULLY BETTER THAN ME. I DON'T THINK I EVER WANT TO DRINK AGAIN! SEB 🌹

A chuckle escaped me. It seemed the night had left a mark on him too.

I responded with a thumbs-up emoji, then wrote:

HI, DEFINITELY NOT MY FINEST MORNING. IT WAS NICE MEETING YOU—HOPE YOU RECOVER SOON!

Then I went to take a shower and make myself breakfast.

Lucky, the little shadow with a voracious appetite, was there to remind me of my duties beyond nursing a hangover. He brushed up against my legs, purring and meowing.

"All right, all right," I grumbled as I went to the fridge. "You're worse than this hangover."

Opening the door, I reached for a tin of cat food. The metallic pop echoed through the kitchen as I peeled back the lid, then I scooped a generous portion into his bowl. He wasted no time diving into his late-morning feast while I turned my attention to my own breakfast.

Opting for something quick yet comforting, I made a toasted cheese and ham sandwich. With my plate in hand, I went over to my laptop—which was still on the dining room table from the last time I'd used it—and settled in front of it.

Lucky, having swiftly devoured his meal, jumped onto my lap with a mischievous glint in his eyes. He eyed my sandwich, and before I could react, he made a daring attempt to snatch a bite.

"Hey, no!" I scolded, pushing the sandwich out of his reach.

He responded with an indignant meow, his paw reaching for another sneak attack.

I sighed, overwhelmed with guilt, and broke off a small piece, offering it to him on the floor. "There you go, but that's it."

Satisfied with his victory, he jumped down and nibbled on his treat.

Turning my focus to the laptop, I powered it on. As it booted up, I took another bite of my sandwich, savouring the taste. I logged into my email, and the usual clutter of newsletters and promotions filled the inbox.

And then I saw it.

There, nestled between the spam and social updates, was *the email*. The one with the outcome of my application. My eyes lingered on the subject line for a moment. I didn't know why I was so nervous. I had stellar grades. Yet for some reason, I was doubting myself.

My heart raced as I clicked on the email. My eyes darted across the screen, searching for the words that would define the next chapter of my life. And there it was, clear as day: *We are pleased to offer you a place in the Bachelor of Finance degree.*

"Yes!" I shot my fist triumphantly into the air. I felt a sense of accomplishment, and I was somewhat proud I'd taken the leap and applied.

Lucky, startled by my sudden outburst, glanced up from his spot on the floor. His green eyes widened, ears flicking back as if to say, "What's going on?"

"Guess what, buddy? Your human is officially a uni student," I said to him.

I went through the process of accepting the offer, then grabbed my phone without a second thought. I should have called Lindsey or my sister, but my fingers had already dialled Shane.

The second he picked up, I didn't even give him a chance to say hello.

"I got in!" I blurted.

There was a brief pause on his end, a stretch of silence that felt like an eternity, before he said, "That's fantastic, Jess! Congratulations!"

"Thank you!" I grinned so hard my cheeks hurt. "I'm so thrilled, but… I'd be lying if I said I wasn't a bit nervous."

"You've got this," he assured me. "But hey, this calls for a celebration, doesn't it? How does Vietnamese takeout sound? I'll drop by with dinner after work, and we can toast to your success."

A smile tugged at my lips. "That sounds perfect."

"I'll see you tonight, future finance guru," he teased.

11

The aroma of Vietnamese takeout wafted through the air as Shane and I settled at the table on the balcony, overlooking the marina. It was an uncharacteristically warm evening and not what I had grown accustomed to in the past month. The heat seemed to hang in the air, refusing to dissipate even though the sun had dipped below the horizon. It was the first day of a heatwave that was meant to stick around for a week.

"It's like we've skipped right to the heart of summer," Shane commented.

I nodded, sipping on a glass of wine. "We're still a couple of months away from that. Who would have thought we'd be getting a preview so early in spring?"

We dug into the delicious array of dishes spread before us.

"So, how was your day?" I asked between bites of my meal.

Shane leaned back in his chair and took a swig of his beer. "It was actually amazing. I closed a deal on a property—and not just any property, but one that's worth several million dollars. The buyer was interstate and ridiculously indecisive, so it was a real challenge to get it across the line." He paused, then added, "But you know the best part? The commission. It's the largest I've ever made."

"Congratulations!"

"Thanks. It's one of those deals that reminds me why I love this job: the thrill of the chase, the negotiation—it's like a game—and the satisfaction of closing the deal."

As dinner wound down, we pushed the near-empty containers to the side.

Shane wiped his hands on a napkin and leaned forward. "The REISA Awards for Excellence Gala is coming up in late October."

REISA—Real Estate Institute of South Australia, I pieced together, recalling brief mentions in the news. It was an event that celebrated the crème de la crème of the real estate world, much like its counterpart in New South Wales that I knew of.

"My agency goes every year. It's quite the spectacle," Shane continued. "A lavish dinner, the awards ceremony, everyone in their finest. I was thinking... how would you feel about being my date for the evening?"

The words landed like a bombshell, and for a moment, I didn't know how to respond. Not because I didn't want to go—I did. I really did. But agreeing to Shane's invitation meant more than a glamorous night out. It meant opening the door of our relationship, letting the world in, and exposing something I'd guarded so carefully. Maybe—just maybe—it was time to let that fear go.

Shane must've sensed my hesitation. "You don't have to decide right now. I thought… it could be fun. I'd love for you to be part of it."

While I had attended galas before—mainly charity events with my parents—this felt different. Charity galas were meaningful and fulfilling, a way to contribute to good causes and have a fun evening. They were nights where philanthropy met socialising, where you could feel the collective desire to make a positive impact. This was different—a night celebrating professional triumphs.

"I'd love to go," I said finally.

"Really?"

"Really." I smiled.

* * *

I reached across the sheets, half expecting to find Shane still beside me, but my hand met nothing but cool linen.

Where was he?

Rolling over, I reached for my phone on the nightstand. It was 6:58 A.M.—too early for him to have gone anywhere, surely. I heard the faint sound of utensils clinking coming from the kitchen.

A smile tugged at my lips. *Of course.*

Sliding out of bed, I put on my silk robe, tied it loosely around my waist, and went to the kitchen. Shane was at the stove cooking while Lucky was perched on the counter, supervising. The sizzle of eggs in the pan and the scent of freshly brewed coffee filled the air.

"Good morning," I greeted, wrapping my arms around Shane in a cosy hug.

"Morning! I thought I'd surprise you with breakfast before heading off to work. Hope you're hungry," he said before kissing me on the forehead.

"Starving, actually," I said.

"Your coffee's ready. Thought you could use a little pick-me-up." He pointed towards the counter.

I slid onto one of the stools at the counter, cradled the mug between my hands, and took a sip that awakened every dormant taste bud with its flavour.

Shane presented a plate of scrambled eggs and toast, followed by a fruit salad. "Bon appétit."

Lucky wasn't forgotten either—Shane placed a small bowl of scrambled eggs on the floor for him before taking a seat next to me with his plate.

"You might have missed your calling as a chef," I teased, taking another bite.

He laughed. "Maybe in another life. For now, I think I'll stick to real estate. But who knows? Maybe one day I might change my mind and open a little café or restaurant."

After breakfast, Shane took care of the dishes despite my protest. And when time came for him to leave for work, we lingered at the door, reluctant to part. His hands slid around my waist, pulling me close as his lips brushed against mine.

"I don't want to go, but I have to," he whispered, his forehead resting gently against mine.

"I'll see you later," I said.

I watched him leave, the door clicking shut behind him. I leaned against the wall, still wrapped in the warmth of our time together. The apartment felt quiet, almost too quiet, after his departure. Lucky must have sensed the change in atmosphere too. He sauntered over and rubbed against my legs, his green eyes looking up at me as if to remind me that I wasn't alone.

I scooped him up and went to get my phone, then sat on the couch. Lucky curled up beside me. Checking my notifications and messages, one alert stood out. My heart sank slightly as I tapped on it—a notification from my bank. Zack's money had been deposited, though it was still pending processing.

The amount was substantial—enough to make most people's chests tighten and their minds fill with possibilities—but for me, it was another reminder of Zack. A gesture of love wrapped in the painful finality of his absence.

I set the phone on the coffee table, staring at it like the weight of the notification might dissolve if I ignored it long enough. But it didn't. Gratitude, guilt, and the hollow ache refused to dull.

I felt as though I was standing on the edge of a chasm, peering out at a future that demanded I leap forward too quickly, too rashly. My apartment, once a sanctuary, suddenly felt like a shrinking space. Its walls inched closer as if to compress my scattered thoughts.

Needing an escape, even if momentarily, I searched for a cigarette and stepped out onto the balcony. The morning sun was climbing higher in the sky, and the warm air was promising another scorcher.

Lighting the cigarette, I inhaled deeply. The smoke curled up into the air, a temporary escape from the emotion clouding my mind.

As I paced the length of the balcony, my thoughts were cast into the depths of memory, reeling with images of Zack—our life, our dreams, the future we'd once imagined. Each one was a haunting echo.

By contrast, what I had with Shane was new and fragile, a delicate bloom pushing through the crack of everything I'd lost. He was my new beginning, my attempt to move on. Yet even as I reminded myself that this was why I'd come to Adelaide—to heal, to start over—the anxiety refused to let go.

By late afternoon, the confines of my apartment seemed to reverberate with the noise of my thoughts. I needed air, space—something to drown it out. So, I decided to go for a walk.

I changed into a pair of shorts and a T-shirt, grabbed my sunglasses and phone, and headed out the door. Minutes later, I was walking along the crowded shoreline. Children were building sandcastles. A group of teens was playing soccer while others were swimming or relaxing on the sand. It was an ideal late afternoon at the beach because the sun was making its descent below the horizon and the temperature was becoming more bearable.

I walked aimlessly for what felt like ages and was about to head back when a black-and-white border collie bounded up to me. With an exuberant leap, it pushed me over onto the sand. Laughing despite the surprise, I sat up and patted it as it wagged its tail, licking my face.

"Well, hello to you too!" I said.

It danced around me, clearly thrilled by its own antics, while I scanned the area to find its owner.

That's when I spotted Seb dashing towards me. "I'm so

sorry," he panted as he reached us. "She's only a year old and gets overly excited when I take her for walks." He extended a hand, pulling me to my feet.

"No harm done," I assured him, dusting off the sand. "She's cute. I didn't know you had a dog. What's her name?"

"This troublemaker?" he said as he grabbed the leash to keep her from darting towards another passerby. "This is Luna. She's a bit of a handful, but I wouldn't have it any other way."

"Well, Luna"—I scratched behind her ears—"you've got quite the introduction strategy. Next time, maybe just a polite bark?"

Seb looped the leash more securely around his wrist. "I didn't expect to run into you here. Are you out for a walk too?"

"It's a great day for it," I replied, glancing at the clear skies and letting the gentle breeze brush against my face—a welcome relief to the thoughts that were plaguing me.

"It is, isn't it?" Seb agreed. "That's why I bring Luna here as much as I can. She loves it, and well, it helps me too." It made me wonder if he was struggling with his own problems, hidden behind his calm demeanour. "So, do you live around here?"

"I do." I gestured vaguely in the direction of the high-rise silhouettes that lined the distant shore, their windows glinting in the waning sunlight. "In an apartment on the marina."

"Fancy," he teased. "Do you have ocean views?"

"Not quite that lucky. But I do have a decent view of the

marina and the park though." I smiled. "How about you?"

"Ocean views? Definitely not," he said. "I rent a two-bedroom unit a few streets down. It's a small place. Nothing grand, but it's close to the shops and tram line, so I don't have to drive everywhere."

He reminded me what I liked about Glenelg. The area felt like a small town, with everything I needed just a stroll away. Unlike Sydney, it offered a simple and more practical lifestyle. Here, the idea of relying on public transport—something I had never considered appealing or even necessary—suddenly struck a chord with me.

Luna tugged on the leash, eager to continue her walk, pulling Seb a few steps forward.

"Luna seems to want to keep moving." He glanced back at me. "Would you like to join us for the walk back?"

"Sure," I said, falling into step beside him. "I was about to head home anyway."

Luna set a brisk pace as we walked along the shoreline.

"Have you lived in Adelaide long?" Seb asked.

"Just a few months," I replied, the breeze catching my hair.

"A few months, huh? What brought you to Adelaide?"

There it was—the question I always dreaded, even when it was asked so casually, like now. I hesitated, not sure how much to share. The truth felt too raw, too personal to drop into a conversation on a beachside stroll.

"A change of scenery," I said eventually. "Needed a fresh start."

"I get that." Seb nodded. "But I don't know if I could leave everything behind to start over again. You're brave."

"Says the guy who backpacked across continents solo." I nudged him.

He chuckled, shaking his head. "Touché. But traveling's different—it's temporary. Moving your entire life somewhere new? That's next level. Do you miss your family and friends?"

"Of course I do," I admitted, the words slipping out with more honesty than I expected. "But they're only a short flight away. I couldn't move somewhere overseas like some people do. That would be too far for me…" I glanced towards the horizon, where the sky was beginning to blush with the colours of dusk.

When we reached Moseley Square, neither of us seemed ready to say goodbye. Our farewell lingered until Seb finally said, "I'll text you," and pulled me into a hug.

As he walked away, Luna running ahead, I watched them until they disappeared into the crowd. "See you," I murmured, though he was already too far to hear.

On the walk home, Seb occupied my thoughts. There was something about him I couldn't shake, and it was pulling me towards him. I wanted to get to know him more, to see him again.

"Damn Lindsey," I muttered as I reached my apartment complex. "Why did she have to introduce me to him?"

The question wasn't serious, of course, but it nagged at me. Seb was the kind of guy who had the potential to upend the delicate balance I was trying to maintain in my life. He was easy to talk to and impossible to forget, and he had this magnetic presence I wasn't quite sure I could resist.

12

As I scrolled through the latest photos from my parents, envy rippled through me. They were in Broome—a place I'd dreamed of visiting for years. One particular photo caught my eye. It was a selfie of my parents on a camel ride along Cable Beach. Mum looked radiant and adventurous, with my dad right behind her, his hand raised in a cheerful wave against the backdrop of the setting sun.

I replied with a heart emoji and set my phone aside as I went back to eating my cereal. Having woken up earlier than usual, I was unable to drift back to sleep. Rather than waste the morning tossing and turning, I'd decided to get an early start to the day and head into the city by tram to find a dress for the upcoming gala. Despite a wardrobe full of options, none seemed suitable for such a formal occasion.

Once I finished breakfast and rinsed my bowl, I moved through my morning routine with purpose—brushing my teeth, combing my hair, dabbing eye cream, and applying a light touch of makeup. After slipping into a summer dress and ballet flats, I grabbed my handbag and phone, ready to step out.

Lucky followed me to the door.

I crouched to give him a scratch behind the ears. "Be good, Lucky."

Outside, the morning was just waking. The sun was peering over the horizon, but the air was already warm, promising another scorching day.

I made my way to Moseley Square where the tramline was, relishing the calm before the city stirred to life. With time to spare, I stopped at Cibo Espresso and ordered a coffee that smelled as good as it tasted. Coffee in hand, I bought a ticket from the machine as the tram arrived.

The doors slid open, and a handful of early risers stepped off. I boarded, ticket still in hand, out of the heat and into a wave of crisp air. It took a few seconds for my eyes to adjust. Rows of seats lined either side. Given the early hour, it was unsurprisingly quiet—only one other passenger sat towards the back. I settled into a window seat.

It was my first time on a tram—or on any kind of public transport. Growing up in Sydney, I'd always relied on cars, whether they were my parents' or my own. Buses and trains had always seemed foreign, like something from another life entirely. Yet here I was, trying something different from what I was used to.

The tram idled at the station for a few extra minutes, giving latecomers the chance to get on.

"Hey, Jessie." Seb's voice pulled me from my thoughts.

Startled, I looked up to see him getting onto the tram, his backpack slung over one shoulder. "Hi." I smiled. "What are you doing here?"

He slid into the seat beside me, setting his bag at his feet. "Heading to uni. What about you?"

"Shopping," I replied before taking a sip of my coffee.

"Shopping?" he repeated. "I've got back-to-back lectures."

"Fun," I laughed.

He tilted his head slightly. "Speaking of lectures, did you ever hear back about your application?"

"Yes, I got in!" I said, unable to hide the thrill in my voice.

"Congratulations," he said. "So, you start next year?"

"Pretty much," I replied. "Plenty of time to mentally prepare myself."

From the streets of Glenelg, the tram travelled through the suburbs, stopping every few minutes. Each stop brought new passengers, each one absorbed in their own life—either on their phone or listening to music, oblivious to the world around them. The closer we got to the city, the more commuters filled the empty seats.

The tram slowed to a halt at the Rundle Mall stop, and Seb and I got off along with a wave of passengers. Traffic hummed past as some of the commuters darted across the road, dodging cars, trying to rush to wherever they were going. Playing it safe, we waited for the lights at the pedestrian crossing.

"Do you mind if I tag along for your shopping trip?" Seb asked, pointing towards Rundle Mall.

"Didn't you say you were going to uni today?" I asked, raising an eyebrow.

"Yeah, but the lectures I have today are a total brain drain. Spending time with you beats them by miles—even though I'm not much of a shopper."

"Won't you get in trouble for skipping? Or, you know, fail?"

The pedestrian lights turned green, and we joined the crowd crossing the road.

"Not unless I make a habit of it," he explained. "This would be the first time I've skipped a day since I started. Everything's online anyway. I'll catch up later."

I gave him a sceptical glance as we reached the other side of the road. "All right, but don't blame me if you end up failing something. I did warn you."

He laughed. "Noted. You'll be the first to say, 'I told you so.'"

As we turned our attention to the shops lining Rundle Mall, reality hit me—they were all closed.

"What?!" I muttered, pulling out my phone to check the time. A bit after eight. Of course. I was too eager to even consider opening hours.

"Nice one!" He laughed.

I rolled my eyes, disappointed by my oversight. "You know, I never thought about the time."

With an hour to spare and nothing better to do before the shops opened, we meandered through the mall while I browsed the latest fashions showcased in the store window displays.

"So, what exactly are you shopping for?" he asked.

"I need a formal dress for a black-tie event I'm attending," I replied. "What about you? Planning to buy anything, or are you just tagging along to kill time?"

"Mostly tagging along," he said. "Figured someone should keep you from blowing your budget on clothes you didn't anticipate buying and you'll probably wear once."

I shot him a mock glare. "Gee, thanks. Your faith in my judgment is touching."

He laughed. "Hey, I didn't say you don't have good taste—just that stores like these are designed to rob you blind."

As the clock neared nine, the mall stirred to life. Store

employees unlocked doors, lifted shutters, and flicked on lights as they entered the stores, preparing for the day's rush. Like a runner at the start line, I felt a surge of excitement. The moment the doors opened to the first store I wanted to look through, we were the first to step in.

"I can already tell this is going to be a marathon," Seb said.

We moved from rack to rack, shop to shop, the hours slipping away as I hunted for the right dress. I told myself to focus on the gala, but my attention kept wandering—casual dresses, blouses, cardigans, jackets. Each piece seemed to whisper, "You need me for your new life." And maybe I believed them, because I didn't resist.

"Another one?" Seb teased as I handed him yet another item to hold.

"Don't judge me," I said. "I haven't done this in ages."

"Really? Could've fooled me," he shot back.

But it was true. For months, I'd avoided shopping sprees, avoided anything that hinted at indulgence or joy. Today felt different. I'd let myself feel like *me* again… and maybe even someone new.

"You do realise this is starting to look like a down payment on a car, right?" he said.

I laughed. "Relax, I'm just looking."

"That's what you said at the other store."

Seb was patient, occasionally checking his phone but

always ready with a lazy nod, a thumbs-up or down, whenever I stepped out of the fitting room.

Eventually, we ended up in a department store with a section dedicated to formal wear. As I sifted through the racks, Seb grabbed a black button-down shirt from a display and held it up against himself.

"Think I could pull this off?" he asked.

"Maybe," I said, disappearing into a fitting room with an armful of dresses.

One by one, I tried them. A pastel-pink floral dress—too sweet. A white-and-navy one—beautiful but not right. Then, there was the last one. A stunning floor-length red silk gown with a high slit. It was a showstopper. I stepped out of the fitting room, feeling a bit like a Hollywood starlet, only to pause when I saw Seb.

He was wearing the black shirt tucked into fitted trousers, sleeves rolled, and a fedora tipped low over his brow. He looked as though he'd stepped out of a time machine straight from the 1940s.

"What the hell?" I laughed.

He grinned, jokingly striking a pose that could've belonged to a mob boss. "What do you think? Does it look old-school gangster or undercover detective?"

"Are you auditioning for *The Godfather*?" I teased.

"Perfect. Then I nailed it."

Standing beside him, our reflections looked straight out of

a classic film noir. He had the easy charm of a vintage gangster; I was the accidental femme fatale. The unintentional coordination of our outfits was almost cinematic—too good to ignore.

I pulled out my phone and snapped a photo. It was the first picture I'd taken in what felt like forever—not with my DSLR, sure, but that didn't matter. What mattered was the feeling it sparked—the quiet thrill of capturing a moment. I couldn't remember the last time I'd felt that.

"So, what's with the outfit?" I asked.

He adjusted the fedora. "We have a uni pub crawl coming up. It's a mafia theme."

"A pub crawl?" I raised a brow. "Can't say I've ever been to one."

"It's a uni thing." He shrugged. "A bunch of us hit every pub in the city during happy hour dressed as old-school gangsters. Cheap drinks, bad decisions, the usual."

"Sounds… chaotic," I said, amused. "And you're inviting chaos dressed like *that*?"

"Of course. Chaos loves a good fedora." His grin widened. "You should come along. It'll be fun. Lindsey and John are coming too, so you'll already know a few people. And you'll get to meet some new ones."

"When is it?" I asked.

"Not this Saturday, but the one after." He looked at me. "Come on, Jessie. You can't say no to dressing up and cheap drinks."

"I don't think I have anything in my wardrobe suitable for a mafia-themed pub crawl," I said, glancing around the store in search of inspiration.

"You'll find something," he insisted.

And with that, we headed back to the racks, combing through rows of dresses until I found a short black dress that fit the theme well. I paired it with a headband, a string of faux pearls, and a vintage-style clutch.

"Now you've got no excuse," he said as we left the store. The mall was busy, with a busker playing guitar while crowds moved in every direction.

"So, where is everyone meeting up on the night?" I asked.

"We haven't nailed down the details yet," Seb admitted. "The group can't seem to agree on anything ahead of time. But I'll text you as soon as we do. It'll probably be last minute, knowing them."

"Sounds organised," I joked.

By the time we'd finished, I was weighed down with shopping bags—far more than I had planned. Seb carried his only purchase—the so-called gangster outfit for the pub crawl—while I looked as if I'd cleared out half the mall. There was no way I could lug all this onto the tram, then carry it from the tram stop back to my apartment without getting too exhausted. So, we opted for a taxi instead.

When we pulled up to the front of my apartment complex, the driver helped unload the shopping bags. Seb hopped out as well.

"Thanks for joining me today," I said to Seb.

"No problem," he replied.

I glanced at the mountain of shopping at my feet. "Guess I went a *little* overboard, huh?"

"Just a bit," he teased. "But hey, you got what you needed. And an extra dress for the pub crawl, so I'd call that a win."

"True," I agreed. "I'm actually looking forward to it."

"Me too. I'll text you the details once the group stops arguing and decides." He opened the taxi door and got back in. "See you soon, Jessie."

"See you." I watched the taxi pull away.

Lucky greeted me with a chorus of meows when I stepped through the door, shopping bags in tow. He wove around my legs as I headed to my room, his tail flicking with just the right amount of attitude to suggest I'd been gone far too long for his liking.

"I know, I know," I said, setting down the bags and scooping him up. "I was out shopping. Had to find something special for the gala. And okay, maybe I bought a bit more than I planned."

As I set Lucky down, he sniffed around the bags like a tiny

detective, tail swishing with curiosity as he investigated the foreign scents clinging to my purchases. I watched him for a moment, amused, before getting to work unpacking.

One by one, I hung or folded each piece neatly in the wardrobe. The red gown looked even more stunning in the soft evening light, and the black dress for the pub crawl had just the right amount of flair to fit the theme. I couldn't help but feel excited about the upcoming events.

Lucky pawed at one of the bags, the crinkling sound drawing my attention.

"All right, all right, I'll feed you before I finish this." I went to the kitchen, grabbed his food, and filled his bowl. "There you go, buddy."

He attacked it as though he hadn't eaten in weeks.

With Lucky taken care of, I returned to my haul, arranging everything neatly. Today was exactly what I'd needed. It was a small step forward in this new version of my life.

I picked up my phone and opened my gallery. There it was at the top—the photo I'd taken with Seb. It captured us perfectly. We looked like a great duo, a modern-day Bonnie and Clyde, minus the getaway car and crime spree. Seeing it reminded me of what I'd been missing from my old life—someone who was fun to be around.

Maybe Lindsey introducing us wasn't such a bad thing after all…

13

The next day, the weather made the decision for me: I was staying home. Rain hammered the windows in torrents, and the temperature had plummeted, a sharp contrast to the heatwave we'd experienced days earlier. The dreary, grey sky seemed to absorb any thought of stepping outside. It wasn't the kind of weather for a walk—or for doing much of anything, really.

So, I figured I'd use the time productively. My mind kept circling back to the money Zack had left me. The funds had finally landed in my bank account, and now it was up to me to decide what to do with them. I could almost hear my father's advice ringing in my ears: "Invest." He also would say, "And remember not to put all your eggs in one basket." Cliché? Sure, but grounded in practicality.

I made myself a hot chocolate, the steam curling up from the mug, then settled into the corner of the couch, my laptop perched on my knees. I opened my browser and began researching different investment strategies, delving into articles and forums about real estate and the share market.

Firstly, I explored real estate. It seemed like a solid option. Adelaide's real estate market was booming, and buying rental properties in promising suburbs could provide a steady income stream. The thought of being a landlord made me pause—managing tenants, dealing with maintenance—but the potential returns were too tempting to ignore. The property market was less volatile compared to other investment options. Plus, I could always hire a property manager.

However, I couldn't ignore the share market either. My father had always emphasized the importance of diversification. Stocks, with their potential for higher returns, tempted me—especially blue-chip ones. These were the established heavyweights of the financial world, companies with reputations for stability and consistent dividends. For someone as new to investing as I was, they felt like a safe place to start, a low-risk way to dip my toes in without fear of losing too much if the markets turned.

Then there were ETFs—exchange traded funds. Instead of picking individual stocks, I could buy into a ready-made basket of assets—shares, bonds, currencies, and derivatives. It would take the pressure off having to choose everything on my own.

As the rain continued to pour outside, streaking the windows with rivulets of water, I opened a spreadsheet on my laptop. One column for real estate, one for stocks, and another for ETFs. I experimented, allocating hypothetical amounts, testing combinations, adjusting, and refining as I went.

Still, daring ideas kept creeping in. What about companies that had just hit the market—IPOs with all their promise and unpredictability? Or even penny stocks? Risky, yes, but the allure of high returns was enticing, and a part of me wondered if taking a chance would pay off. My father's advice came to mind again, and I reminded myself to be cautious, ensuring that the bulk of my investments were in stable, reliable options.

I didn't intend to invest all the money. A quarter of it would sit safely in a high-interest savings account—there for emergencies, for the "just in case" moments life inevitably throws at you—and some of it, I wanted to give to charity. I wasn't sure which one yet, but I knew I wanted the donation to matter. My parents donated regularly—not for praise, but because it was simply part of who they were. That was something that had always stayed with me.

Hours slipped away without me noticing. The rain outside turned from a steady downpour to a light drizzle, and the faint glow of the late afternoon crept in through the clouds. I looked up from my laptop, realising how long I'd been sitting. My stomach growled in protest, reminding me I hadn't eaten since breakfast. I got up, stretched, and made myself a quick snack—a toasted sandwich. Simple, but satisfying.

As I chewed the last bite of my toast, my thoughts turned to Shane. I hadn't heard from him in a few days, which wasn't entirely unusual. He had a way of throwing himself into work, sometimes to the point of disappearing for a while. It didn't bother me; I admired his ambition and focus.

Thinking about him made me realise I needed someone to help me navigate the labyrinth of investment properties. Lindsey crossed my mind first—mostly because she was my friend and I knew she would love to help—but she probably wasn't the right person to guide me since she wasn't working in real estate anymore. Shane, on the other hand, was still in the thick of it. Real estate was his world, and he'd even earn a commission from each purchase if I bought from his listings.

I grabbed my phone and dialled his number. As the line rang, I hesitated. This wasn't just a casual call. It meant revealing more about my finances than I had when buying my home. Then again, he already knew I came from a wealthy family, so it wasn't as if the idea of me having money would surprise him.

"Jessie, I was going to call you," he said. "Sorry I haven't called. Work's been insane—people are losing their minds over property right now. Prices are skyrocketing, and I've closed three sales this week alone."

"Wow, three? That's amazing! Congratulations," I said, happy for him.

"Thanks! What's up? Everything okay?"

"I need some advice," I admitted. "I'm thinking about buying some investment properties. Can you help me?"

There was a pause on his end, the kind of silence that let me picture him processing what I'd said. "Sure, I can. I'll come over shortly."

It didn't take him long to arrive. When I opened the door, my heart flipped. He was dressed in a crisp button-down shirt and tailored pants, looking every bit the professional. Meanwhile, I was in my leggings and a cosy jumper, feeling a bit underdressed but comfortable.

He greeted me with a kiss. "Hey, you. Ready to talk business?"

We settled at the dining room table, where he set up his iPad, instantly switching into work mode. "So, how many properties are you thinking of buying?"

"I'm not sure yet," I admitted. "I've been researching, and I think a mix of residential and commercial might be good. Maybe start with three or four properties."

Shane nodded, tapping on his iPad. "That's a smart approach. Diversification is key. Residential properties are generally safer and easier to manage, but commercial properties can offer higher yields. It's about finding the right balance."

"How do I even start? Do I look at locations first? Or should I focus on rental demand?" I asked.

"It's a mix of both," he explained. "Location is everything. You want areas with strong growth potential or consistent demand. For residential properties, think about proximity to schools, transport, and amenities—stuff renters value. Also, what type of renters you will get in that area. Commercial properties are a bit trickier. You'll want to look at things like long-term leases, tenant reliability, and even the type of businesses the area attracts."

I nodded, soaking in his words as he turned his iPad towards me, pulling up a list of current properties his agency was selling. Shane's expertise shone through. He didn't only explain the basics; he broke down market trends, potential growth areas, and the pros and cons of every option.

"We can start by looking at a few properties here in Adelaide," Shane said, scrolling to a highlighted map of the city. "But I'd also suggest considering other cities, like Perth and Brisbane."

He tapped on a property listing south of Adelaide. "This one's a good contender—it's close to the beach, has modern renovations, and already has tenants. That means rental income starts the day you close. And don't worry about the market being hot right now; high rental demand makes it a good time to buy."

"That does sound promising," I said, my nerves easing a little.

"We can check it out this weekend," he added. "I've already got a few times in mind for viewings. Some properties are closer to the city, and a couple are down south. I'll lock in the appointments tomorrow."

"Sounds like a solid plan," I said.

As we continued exploring, Shane flipped to a property in Brisbane. "Take a look at this one. It's in a rapidly growing neighbourhood. Great schools nearby, shopping centres, public transport—it ticks all the boxes. The rental yield is solid, and property values in the area are predicted to increase in the next few years."

I leaned in, studying the photos of the house on his iPad. It was a modern property with a spacious yard. "It's nice."

"Exactly," Shane agreed. "Families are more likely to stick around long-term, which means steady rental income."

We moved on to another listing, this time in Perth.

"This one's interesting," Shane said, pausing at a beachside property. "It's a bit older but has been recently renovated. It's close to the beach and not far from public transport. That's always a major draw for tenants."

I raised an eyebrow. "You make this sound almost too easy."

He laughed. "It's all about doing the research. Once you've got the right property, it kind of runs itself."

"It's going to be a busy weekend," I said as we wrapped up our discussion.

Shane had jotted down all the properties we planned to view and was heading back to the office to make the necessary arrangements.

"And remember, I'm here for you. Whatever you need." He kissed me. "I'll be back in a couple of hours."

* * *

The next morning, after Shane left for work, I stepped onto my balcony, holding a mug of tea to ward off the chill. Though the rain had cleared, the sky remained overcast, and the cold wind sliced through my jumper.

I intended to spend the day delving into my investment plan. Real estate was already in motion thanks to Shane's guidance. Now it was time to face the share market—a completely different beast. If I wanted to make informed decisions about my future, I needed to take control, and that meant figuring out which companies were worth the risk.

Back inside, the ducted aircon was pumping out warm air. I took a seat at the dining table with my tea beside me and my laptop ready to guide me through hours of research. I wasn't venturing into entirely foreign territory—my father had instilled in me a basic understanding of how to invest, and I was determined to put it into practise and manage this aspect of my finances myself.

Hours passed as I sifted through information on the ASX website, comparing company performance, reading financial news, and analysing stock charts. It was a meticulous process, but I found a strange satisfaction in it. The process made me feel more comfortable about my decision to pursue a degree in finance.

By early afternoon, I'd made my decision. I opened an investment account with my bank and carefully selected a range of companies to invest in. My strategy was clear: balance the risk by spreading my money across various sectors. With a few clicks, I'd purchased different stocks. The confirmation emails from the bank arrived promptly.

I closed my laptop and stretched my legs, wandering over to the window where Lucky was sitting. The wind had picked up, rustling the tree leaves outside. Despite the gloomy weather, I felt a flicker of optimism I hadn't felt in a long time.

14

Over the next several days, I viewed properties with Shane in Adelaide before jetting off to Perth and Brisbane to do the same. Each city presented its own unique opportunities. I put in offers on six investment properties—two residential in each city, except in Brisbane, where one of them was a commercial property with promising potential.

All the offers were accepted.

It was official—I was now a property investor.

Shane suggested we celebrate, and when he arrived at my apartment, he brought a bottle of Armand de Brignac Champagne. Extravagant and over the top, but I didn't mind.

"It feels surreal," I said, pacing the living room, sipping on the glass of champagne. "I can't believe I bought six properties. Six."

Shane, lounging on the couch with his glass in hand, watched me with a grin. "Having second thoughts?"

"No, not at all," I said. "It's just... a lot to take in. I feel like I've aged twenty years in the span of a week, like I went from twenty-two to forty-two overnight."

"Look at it this way—you're setting yourself up for life. You could retire early. Hell, with the rental income you're about to pull in, you wouldn't even need to work."

"Well, I could've done that without investing." I swirled the champagne in my glass. "When I think about it, it doesn't feel like an achievement—not in the way it does for most people. They save for years, working hard and taking risks to slowly build their portfolios. I didn't do that. I was handed the capital. It's... different."

"It doesn't matter how you started. What matters is what you're doing with it. You're not blowing your money on stupid stuff. That's something to be proud of. Do you know how many people would squander that kind of money in a heartbeat? You're building something here—something real."

I bit my lip. Maybe he was right. Maybe it didn't matter how I got here as long as I made the most of the opportunity.

However, I couldn't shake the feeling that I was playing a different game entirely.

"I know you said you didn't want to manage the properties yourself, but are you sure you don't want to?" he asked. "I mean, I could help you or even manage them for you until you could do it yourself."

I appreciated his offer—I really did—but I didn't need the stress, and more importantly, I wanted to have some boundaries. It wasn't just about keeping things simple—it was about maintaining my independence and making sure our relationship didn't blur into professional territory.

"Nah," I said. "It will be easier for the local real estate agents to manage them."

He nodded, accepting my decision without pushback. "All right, if that's what you want."

* * *

The next morning, my phone buzzed with a text from Seb.

Morning, Jessie. Meeting at The Little Pub on Hindley Street at 6 p.m. Seb. x

Simple and straightforward, just like him. Very last minute, but the thought of seeing Seb again brought a smile to my face. It had been over a week since we'd last hung out.

"What are you smiling about?" Shane's voice cut through

my thoughts. I glanced up to see him half-dressed, buttoning his shirt in front of the mirror. His phone was going off on the nightstand—no doubt a client.

"Nothing," I said quickly, locking my phone and dropping it on the bed beside me.

He shot me a look, one eyebrow raised. "That doesn't look like nothing."

I sighed, deciding honesty was better than dodging his curiosity. "I've been invited to a pub crawl tonight."

"A pub crawl?" He grinned. "Where's my invite?"

"Uni students only," I teased, stifling a laugh.

"I could *pretend* I'm a uni student," he said.

I folded my arms and stared at him. "Really? You'd want to spend the night surrounded by a bunch of rowdy uni students?"

"What? It sounds like fun!" he insisted. "I'm sure they're only a few years younger than me."

I laughed. "Maybe next time."

"Well, have fun," he said, leaning down to kiss me goodbye. "I'll call you tomorrow."

And just like that, he was out the door, already dialling his phone as work consumed him again.

The day passed quicker than I expected, and before long, it was time to get ready. It felt like ages since I'd dressed up for a night out even though it hadn't been a month since Lindsey's birthday. There was something about the process of getting ready—styling my hair into loose waves, applying my makeup, slipping into my short, black dress—that excited me.

I added the finishing touches to my look—a pearl necklace, a headband, and a pair of black heels that screamed femme fatale. Stepping back from the mirror, I checked every detail, ensuring nothing was out of place. Satisfied, I grabbed my bag and headed out the door.

After catching a taxi into the city, I was dropped off right in front of The Little Pub. Tables were scattered at the front, many already occupied. It didn't take long to spot Seb near the entrance. His mafia-themed outfit—black pants, a black shirt, and a fedora tipped at just the right angle—made him stand out.

"Jessie!" Seb called, waving me over even though I'd spotted him first.

He wasn't alone. Lindsey stood beside him in a chic gold dress that hugged her body, paired with strappy heels that gave her an edge. John was dressed in a sleek all-black ensemble—a fitted blazer, shirt, and trousers.

As I got closer, I noticed how many people were joining us on the pub crawl. It looked as if Seb's entire class had shown up—at least twenty people, maybe more. The guys were decked out in suits and ties, some with suspenders or fedoras to fit the mafia theme, while the girls wore colourful dresses, embodying the concept of either gangster wives or gangsters themselves.

"Hey!" I greeted Seb with a hug. "You look great."

"You too," he said, giving me a quick once-over. "Ready for a fun night?"

"Absolutely," I cheered.

Seb did his best to introduce me to everyone, though I knew there was no way I'd remember most of their names. There were too many faces—though a few I recognised from Lindsey's birthday.

Before we started our night, someone suggested taking photos, and within minutes, we were snapping group shots and selfies. People struck dramatic poses, playing up the gangster theme with mock-serious expressions, finger-gun gestures, and cheeky smirks.

Lindsey looped her arm through mine as the group went inside. "Let's get the night started."

The pub was packed. Music thrummed in the background, laughter and conversation wrapping around us. The venue itself was dripping with charm—wooden interiors that gleamed under the dim glow of pendant light fixtures and walls adorned with old photographs of the city.

"Drinks first." Lindsey pulled me towards the bar.

We squeezed into a gap just big enough to get the bartender's attention. Drinks were half price, and vodka seemed to be the crowd favourite, so I decided to go with the flow.

Our group had settled into a corner, and we joined them

with our drinks. I took a moment to soak it all in. A strange but welcome sense of belonging swept over me.

As the night unfolded, we moved from one pub to the next, each new spot adding its own vibe to the adventure. Once happy hour was over, many went home. The few that stayed behind were huddled around the bar at yet another pub. Seb bought Lindsey, John, and me three vodka shots each. We lined them up in front of us.

"All right, let's see who's got the guts," Seb challenged.

"Seriously? Three?" I laughed.

"Go big or go home," he said, raising his first shot with a playful smirk.

"Cheers!" Lindsey chimed in, clinking her glass with ours.

We'd already had plenty to drink by this point—vodkas, cocktails, whatever had been shoved into our hands—so adding three shots on top of that was practically begging for trouble, but drunk logic remained undefeated.

The first shot went down smoother than I expected, though it burned all the way to my stomach.

Lindsey gagged dramatically beside me. "Nope—*nope.* Absolutely… *nope.* I'm *done.*" She slammed her empty glass on the counter, her face twisted in disgust. "Whyyy does it taste like fire and regret?"

John snorted. "That was one shot."

"One too many," she insisted.

I somehow got all three down, though the last one was already staging a rebellion in my stomach. "I-I think I'm doooone."

"Lightweights," Seb teased.

"Time for me to head off," I announced, the words slurring slightly.

Lindsey waved me off with a sloppy smile, her hand resting on John's shoulder as she tried to maintain her balance. Seb gave me a questioning look, but I didn't give him a chance to argue. I hugged everyone and stumbled my way out of the pub.

The cold night air hit my flushed face. I took a deep breath, trying to steady myself. The streets were quieter now, so I headed towards the taxi rank in front of the pub. Just as I reached for the door of a taxi, a voice called out behind me.

"Jessie!"

I turned, startled to see Seb running towards me.

"Wait," he said, catching up to me. His eyes were slightly glassy from the vodka. "Thanks for coming out tonight. It was awesome having you here."

Before I could respond, he moved closer, and in one swift, unexpected motion, he kissed me. I froze. Then as the warmth of the connection washed over me, I kissed him back. It wasn't just good—it was *perfect*. The kind of kiss that made the world around you disappear.

But the world didn't disappear—not for me. Reality hit me

and the truth rushed forward—Shane.

I gently pushed Seb back, breaking the kiss. "Seb…" My voice was barely above a whisper. My heart twisted, torn between the undeniable chemistry I felt in that minute and the unspoken truth hanging between us. "I can't."

His brows furrowed. "Why?"

I opened my mouth to explain, to tell him about Shane, but the words caught in my throat. How could I say it without making everything more complicated? Without risking losing Seb not just as a potential partner, but as a friend?

"I'm sorry," I murmured. It was all I could manage.

Without waiting for him to respond, I climbed into the taxi and closed the door, leaving Seb on the curb.

I gave the driver my address, and as we pulled away, I glanced through the rear window to see Seb's silhouette illuminated by the streetlights.

He looked confused. Hurt. And maybe a little lost—just like I felt.

The ride home was a blur. The city's lights streaked past the windows in fractured flashes, mirroring the chaos swirling inside my mind.

Seb. Shane. That kiss.

When the taxi stopped outside my building, I paid the driver and got out, my heels unsteady beneath me as I walked to the entrance. I stumbled through the foyer, my heels clicking against the tiled floors. The familiar surroundings offered a small measure of comfort as I stepped into the elevator. The ride up felt agonizingly slow. I leaned against the cool metal wall.

Inside my apartment, I took off my heels. Pulling my phone out of my handbag, I tossed the bag onto the couch.

Lucky shot upright with a sharp hiss, startled. I hadn't realised he was there—but thankfully, I'd missed him.

"Sorry, dude!"

Without bothering to turn on the lights, I picked him up and carried him to my bedroom. Moonlight spilled through the curtains, painting faint shadows on the walls. I set Lucky down and collapsed onto the bed. Every muscle in my body felt drained.

The events of the night replayed in my mind.

Seb's kiss.

His words.

The look on his face when I walked away.

I knew he liked me more than as a friend.

As I was about to close my eyes, my phone buzzed in my hand. The screen lit up, casting a soft glow across the room. My heart lurched when I saw Seb's name on the screen.

I'M SORRY IF I OVERSTEPPED. I HOPE YOU'RE OKAY.

I stared at the message, my thumb hovering over the screen. What could I say? What was there to say that wouldn't make this mess even messier? The truth? A lie? Some half-hearted attempt to brush it off?

After what felt like an eternity, I finally typed back: IT'S OKAY.

A moment later, his reply came: a single heart emoji.

I stared at the screen. It was simple. Sweet. Loaded with everything we weren't saying.

Without thinking, I sent back a heart emoji.

The moment I hit Send, a surge of emotion hit me—longing, guilt, confusion. It was suffocating.

I dropped the phone onto the bed and stared at the ceiling. I couldn't stop thinking about Seb. His smile, the way he listened, and that kiss—it all felt so right and yet so wrong.

My thoughts drifted to Shane. Stable, reliable Shane. He cared about me, and I cared about him too. But was it the kind of relationship that lasts—or something I'd reached for when I was drowning? Maybe he'd been the first man to show up after Zack, the first to make the silence less unbearable. Had I mistaken comfort for connection?

A part of me wondered what Zack would have thought about me being with the Shane. He'd never been a fan of him back in school. They'd crossed paths at parties, sure, but they didn't hang out. Zack drove him home a few times when he was too drunk—mostly because I'd asked him to—but he always found his reckless behaviour annoying. And even though Shane had changed since then, knowing that didn't make me feel any less confused.

My phone buzzed again, snapping me out of my thoughts. I reached for it.

Another message from Seb.

GOOD NIGHT. SWEET DREAMS. 

Despite the confusion gripping me, I smiled. There was something about him, something that felt alive in a way I hadn't felt in a long time.

I typed back quickly:

GOOD NIGHT! X

I woke up with a pounding headache, the remnants of the previous night's alcohol still coursing through my system. Blinking against the sunlight streaming through my window, I groaned and dragged myself out of bed, then shuffled into the kitchen.

Coffee first. Survival depended on it.

After making a cup of coffee, I filled Lucky's bowl with food and sat on the kitchen counter. He immediately darted over, purring like a tiny engine.

"You're the only one enjoying this morning," I muttered, rubbing my temples before taking my first sip of coffee.

As the caffeine worked its magic, I scrolled through the photos on my phone, reliving moments from the mafia-themed pub crawl. There were heaps of group shots, all of us grinning as if we didn't have a care in the world. One photo showed Seb and me, his arm casually draped over my shoulder, both of us in our gangster outfits. Another had Lindsey and me striking ridiculous poses with fake guns that we got from someone.

I'd taken more photos than I had in ages.

With a sigh, I set my phone aside and went to get the camera I'd brought back from Sydney. It had been stashed in my bedside table drawer for months, untouched. The last set of photos on it were from my final days with Zack. I'd avoided them, convinced that revisiting those moments would rip open old wounds. But today, something inside me wanted to see them, as if they would somehow bring clarity to my life.

I powered on the camera, my fingers trembling as the screen flickered to life, illuminating the images frozen in time. The first photo appeared—Zack, happy. My breath caught as I flipped through the photos. Each one was a punch to the gut. Zack and me at the music festival with friends. Zack laughing. Zack seated at his beloved grand piano, fingers poised over the keys as if mid-composition. And then, one that stopped me cold—his hands held up, forming a heart.

Lucky jumped onto the counter, purring softly. I ran my hand over his fur, taking a deep breath to steady myself.

Neither Shane nor Seb could replace Zack. I'd known that, of course. But staring at these photos, it was painfully clear how much of my heart still belonged to him. And then there was the nagging feeling about Shane—that I'd rushed into something with him, grasping for comfort, for a distraction from the void Zack had left behind.

The camera beeped softly as I shut it off, setting it aside.

My phone buzzed on the counter. It was a message from Lindsey.

MORNING, YOU ALIVE? 😄 LAST NIGHT WAS WILD! WANT TO GRAB BRUNCH?

I laughed and texted back.

BARELY, BUT YES! BRUNCH? SOUNDS LIKE A PLAN.

In seconds, she responded.

SEE YOU IN THIRTY AT MOSELEY SQUARE.

Swapping my pyjamas for black jeans and a cardigan, I headed out to meet Lindsey. The walk was short, and I spotted her waiting for me, looking as rough as I felt. Her hair wasn't styled, and her face was makeup free, a clear sign of a tough morning. If I thought I looked bad, Lindsey looked worse.

"I'm *never* drinking again!" she groaned.

"How long did you stay out after I left?" I asked, falling into step with her as we walked towards The Moseley.

"An hour longer," she admitted with a wince. "That vodka shot on top of everything else we drank? Never again. I spent half the morning with my head in the toilet. I don't know how you handled those drinks."

"I didn't," I confessed. "Believe me, I wasn't feeling great either."

We entered The Moseley. The place was packed with the late-lunch crowd—families chatting over pizza, couples sharing cocktails, and groups of friends looking just as hungover as we were.

We found a free table near the window and ordered soft drinks and pizza—because, really, what's better hangover food than pizza?

As we waited for our order, Lindsey leaned back in her chair. "Last night was fun, but I don't think I've ever hated vodka more in my life."

"Lesson learned," I said, "stick to wine next time."

She snorted. "Noted. Although, if I'm being honest, I'll probably ignore that advice the next time we go out." I smirked, but my amusement was short-lived when Lindsey turned on me with an accusing look. "Seb wasn't too cheery when you left last night. He bailed shortly after you did."

"Really?" I asked, trying to sound casual.

"Yeah. Jessie, come on. He likes you." She leaned forward.

I bit my lip. Of course I knew Seb liked me—it was obvious when he'd kissed me. And God, that kiss. The memory of it flickered through my mind like a forbidden spark. But there was Shane. And even just *thinking* about Seb, let alone the kiss itself, felt like a betrayal.

I fiddled with the edge of my napkin, avoiding Lindsey's gaze. "I'm… I'm not looking to be in a relationship right now," I lied.

Lindsey frowned, clearly unconvinced. "You don't like him, then? You could have just said that."

"No, it's not that at all," I blurted too quickly.

Her eyes narrowed. "Then what's the issue? Seb's great. He's fun, he's sweet, and let's be real, he's hot as hell. What's holding you back?"

I swallowed hard. "It's complicated," I said quietly, hoping that would end the conversation.

Lindsey wasn't having it. "What's complicated about it, Jessie? If you like him, why not go for it?"

At that moment, the waiter arrived with our pizza, placing the steaming dish between us. I used it as a distraction, grabbing a slice and taking a bite even though I had no appetite. The gooey cheese and tomato sauce tasted like cardboard.

"Look, even if you don't want a relationship, what's stopping you from having some fun?" she said, a devilish grin spreading across her face.

"Lindsey!" I exclaimed, nearly choking on my pizza.

She had a way of simplifying things, turning emotional mayhem into something casual, almost careless. But this wasn't just about fun. This wasn't a harmless fling waiting to happen.

There was too much at stake—Shane, Seb, my friendship with her. One wrong move, and I'd risk breaking hearts, including my own.

I put down my slice and met her gaze. "He kissed me."

Her eyes widened, her jaw dropping mid-chew. "He *what*?"

I sighed, letting the words tumble out. "Last night, before I got into the taxi… It just happened. One minute we're talking, and the next…"

"And? What did you do? Did you kiss him back? Tell me everything!" she asked.

"I pushed him away," I admitted. "I told him I couldn't. And then I left."

"Why? I thought you liked him?"

I hesitated, the truth wedged in my throat. I wanted to tell her about Shane, to finally admit the real reason why I couldn't let things progress with Seb. But instead, I deflected. "Like I said, it's complicated, and I need time to figure things out on my own first."

It hurt knowing I wasn't being truthful, but I wasn't ready to open that door yet.

After we parted ways, I lingered in Moseley Square, unwilling to head home just yet. My thoughts were consumed by the kiss with Seb and the denial. Without really thinking about where I was going, my feet carried me down an alley that opened up onto the beach.

The ocean stretched out before me, its waves crashing against the shore. I wandered to a spot on the limestone wall that overlooked the water and sat on it. The wind tangled my hair, whipping it in every direction.

I wondered if Seb was out with Luna somewhere along the beach. The idea of bumping into him again sent an unexpected flutter through my chest. But as I scanned the shoreline, there was no sign of him. The beach was mostly deserted, except for a couple walking hand in hand in the distance. Maybe Seb was at home, recovering from the previous night.

My phone buzzed and I pulled it out of my pocket, glancing at the screen—a message from Shane.

DID YOU HAVE FUN LAST NIGHT?

Fun. That word seemed so far from the guilt brewing inside me. I stared at the message before liking it and sending a thumbs-up emoji. Words felt too complicated right now. Too risky.

With the phone still in my hand, I opened the gallery and swiped through last night's the photos again. Seb looked so good and that kiss… It replayed in my mind like a scene I couldn't stop watching.

I needed a distraction.

Opening the camera app, I aimed the lens towards the jetty that stretched out into the water, silhouetted against the sky. I snapped a few shots of the Ferris wheel and the waves crashing against the shore, then turned the camera on myself. I forced a smile that felt awkward at first, but I held it anyway, hoping it would make me feel better.

But no matter how many photos I took, my thoughts circled back to Seb. It was as if he had me hypnotised. Before I could talk myself out of it, I opened our message thread and typed a quick text.

HEYA, HOW ARE YOU FEELING?

He responded in seconds with a photo of his TV screen showing a zombie movie.

LIKE THE LIVING DEAD BUT SURVIVING. HOW ABOUT YOU!?

I smiled and snapped a photo of the beach, the waves rolling in, and sent it with the caption:

NOT TOO BAD. CHILLING AT THE BEACH.

A moment later, my phone buzzed again. This time it was a photo of Luna sitting at his door.

LUNA IS EAGER TO GO FOR A WALK.... BUT WE'RE NOT HEADING OUT TODAY.

I chuckled softly, imagining Seb sprawled on his couch in recovery mode.

POOR LUNA. CATCH UP SOON?

I typed, hesitating for a second before hitting Send.

His reply was almost instant.

DEFINITELY.

The single word felt like a small promise in the middle of

the tangled web I'd created for myself.

I took one last photo of the view, then tucked the phone back into my pocket and headed home. The wind was getting colder, cutting through my cardigan, and I wasn't keen on turning into a human ice block.

15

The urge to see Seb again was overwhelming, a craving that seemed to grow with each passing hour. I'd attempted to push it away by spending time with Shane, hoping that immersing myself in our relationship would help.

We had dined at our favourite spots, strolled along the beach, and Shane had stayed over a few nights in a row. One afternoon, we spent hours hiking through the Adelaide Hills. Shane was everything I should have wanted and more. Yet no matter how much I tried to focus on our moments together, my thoughts crept back to Seb like an obsession.

And at night, as Shane lay beside me, his arm draped over my waist, I found myself staring into the dark, feeling conflicted. With Zack, I hadn't been interested in other guys. Zack was my

world, and my heart never strayed. But with Shane, things felt…
different. I liked him, I really did, but I wasn't sure if I loved
him—or if I could love anyone again, for that matter. And then
Seb had entered my life, and it was as if he'd flipped a switch I
hadn't even known existed. One that drew me to him in a way I
couldn't explain. Whatever this pull towards Seb meant, I couldn't
keep running from it. Ignoring it wasn't working. If anything, I
needed to face it—sooner rather than later.

The next morning, as soon as Shane left for work, my mind
veered straight back to Seb. I hated how automatic it was—like an
addiction. I hadn't seen Seb in a week, though we'd been
messaging back and forth. His texts were casual, but there was no
mention of wanting to catch up. I debated messaging him to meet
up for lunch but stopped myself. It felt too obvious—too forward.
What if the reason he hadn't asked yet was because he didn't want
to?

Then an idea struck me—innocent, or so I told myself. I
could "accidentally" run into him during one of his beach walks
with Luna. He was usually there at some point in the day, and if I
happened to be there too, well, it would just be a coincidence,
wouldn't it? The thought sent a jolt of anticipation through me. A
coincidence, I told myself again, though I wasn't fooling anyone.
Least of all me.

Hours later, I got ready, carefully selecting my outfit—
black shorts, a fitted T-shirt, and sandals. Casual, yet flattering.

The kind of outfit that said I was a beach regular, nothing out of the ordinary, rather than someone with a hidden agenda.

I tied my hair back into a loose ponytail, keeping it effortless. Then I stepped in front of the mirror for a final once-over. There I was—a woman supposedly ready for a stroll along the beach, nothing more, nothing less. It was a façade, of course, but for a moment, I almost believed it myself.

I timed my departure for late afternoon, the time I'd previously seen Seb and Luna. The sun was beginning its slow descent, and the air was much cooler. It was an ideal hour for a beach walk—or for a casual "accidental" run-in.

The beach was alive with activity: joggers pounding along the shoreline, kids chasing one another, and dog walkers weaving through the tide line. I blended in easily, just another person enjoying the fading light of the day.

I kept my pace steady, my eyes discreetly scanning the stretch of coastline. I told myself I wasn't looking too hard, but with each step, my hopes faded.

No sign of Seb.

No Luna bounding across the sand.

My heart sank and disappointment set in the farther I walked. Maybe they weren't out today. Or worse, maybe I'd miscalculated and already missed them.

I stopped walking, glancing down at my outfit. The idea suddenly felt ridiculous. Here I was, dressed for a walk, wandering along the beach like some lovesick teenager.

What am I doing?

The question echoed in my mind, impossible to ignore. Sitting on the sand, I let the cool grains seep between my toes. I was in a relationship with Shane, yet I was captivated by the thought of someone else. It was unlike me.

I stood up, brushing the sand from my shorts, and headed home.

* * *

I spent most of the morning vacuuming and mopping the floors. Cleaning was a therapeutic outlet for me, a way to vent and bring order to my home and mind without needing to open my mouth. By the time lunch rolled around, the apartment sparkled and I was ready for a break.

I made myself a sandwich and stepped out onto the balcony, letting the afternoon breeze wash over me. The suffocating heat from the previous days had eased off, making it more bearable to sit outside at noon. Settling into my favourite chair, I took a bite of my sandwich.

As I sat there, my mind replayed the events of the previous day, my failed attempt to run into Seb at the beach. Maybe I'd had the time wrong or he'd changed his routine, going earlier or later. Determined, I was going to try again today, but earlier this time.

I headed out for the walk after three o'clock, wearing similar clothes to the day before to keep up the pretence that it was what I did daily. Walking along the shoreline, I gazed around in search of Seb and Luna. The crowds were the same—joggers and dog walkers as well as a few swimmers. None of them were Seb and Luna.

The familiar twinge of disappointment swept through me. Had I missed them again? Or maybe he'd decided to skip today altogether?

I was on the verge of giving up, ready to turn back and accept defeat for the second day in a row, when a speck of movement in the distance caught my eye. My heart skipped a beat. There, bounding across the sand, was Luna, her black-and-white fur unmistakable, even from afar.

And then I saw him—Seb, emerging from behind a group of beachgoers.

The second he saw me, he raised his hand, waving. My feet moved of their own accord towards him, closing the distance.

Luna reached me first, her tail wagging furiously as she jumped up, clearly happy to see me again. I stroked her long, soft fur and seizing the opportunity to steady my racing heart.

"Jessie! What a surprise to see you here," he said.

"Likewise, but I do like to go for a walk every day," I lied.

Seb nodded. "That's awesome. Luna gives me a reason to walk daily, though I hit the gym on weekends… but I've been neglecting my membership recently—and the walks.”

I laughed. “Well, you weren’t exactly in any shape to go to the gym after last weekend.”

“Guilty as charged. That was a rough night.” Before I could respond, he asked, “Do you want to come to dinner with me tonight?”

His question hung in the air.

“Dinner?” I repeated, trying to buy time to process the idea.

“Yeah, unless you have other plans,” he said as Luna bolted, the leash slipping from his grip as she darted after a seagull. He took off after her, leaving me to gather my thoughts.

The truth was I wanted to say yes. I wanted to spend more time with Seb, even just as a friend. Not to feed the feelings, but to figure out why I was drawn to him and to see if this fixation would fade once I knew him more. It had to, didn’t it?

And yet, deep down, I wasn’t sure if I entirely believed that. I felt as if I was tiptoeing along an invisible line that separated friendship from something more.

Seb returned, slightly out of breath, Luna’s leash firmly back in his hand. “So,” he said, his cheeks slightly flushed, “what do you think?”

I hesitated, my heart waging a silent war with my head. “Dinner sounds nice,” I finally said, clinging to the notion that I’d get this obsession out of my system.

His face lit up. "Great! There's this Italian place on the marina I've been wanting to try. How about we meet there at seven?"

I knew exactly the restaurant he was talking about. Shane had taken me there on our first date—the one near my place. The food was great, but the idea of going there with Seb felt like crossing that invisible line, a move I wasn't sure I could come back from.

I glanced at Luna, who was now happily digging in the sand. Brushing away the negative thoughts, I said, "Sounds good to me."

We headed back to Moseley Square and said our goodbyes before going our separate ways.

The second I got home, I went straight to my walk-in wardrobe to pick out an outfit for the evening. I wanted to look good but didn't want to overdo it. After all, we were only friends, and I needed to keep it that way. At least, that was what I kept telling myself.

I riffled through my clothes, finally settling on a blue-and-white dress. Slipping it on, I smoothed out the fabric and adjusted my hair in the mirror. Satisfied, I stepped back and took a deep breath.

As I waited for the time to pass, my phone buzzed on the counter—Shane.

HEY, HOW'S YOUR DAY GOING?

I stared at the screen, my chest tightening. I didn't want to lie, but telling him I had dinner plans with Seb wasn't an option either. What would I even say? That it wasn't a date even though it was a date? That I didn't know why I was going, only that I couldn't seem to stay away?

I typed back a quick response.

GOOD, JUST KEEPING BUSY. HOW ABOUT YOU?

The reply came almost immediately.

BUSY TOO. CAN'T WAIT FOR THE AWARDS NIGHT. X

I liked his message.

When the clock neared seven, I grabbed my handbag and headed out. The short walk to the restaurant was nerve-racking. What was I even hoping for tonight? For my feelings to fade? Or for something else entirely?

I spotted Seb waiting at the front of the restaurant, leaning casually against the wall. Even in a simple shirt and jeans, he looked effortlessly handsome. The sight of him made my heart race, and for a second, I wondered if he could hear it hammering as I approached.

"Jessie." He greeted me with a hug.

"Hey," I replied, feeling heat rise to my cheeks.

He held the door open as we went inside. The restaurant was as cosy as I remembered, but this time, there were fewer people. We were seated in the middle of the venue, a spot I normally wouldn't have minded, but tonight it felt like a spotlight.

My gaze darted around the room as my anxiety rose. This was Shane's favourite restaurant—our place—and here I was, sitting across from someone other than him. If Shane happened to walk in and see me here with Seb… I couldn't even begin to imagine the fallout.

I shouldn't have agreed to this—not here. It felt wrong, but it was too late to back out now. I was already seated, already committed to the dinner, and running off would only make things awkward.

Seb must've noticed my unease because he leaned in and asked, "Everything okay?"

I nodded, plastering on a smile. "Yeah."

The waiter came over and we placed our orders—I opted for a vodka and lemonade while Seb went with a whiskey and Coke, and we both went for the same pasta dish. The drinks arrived swiftly, and I took a long sip of my vodka, hoping the alcohol might take the edge off my nerves.

As we waited for our meals, Seb glanced around the restaurant. "You know, I don't usually go to places like this."

"Really? Why not?" I asked.

He shrugged. "I never really had anyone to go with before, and when I was travelling, I was always on my own. So, it was mostly street food and little cafés, working within a tight budget. I mean, it's nice, but I didn't see the point in sitting at a restaurant like this by myself."

I tilted my head. "That's such an adventure though. Travelling solo."

"It was," he said. "But it's also… different. You can have the most incredible view or the best meal, but when there's no one to share it with, it loses something, you know?"

"I know what you mean," I said, swirling my straw around my glass. "Some experiences are just better when they're shared."

The waiter arrived with our food, setting steaming plates of pasta in front of us. I took a sip of my drink—more of a gulp, really—finishing the vodka in one go. I glanced at my plate of pasta, the rich aroma of tomato and basil wafting up to me. It looked incredible, but I was unsure if I even had an appetite.

"Not hungry?" Seb asked.

"I am," I lied, spearing a forkful of pasta, and took a bite.

He didn't press. Instead, he leaned back in his seat, tapping his fingers lightly on the table. "You wouldn't believe what happened the other day."

I looked up, grateful for the distraction. "What?"

"A mate of mine talked me into doing a drive-home radio segment with him."

I blinked. "Wait, like… actually on air?"

Seb laughed. "Yeah. Total chaos. The guy he usually does the show with started a full-blown argument live on air. Not a funny bit—like a real fight. Then he stormed out mid-segment and quit on the spot."

My eyes widened. "No way!"

"Oh, it gets better," Seb said. "Everyone listening thought it was some scripted stunt, but when they realised it wasn't, it blew up online. Management panicked and was ready to pull the show until they found a replacement. My mate freaked out and called me."

"Why you?"

He shrugged. "He needed someone he wouldn't fight with on air. And someone who knows music. We've known each other since high school—we were in a band back then with a few friends."

"You were in a band?" My heart reacted before my mind did, and the words slipped out.

"Yeah. We mucked around with gigs here and there. I played the guitar. It was never anything serious. It was fun but not a career path. Too hard to break into the industry unless you've got money or connections."

A sharp ache tightened my chest.

Music always reminded me of Zack. Different instrument or not, Zack would've liked Seb. Or at least, he would've understood him in a way that made the thought sting.

I forced a smiled even though I was dying on the inside.

Seb kept talking, unaware of where my mind had gone.

"The station offered me a contract until Christmas. After New Year's, they're revamping the drive-home block, so there's a chance I might get something longer-term but perhaps a different segment."

"That's… actually really cool," I said before flagging down the waiter for another drink.

"How are you going to manage that with uni and the internship?" I asked.

"Thankfully it's only two days a week, but yeah… I've had to shuffle things around."

A reluctant laugh escaped me. "That… actually makes a lot of sense."

It did. And it explained why I hadn't seen him with Luna at the beach the previous day. The time fit perfectly—he must have been at the station.

Once we finished our meals, we had a few more drinks and signalled the waiter for the bill.

Seb reached for it immediately.

"Let's split it," I insisted. "It's only fair."

"No way," he said, shaking his head. "I've got it."

I raised an eyebrow. "You sure?"

"Positive." He winked. "I invited you, remember? Next time, it's on you."

"Deal," I said before tipping back the last of my drink.

We went out into the cool night air, the marina lights casting a warm glow around us. Seb walked me to the front of my apartment complex and glanced up at the building.

"This is a fancy place," he said.

"I guess so." I laughed softly. "Thanks for tonight. I... I had a really great time."

"No, thank *you* for saying yes." He moved in closer.

Before I could fully process what was happening, his lips were on mine. The kiss was soft yet deliberate, as though he'd been holding himself back all night and couldn't wait any longer.

I pulled away. But then, without thinking, I leaned into him, kissing him back with a passion that surprised even me. His arms slid around my waist, drawing me closer. I didn't want to stop. For a few seconds, everything else faded away—the guilt, the confusion, the world itself. It was just Seb and me, lost in a moment that felt inevitable and forbidden.

But reality crashed back in, and I knew I couldn't let this continue, as much as I wanted it too. I broke the kiss, my heart pounding.

"I... I can't," I stammered, barely able to look him in the eye. "I have to go."

He didn't try to stop me, but I felt his eyes on me as I hurried towards the entrance. My thoughts were a jumbled mess, and I didn't dare look back. I couldn't tell him about Shane, about the relationship I was supposed to be in, the one that made this kiss feel so utterly wrong. But I couldn't deny the truth either—I liked Seb. I *really* liked him. More than I wanted to admit.

By the time I reached the elevator, my hands were

trembling. I jabbed the button, willing the doors to open faster. As I stepped inside and the elevator began its ascent, I rested against the cool metal wall.

The second I was inside my apartment, I closed the door and leaned against it, sliding down until I was sitting on the floor.

Seb deserved more than this—more than stolen kisses and half-hearted attempts at friendship. I knew he wanted something deeper, and truthfully, so did I. But I couldn't give him that. Not while I was with Shane. And as much as I didn't want to betray Shane, I already had.

I buried my face in my hands. Things couldn't stay the way they were much longer. I was at crossroads, and no matter which path I chose, someone would end up hurt.

16

The day of the REISA Awards had finally arrived, and I found myself standing in front of the mirror in my floor-length gown. It was a vibrant red, hugging my figure in a way that was elegant. I'd paired it with black high heels and taken extra care with my makeup—a cat eye and a swipe of deep-red lipstick to match the gown. My hair was styled in soft waves.

On the surface, I was ready for the night ahead. Inside, though, I wasn't so sure.

Shane had invited me to his house before the event—he was driving us into the city. This would be the first time I'd seen his house, and a flutter of curiosity went through me when I was in my car, typing the address he'd texted me into my GPS. The location wasn't far from my apartment, situated on the north side of Glenelg near the beach.

The drive was quick, and as I pulled up in front of the modern two-storey house, I was taken aback. The house was impressive—an architectural masterpiece with clean lines, floor-to-ceiling windows, and an underground garage. The way it was positioned gave it an unobstructed ocean view, and the faint glow of the sunset reflecting off the windows only added to its allure. This wasn't just a house—it was a statement. Easily worth several million dollars.

I parked my car in the sloping driveway and climbed out, heading towards the oversized front door. Before I could knock, the door opened.

And there he was.

Shane stood in the doorway wearing a black suit, exuding the confidence of a secret agent on a mission. He was an image of success, and even the absence of a tie didn't make him less commanding or more approachable.

His eyes swept over me, and a smile spread across his face. "Wow, you look absolutely gorgeous."

"Thank you," I replied. "You're not looking too bad yourself."

He stepped forward, closing the space between us, and kissed me softly. "Come in."

The interior of his home was just as impressive as the exterior, if not more so. The space was impeccably modern, with an open-plan kitchen that flowed seamlessly into a spacious living and dining area. The furniture was minimalist yet luxurious, with neutral tones that felt as though they belonged in a magazine spread. Floor-to-ceiling windows offered an uninterrupted view of the beach across the road while, in the backyard, the pool had colourful lights, adding a touch of luxury to the small outdoor area. It reminded me of a small version of my parents' house in Sydney.

"Your house… It's lovely. Quite the view."

"Thanks," Shane said. "Just finished some extensive renovations. The place had a dated interior when I bought it, so I had it gutted and renovated to match the exterior. Modernised everything."

"You've done a great job."

"Let me show you around," he said.

He led me through the first floor, pointing out the thoughtful details of the renovation, then went to the elevator—a feature I hadn't noticed or expected.

"An elevator?" I raised a brow, half joking. "Of course you'd have an elevator."

He chuckled. "What can I say? It's practical in a house like this."

The ride to the second floor was swift.

"The bedrooms are all up here," he explained as the elevator doors slid open. "Four in total. The master suite's here."

He opened double doors to reveal a spacious room with a private balcony overlooking the ocean. The décor was just as polished as the rest of the house.

As we continued the tour, Shane brought up the financial aspect of his house. "I have a mortgage on this place. Had hoped to pay it off sooner, but the funds from a side project fell through, so I'm left with rather large payments." His honesty was refreshing and a contrast to the lavish lifestyle his house suggested.

"Still, it's incredible," I said. "You should be proud of what you've done here."

When we returned to the ground floor, he scooped up his wallet and phone from the kitchen counter. "Ready to see the rest of the place before we head off?"

"Lead the way." I was interested to see what else his home had to offer.

We stepped into the elevator again, and it whisked us down to the underground garage. The doors slid open to reveal much more than just a place for him to park his cars.

He showed me through the area. "That's the storage room." He pointed at a door. "Not much to see. It's pretty much empty... And this"—he opened another door—"is my personal gym."

I peered in to see various workout equipment spread out through the room—a treadmill, weights, a bench press, and even a punching bag. It was the kind of setup that would make any fitness enthusiast jealous.

"Do you actually use all of this?" I asked.

He laughed. "I try to. Sometimes work gets in the way, but it's nice having it here when I do find the time."

The next stop, however, was the real showstopper. At the far end of the garage was a temperature-controlled room—a wine cellar. Shelves lined the walls, each holding bottles of wine, whiskey, and spirits of all kinds. It was an extensive collection, meticulously organised.

"What a collection," I remarked as I stepped inside. It could easily rival my parents' collection back home.

"It's nice to have options when friends come over." He grinned. "I'm always on the lookout for something unique to add to the collection."

"You've definitely nailed it." I ran my fingers lightly over the edge of a bottle. The wine lover in me couldn't help but feel impressed.

After one last glance around, we left the wine cellar and headed to his Merc. We climbed in, and within twenty minutes, we were at the venue near the city.

When we entered the foyer, it was filled with elegantly dressed attendees gathered in clusters, glasses of champagne in hand. Their chatter and laughter set the atmosphere as they indulged in pre-dinner drinks and the canapés that were being served.

No sooner had we stepped through the door than Shane was recognised by his colleagues. They waved and called him over.

He introduced me to them one by one. "Jessie, this is Kylie. She's a sales associate."

Kylie was the person I'd seen when I first stepped into the agency with Lindsey. She was the one with the artificial appearance, having overdone Botox and fillers.

"Nice to meet you," I said, shaking her hand.

"And this is Mitch," Shane continued, introducing a young guy who radiated confidence. "He's a sales agent and one of the best. He sold over twenty houses this year."

"Great to meet you, Jessie," Mitch said with a nod.

"And last but not least, Greg and his wife, Cindy," Shane finished, gesturing to a man and woman in their fifties. "They're the owners of the agency."

"Pleased to meet you, Jessie," Greg said warmly as we shook hands. "Shane speaks very highly of you."

"That's kind of him," I replied.

As we chatted, a photographer moved through the crowd, his camera flashing as he captured moments of the evening. When he approached us, Shane slipped an arm around my waist, pulling me closer as we posed for a photo with his team. The flash went off, and I couldn't help but wonder where the photo might end up. Would it be on some real estate newsletter, social media, or both? And more importantly—did I look okay? Or, heaven forbid, did I blink?

Moments later, the grand doors to the main event space opened, and the crowd filtered inside. Shane took my hand, guiding me through the maze of round tables spread evenly across the room. The space was stunning—white tablecloths adorned with elegant floral centrepieces, soft lighting casting a glow over everything.

Once we reached our designated table, we settled into our assigned seats. The table gradually filled as more of Shane's colleagues and their partners arrived, greeting each other and introducing themselves to me.

Waiters glided between tables, balancing trays of champagne like seasoned acrobats. I reached for a glass, having missed the chance to secure one when we were in the foyer.

Shane pulled out his phone and held it up. "Smile," he said, snapping a photo of the two of us. "It's going to be a fantastic night."

"Are you up for any awards tonight?" I asked, wondering if he had been nominated. He hadn't mentioned anything to me earlier.

He shook his head. "Not this year, but our agency is nominated."

The evening was alive with performances and entertainment before dinner was served and the awards were presented. The room buzzed with excitement as nominees were announced as they progressed through each category. When the Residential Agency award was called, Shane's colleagues straightened in their seats. When the winner was announced, it wasn't their agency, but they still cheered and applauded.

Greg raised his glass. "To all the hard work this year," he said, then went on to encourage his team to stay focused on the bigger picture. "There's always next year." He winked.

As the formalities came to an end, the lights dimmed, the music grew louder, and the dance floor came alive. Groups of attendees spilled onto the floor.

Shane stood and extended a hand to me. "Come on, let's dance."

We joined the crowd on the dance floor, where the DJ played a mix of classics and modern hits. As we danced, I found myself enjoying the evening. Around us, his colleagues and their partners moved with the same energy, celebrating the night in full swing.

Time slipped away, the hours blending into one another as champagne flowed freely. I lost count of how many glasses I'd had, which left me more than tipsy, unlike Shane. He was mindful of the drive home and limited his drinking.

We left the function before midnight. The cold night air

sobered me just enough to make the walk to Shane's car. He opened the passenger door and helped me in. The drive back to his place was a drowsy haze.

By the time we arrived, I was barely awake. Shane helped me out of the car, his hand on the small of my back as we made our way to the elevator and up to his bedroom. I kicked off my heels, stumbled towards the bed, and climbed in without bothering to take off my dress. The softness of the mattress enveloped me, and before I could even think about saying good night, sleep overtook me.

I stood barefoot on the golden sand of Glenelg Beach, watching the sunlight shimmer across the ocean. Everything felt vivid, almost too real, the waves crashing against the shore… and then I saw him.

Zack.

He stood a few metres ahead of me, his figure outlined against the glowing horizon. My breath caught in my chest. He looked exactly as I remembered. How was this possible?

"Zack …" My voice cracked. "I'm in Adelaide, would you believe it?" I said to him. "It's a fresh start."

He didn't respond. His gaze remained fixed on the horizon. His mind seemed to be somewhere else. Something about him felt… off. Different.

"Zack?" I called, stepping closer.

Still no response. He didn't even look at me. Instead, he advanced along the water's edge without leaving a single imprint in the sand.

"Zack?" I followed him. The sand was wedging itself between my toes, and my feet were sinking. I was struggling to reach him. "Where are you going?"

He didn't answer or look back.

"Zack!"

This time he stopped, and I managed to catch up. He turned to face me and said, "Be careful."

I froze. "Careful? Careful of what? What's that supposed to mean?"

He didn't explain. He just turned and walked away. And before I could call after him again, his figure faded— disintegrating into the air like smoke caught in the wind.

"Zack!" I dropped to my knees. My chest heaved, my hands digging into the sand as I watched him vanish completely. "Zack, come back!"

My cries echoed into the emptiness around me. The beach stretched endlessly in all directions, but I was utterly alone. The once-lively shoreline had transformed into a desolate place.

"Jessie!" someone called out.

Seconds passed. Then I heard my name again.

I looked around, squinted against the harsh light, wondering where the voice was coming from. There was no one—

nothing but the empty beach and the endless horizon. I raised a hand to shield my eyes, but it didn't help. The brightness intensified, overwhelming everything until the world disappeared in a blinding flash—

"Jessie!"

The voice jolted me awake. My eyes flew open, the dream dissolving like mist as I sat up abruptly. The soft light of the bedroom replaced the blazing sun, and I blinked in confusion, trying to ground myself in reality.

Shane was sitting beside me on the bed, his brow furrowed with concern. I realised he'd turned the overhead lights on.

"You were dreaming," he said.

I took a shaky breath, my heart still racing. "It felt so real," I whispered, running a hand through my hair.

Shane tilted his head slightly, studying me. "You were calling out Zack's name."

My stomach tightened. I hadn't even realised I'd said Zack's name out loud. Heat crawled up my neck, part embarrassment, part guilt. "I… I didn't realise." I picked up my phone to check the time. It was 4:17 A.M. "Did I wake you?"

He nodded. "Yes, but it's okay. Go back to sleep." He switched off the lights, plunging the room back into the quiet comfort of darkness.

I closed my eyes and tried falling asleep, but my mind

wouldn't quiet. Zack's words—*be careful*—echoed over and over.

That's when I realised I was still in my dress. The fabric felt tight around my body, the once-sleek gown now crumpled and restrictive.

I glanced at Shane, who was sitting back now, his bare chest catching a faint sliver of the moonlight filtering through the curtains. He had already changed into his boxers, having shed the formal attire of the night before he'd come to bed. His hair was slightly messy, his body relaxed in a way that made me ache for that same comfort.

"I'm still in my dress," I mumbled, sitting up and running a hand over the silky fabric, suddenly desperate to be rid of it.

"You just noticed?" he asked.

"It's been a long night," I murmured, tugging at the edge of the gown. "Can you unzip it for me?"

Without hesitation, Shane shifted closer, the bed dipping under his weight. His hands brushed against my back as he reached for the zipper. His touch lingered for a second before he gently tugged it down, the sound of the zipper cutting through the silence of the room.

"There you go," he murmured.

"Thanks," I whispered, slipping the dress off my shoulders and draping it over a nearby chair.

As I climbed back into bed, I couldn't help but glance at him. He was already lying down, his head resting against the pillow, watching me.

"You okay now?" he asked.

"I will be," I murmured, settling under the covers. The words felt like a promise I wasn't sure I could keep.

Shane reached out, his fingers brushing a strand of hair away from my face. "I love you." He then pulled me closer and kissed me.

His words stopped me. Not because they were unwelcome, but because I hadn't expected them. This was the first time anyone other than Zack had said them to me. Hearing them now hit something deep and fragile inside me.

Did he truly mean it? Or was he trying to comfort me, knowing I'd dreamt about Zack?

I opened my mouth, searching for something—anything— to say back, but the words wouldn't come. My throat tightened. My mind scrambled. Panic fluttered in my chest, not because of him, but because of what those three words demanded of me. I wasn't sure I was ready to give him the same words I'd once given Zack. Not yet.

The silence stretched until I felt I had no other choice but to say it back.

"I love you," I whispered.

It wasn't a lie, but it wasn't the whole truth either.

Shane seemed satisfied with my response.

In the safety of his embrace, I couldn't escape the lingering shadow of Zack's warning.

Be careful.

The words haunted me.

Be careful of what?

Was Zack trying to tell me something? Warn me about Seb? About Shane? Or was this all about me—my own choices, my own heart?

It was unsettling, as if Zack had reached out from wherever he was to deliver a cryptic message I didn't know how to decipher. The question was clawing at the edges of my mind.

Maybe my subconscious was dredging up buried grief and unresolved feelings. After all, dreams were nothing more than jumbled pieces of our deepest fears and desires warped into nonsensical storylines.

I glanced at Shane. He'd drifted off to sleep beside me, his arm still draped over me.

I closed my eyes.

It was just a dream.

And yet... it hadn't felt like *just* a dream.

17

The next morning, I made my way home. I needed to check on Lucky, swap out my dress for something less *yesterday*, and reset my mind. I'd promised Shane I would return in the evening; he was planning to cook dinner for us.

As soon as I stepped into my apartment, Lucky greeted me with an impatient meow, weaving between my legs as if I'd abandoned him for years instead of a night. I picked him up, pressing my face into his fur and letting the familiar scent ground me. *It was just a dream. Just a stupid dream.* I wasn't going to let it spook me.

After ensuring Lucky was fed and my apartment was in order, I freshened up, slipping into something more casual. But despite my best efforts, I couldn't shake the unsettled feeling triggered by Zack's warning.

By the time six o'clock rolled around, I'd pushed aside the thoughts, determined to enjoy the evening. I drove to Shane's place, parked in his driveway, and headed up the steps to the front door. I lifted my hand to knock but stopped. The door was slightly ajar.

Shane knew I was coming. Maybe he'd left it open so I could just walk in? That made sense.

I pushed it opened without a sound and entered the corridor but paused when I heard voices in the living room.

Shane's voice…

And a woman's?

An instinctive thought flashed through my mind: *Is he cheating on me?* But when the woman spoke again, I recognised her voice—Olivia.

My stomach dropped for an entirely different reason.

"You thought I wouldn't find out, didn't you?" she shouted.

"What are you talking about? Olivia, you're—this is insane." Shane sounded strained.

My heart raced. Olivia? Here? With him?

"Oh, stop denying it, Shane. You know exactly what I'm talking about," she snapped. "How long did you think you could blackmail my husband for?"

Blackmail?

My breath caught. Olivia had more than once suggested Zack was blackmailing Mark. Now she was accusing Shane? Was she pointing fingers at everyone I'd ever been close to, or… had Shane actually done something?

I pressed myself against the wall, pulse drumming in my ears.

Shane had denied knowing Mark, denied knowing Olivia. Had he lied?

A sense of dread washed over me. "Oh, God!" The words slipped out before I could stop them.

A million questions invaded my mind—none of them with answers I wanted.

"How long did you think you could hide the truth?" she demanded.

"Olivia, don't be stupid."

She let out a short, humourless laugh. "You really think I believe my husband's death was an accident?"

My eyes widened.

"I know you were behind that car accident."

I clamped a hand over my mouth. *Behind the accident?* The words didn't fit. They twisted everything I thought I knew into something dark and wrong.

Careful not to make a sound, I leaned forward far enough to steal a quick glance into the room without being seen. I didn't want either of them to know I was there.

Olivia stood in the centre of the living room, dressed in black jeans and a fitted jumper, her dark hair tucked beneath a beanie. She didn't look like a typical street thug, but she was just as scary.

Then I saw the gun.

My knowledge of firearms was limited to what I'd seen in movies, but I didn't need to know the make or model to know it was real. And knowing Olivia and her recent state of mind, she wouldn't have bought it legally. Just cash, a shady exchange, and bought out of the boot of some guy's car in a back street of Sydney.

Shane was a few steps away from her—too close, far too close. One twitch of her finger and he was a bullet away from a coffin.

I gasped, stumbling back. *Stay calm*, I told myself. My heart was beating so loudly I was sure they'd hear it.

I moved on instinct—out the front door, down the steps, fumbling for my phone in my handbag. My hands shook so violently I almost dropped it.

I dialled triple zero.

"Police," I blurted as soon as the operator answered. I forced myself to speak clearly, giving Shane's address, explaining that there was an intruder with a gun in the house. "Please, you have to hurry. She's going to kill him."

When the call ended, I stared at the house. Every part of

me screamed to run, to get in my car and drive far, far away. But Shane was still inside. If I left and something happened to him, I couldn't live with myself.

I had been told to stay outside and wait for the police, but me being me, I didn't listen. I crept back inside, moving as quietly as I could.

"You stole millions from my husband!" Olivia's voice was ragged with fury. "And when he refused to give you more, you were terrified he'd expose you—so you had him killed."

The words hit me like a blow.

Millions?

Murder?

Shane?

They didn't fit. They didn't belong anywhere near the man I thought I knew. The very idea that he could be involved in something like that was hard to fathom. The Shane I knew— ambitious, driven, successful—he would never blackmail someone, let alone orchestrate a death.

Would he?

Could he?

Or was Olivia spiralling so deeply that she was seeing betrayal everywhere?

"So, what? What now, Olivia? You planning on killing me?"

Olivia didn't hesitate. "Blood for blood."

The click of her shifting grip on the gun jolted me into motion—pure instinct overriding every shred of sense.

"Stop!" I burst into the room before I could think.

Olivia spun towards me. A split second. A flash.

Then—

Bang.

The gunshot exploded through the room, deafening.

The force of it knocked me back. A scream ripped from my throat as searing pain tore through my shoulder.

I'd been shot.

I pressed my hand against the wound, but all I felt was warm, sticky blood. My fingers and palm were drenched in it— *too much of it*. It seeped out onto my dress in slow, heavy rivulets.

"No!" Shane's voice cracked somewhere far away— distant, panicked, muffled, as if I was underwater.

Olivia's eyes went wide. "Oh my God! What are you doing here, Jessie? Sneaking up on me? Are you insane?" She jerked the gun toward me, her hands shaking violently. "This is between me and your boyfriend."

Shane lunged, trying to wrestle the weapon from her hand.

Olivia shouted as they fell over the coffee table, smashing the glass.

A deafening bang tore through the room as she fired another shot—which missed Shane and hit the wall. A wave of nausea rolled through me. My mind scrambled for focus, but all I could hear was Zack's voice—his warning.

Be careful.

Oh, God.

He had been warning me about this.

A premonition, a message. And I had brushed it off as a dream.

My chest tightened. I was drowning in pain, in fear, in regret.

Why didn't I just wait outside?

My legs buckled beneath me. My strength vanished.

The world around me tilted.

Somewhere in the distance, voices—Shane shouting, Olivia yelling.

Then…

Police stormed the house, voices booming commands I couldn't fully process.

"Police! Drop the weapon!"

"Hands where we can see them!"

More shouting. More chaos. Olivia screaming something I couldn't make out. Shane yelling my name.

But it all sounded warped, stretched thin, faded.

Darkness edged into my vision.

My last conscious thought was of Zack.

I'm sorry.

Then, darkness…

18

Consciousness returned in fragments, a gradual emergence from the abyss of darkness. My eyelids felt heavy, but I forced them open.

A ceiling. Plain, grid-like panels.

I was in a hospital.

I inhaled sharply, only to have pain lance through my shoulder.

A voice pulled me from my thoughts.

"You're awake. Good."

I turned my head—slowly, stiffly—towards the voice. A nurse stood beside my bed, adjusting buttons on the vitals monitor.

She smiled. "I'll go get the doctor. He wanted to speak with you as soon as you regained consciousness."

I tried to respond, but my throat was dry, raw. Only a faint croak escaped.

"Oh, dear. Let me get you some water." The nurse reached for a jug on the overbed table, poured a small cup, and held it out to me.

"Thank you," I rasped before she left.

Minutes later, she returned, this time with a doctor in navy scrubs.

"Jessie, I'm Michael Tan, your doctor. It's good to see you're awake."

The nurse rolled in a mobile workstation and scanned my wristband. "Can you confirm your name and age for me? It's part of the hospital protocol, just making sure our records are correct."

"Jessie Florence. Twenty-two." My voice was still hoarse but at least audible now.

She nodded, then glanced at the vitals monitor and typed away on her laptop.

Having zoned out, I hadn't been listening to what the doctor was saying. "What happened to me?"

Dr. Tan met my gaze. "Yesterday, you were shot in the shoulder and brought to the hospital."

His words took a few seconds to sink in.

Shot.

Flashes of memory surged back—the gunshot, the searing pain, and Olivia's anguished face.

It wasn't a nightmare.

"It actually happened...? I... I collapsed?" The question was barely a whisper.

Dr. Tan nodded. "Yes. You lost consciousness after hitting your head on the floor. When you arrived in the emergency room, we stabilised you, cleaned the wound, and performed a CT scan on your shoulder and head. We ruled out any serious head injuries and assessed the bullet's position and injuries from it."

"The bullet was lodged inside me?"

"Yes. The surgeon successfully removed it and repaired the damaged muscles. You're very lucky. It was a clean wound, and thankfully, it wasn't life-threatening."

Relief washed over me. I'd narrowly escaped a grimmer fate.

I tried to move my left arm into a more comfortable position, but the second I did, searing pain shot through me, leaving me breathless.

I winced. "Please tell me this pain will go away fast."

Dr. Tan offered a small, reassuring smile. "It may take a week or two for the worst of it to ease. The bullet penetrated your skin and muscle, which is why you're feeling so sore. You'll have a scar, but the good news is, the damage wasn't severe."

A scar. The thought hadn't even crossed my mind.

Great.

"Would you like some more pain relief?" Dr. Tan asked.

"Yes, please,"

"I'll organise that now." He stepped out of the room.

The nurse finished her notes on the computer while I tried to adjust myself into a more comfortable position.

Minutes later, Dr. Tan returned with a small plastic cup containing three tablets. "I have two paracetamol tablets and an Endone for you," he said. "This'll help take the edge off the pain." After the nurse reconfirmed my details, a hospital protocol, he handed them to me along with the cup of water I had on the overbed. I swallowed the pills, my throat still raw.

"Do you know when I'll be able to go home?" I asked, worried Lucky was alone in my apartment, probably starving and wondering why his human had been gone for so long.

"You're under observation, and everything looks stable. If there are no complications, you should be okay to head home this evening," he said.

"Oh, okay. That's good." I was relieved. I'd never liked hospitals.

"If you need anything, just press the call button," he said, pointing at a small remote attached to the bed. With a final reassuring nod, he left the room, followed by the nurse, who wheeled out the mobile workstation after him.

I lay there trying to piece together the fragments of last night, the reality of it all feeling like a bad dream, when two police officers entered the room. Their presence brought the events of the night sharply into focus.

Here we go.

"Miss Florence?" The taller of the two spoke first. "If you don't mind, we would like to get a statement from you about the incident last night." He was holding an iPad.

I wasn't keen to give them a statement, but I knew it would help them with the case.

Nodding slightly, I shifted upright, the pain in my shoulder making the movement difficult. As I recounted the events, my words felt detached, like I was narrating a scene from a movie. I kept it vague, deliberately omitting certain details—I was already more entangled in this mess than I wanted to be.

"I'm not entirely sure why Olivia was there," I said carefully. "It seemed to be something between her and Shane."

The officer tapped something on the iPad. "And you had no prior knowledge of any conflict between them?"

No prior knowledge? Shane had denied knowing Mark and Olivia when I told him about Olivia confronting me and her accusations. He had looked me straight in the eye and lied.

"No."

They wrapped up their questions and thanked me for my time, then left.

Olivia was going to face serious charges for assault and firearm offenses. The law wouldn't overlook something like this. And yet, I didn't know how I felt about her getting charged and the possibility of her going to prison.

She'd shot me—that alone should've made me want to see her punished, to want justice. But I wasn't angry. Not in the way I should've been.

She hadn't been in her right mind—not since Mark's death. She was a grieving widow who had finally snapped, clinging to the last threads of her sanity, and I'd stepped into the crossfire of a situation that was never really about me. I wasn't her target—I was collateral damage. And instead of rage, I felt sorry for her and hoped they would consider her mental state.

Shane dropped by the hospital to see me. He looked disconcerted, not his usual composed, self-assured self. In his hand was my handbag.

Only then did it hit me that it must have been left behind at his house when the paramedics took me away.

He set it on the overbed table. "I stopped by your apartment to feed Lucky."

"Thank you," I said, knowing it was one less thing for me to worry about.

He pulled up a chair beside my bed. "I can't believe you did that... stepped in like that. That bullet was meant for me."

I knew that. "Believe me, I won't be doing anything like that again."

The thought lingered—if I hadn't returned when I did, Shane would be dead. No one would have known the truth. No one would have known why he was killed or who had pulled the trigger. My presence had changed everything—his fate, Olivia's, and mine.

Shane looked down and told me the news had picked up the story. The shooting, his name and mine, our life—plastered across headlines, discussed by strangers.

Because of him.

Finally, I mustered the courage to confront the elephant in the room. "So, why did you lie to me? You told me you didn't know Mark."

The silence that followed was suffocating.

"How did you even know him?" I pushed.

Shane rubbed the back of his neck. "He bought land for a development project through the agency I worked at in Sydney."

"That doesn't explain the lie," I said.

He looked away.

"Why did you lie about knowing them?"

There it was again—silence. The one thing that made me believe everything I overheard Olivia say to him.

"She's telling the truth, isn't she?" My voice wavered, but the question cut through the silence. "You blackmailed her husband. How much money did you take from him? Enough to put a deposit down on that mansion and renovate the whole place? And what about the car accident—did you have something to do with that too?"

"She's crazy," he snapped, too fast. Too sharp.

"You didn't answer my questions."

Our eyes met, and for the first time, he appeared concerned. "Jessie, this is between me and her. Not you. I'm not discussing this with you, okay? So, it's best if you stay out of it."

It was the kind of answer people gave when the truth was poisonous—when saying it aloud would make it real.

And he was right about one thing: it was best if I stayed out of it. I didn't want to know more than I already did. I didn't want to be dragged deeper into something criminal and ugly that had nothing to do with me—something that had nearly cost me my life.

But I also knew exactly what he was doing.

He wasn't protecting me.

He wasn't even denying it.

He was shutting me out because the less I knew, the safer *he* was. The less I could repeat and the fewer details I could share with the police when asked. Because if it came down to Olivia's word against his, my silence—my ignorance—would only strengthen his defence.

He knew that.

And the realisation hit me hard.

I didn't trust him. Not anymore.

I was scared of him—of this version of him I hadn't known existed. This was the real Shane. Not the charming agent. Not the man who told me he loved me. Not even the reckless drunk guy from high school. But someone who could lie without hesitation, who wanted wealth badly enough to cross lines most people never would.

Shane stood abruptly, adjusting his jacket. "I've got to head to an open house. I'll come back later."

I didn't respond.

I watched as he walked out the door, disappearing into the corridor as though nothing had happened. And suddenly, the room felt emptier, the silence louder.

His visit hadn't brought closure. It hadn't even brought clarity. It had only left me feeling… done. With him. With his lies. With the realisation that the man I had been with was a stranger.

Reaching into my bag, I pulled out my phone, only to be greeted by a cascade of missed calls and unread messages: my parents, my sister, Conrad, Lindsey—even Seb. News of the shooting had spread. The thought of my private nightmare becoming public knowledge was a bitter pill to swallow. I wasn't ready for the questions, the sympathy, the scrutiny.

But I needed to talk to someone.

I decided to call my sister first.

She picked up immediately. "Jess! Oh my God, I've been so worried. Are you okay? What exactly happened?"

"I'm okay," I assured her. "I'm in hospital. They'll be releasing me soon."

I gave her a rundown of everything that had happened, revealing more than I had to the police.

When I told her what I'd overheard, her reaction was instant. "Shane was the blackmailer? Are you serious? That is insane! And to think we all thought Olivia was crazy."

Her disbelief mirrored my own.

"That's beyond greedy," she added. "And dangerous. Honestly, it scares me."

"It scares me too," I admitted. "I don't even know how to feel about any of it. I moved from Sydney to get away from everything. To find happiness. To free myself of pain. And somehow, I've ended up in someone else's mess."

"You need to do what feels right for you," she said.

What feels right…

The words stuck with me. Because the problem wasn't that I didn't know what felt right—the problem was that I did.

And what felt right was walking away from Shane completely. But the thought of ending things brought a new kind of fear. It had nothing to do with heartbreak or being alone—I feared how he would react. What if he didn't take it well?

Pushing the thought aside, I shifted the conversation. "Enough about me. How are you? How's the pregnancy going?"

"Oh, I'm doing okay, aside from the morning sickness," she said. "It's been a bit of a rollercoaster emotionally. It doesn't help not having anyone here for support."

"I know it's been tough with him out of the picture," I said. "Just remember, our parents will be back around Christmas—that's only two months away. Once you tell them, they'll be there to support you."

"I know," she said. "I'm just not looking forward to breaking the news to them."

We talked for a little longer before ending the call, but as soon as I set my phone down, I knew I had another conversation to face—one far more difficult.

Bracing myself, I dialled my parents. The moment they answered, their voices were laced with concern.

"Jessie, we heard about the shooting," Dad said, his words rushed. "We were so worried. It's unbelievable that Olivia would do something like this."

I took a deep breath, forcing a calm I didn't fully feel. "I'm okay, really. It was terrifying, but I'm safe. Olivia wasn't trying to hurt me—it was an accident."

"*Accident?*" my father's voice boomed. "Jessie, she *shot* you! She could have killed you."

I flinched at the bluntness of his words.

"I knew she seemed stressed before we left on our trip," he continued. "Mark's death has hit her hard, and with us retiring after this next construction project—the Baltimores too—it didn't help. But none of that excuses what she did."

I'd expected my parents to retire at some point, but I hadn't realised it would be so soon. Before I could react to that news, Dad must have switched the phone to speaker, because Mum's voice came through next. "Jessie, what are you doing in Adelaide? Where's Zack? And when did you start dating Shane?"

It was time for me to reveal the part of my life I had kept hidden from them. "Mum, Dad, there's something I haven't told you." My voice trembled. "Zack… died a month after you both left on your trip."

Silence.

Then finally, Dad spoke, "Oh my… Jessie. I'm so sorry. Are you okay?"

"Yes and no," I admitted. Zack had been my world—they knew that. We'd been together for years and friends since I could remember. "I'm still devastated, but I'm trying to move forward."

"Why didn't you call us?" Mum asked. "We would have come back immediately if we'd known."

"I didn't want to tell you sooner for that very reason," I confessed.

"I'm surprised no one called to tell us," Dad said, sounding puzzled.

"I asked Alesha and the Baltimore family not to say anything. Everyone else probably assumed you already knew. I didn't want to interrupt your trip. You both deserve to enjoy your holiday without having to worry about me."

"Jessie," Dad said, "you're never a burden. We're your

parents. We're here for you no matter what. You and Alesha are more important to us than a trip, and so was Zack."

I closed my eyes for a second, absorbing his words. "I know."

For the first time since Zack died, I wished I had told them sooner.

I took a deep breath before finally answering Mum's original question. "After Zack… I couldn't be in Sydney anymore. Everything reminded me of him. I wanted a fresh start. The only way to create a new life for myself was by moving. So, I made a split-second decision to go to Adelaide. I bought an apartment. I got into uni." Saying it aloud made me realise how much I had changed in the past few months. This hadn't been running away— it had been survival.

And then, there was Shane.

"And, well… Shane is"—I hesitated. *Was?*—"was my boyfriend."

Was. The word felt wrong the second it left my lips. For the first time, I allowed myself to truly feel it. My relationship with Shane was over.

It wasn't just the blackmail, or the lies, or walking into his house to find Olivia pointing a gun at him, or the fact that I had almost died because of him. It was everything.

I had been holding onto something that was never real in the first place.

Mum's voice broke through my thoughts. "Was?"

"I'm going to break up with him," I said, the words coming easier than I expected.

I had been clinging to the idea of Shane—to the distraction he provided from my grief—but I didn't love him. Not in the way he wanted. Not in the way I once loved Zack. That was why saying *I love you* had felt impossible. I'd forced the words out because I didn't want to hurt him.

Silence stretched on the other end of the line.

"Okay," Mum said. "Do what feels right for you."

"I just want to focus on myself for now." And I meant it.

"That's great," Mum said. Then her tone shifted, lighter, teasing. "And did I hear right? You got into uni? I'm so proud of you, Jessie. But I can't believe you moved to another state without telling us."

"I'm not that far away," I said, attempting to keep things positive.

Dad chimed in. "I'm impressed you did all that. What will you be studying at uni?" In a hopeful half whisper, he added, "Please be finance, please be finance."

A small chuckle escaped me. "Finance."

"Are you serious?" Dad practically shouted. "That's fantastic! I was giving up on the idea that one of my daughters would become a banker. You've done me proud, Jessie."

His reaction made me smile despite everything.

As the conversation drifted back to my current situation in hospital, Dad said, "We want to come see you in hospital."

"There's no point," I said. "I'll be out before you could even get here. Don't worry about me. Just enjoy the trip. We'll catch up at Christmas." Eager to steer the topic away from me, I asked them, "So, where are you right now?"

"We're in Perth," Mum said. "Heading to Wave Rock next."

"We'll send you and Alesha photos like we always do," Dad added.

As the call was coming to an end, Dad said, "Try to stay out of the media spotlight, okay?"

Of course. My parents had always kept a low profile. They hated journalists, especially when articles popped up about their construction ventures and wealth. They didn't like or want the attention.

"I promise I will," I said, meaning it. "I love you both." Hearing their voices, knowing they were there for me—it was a comfort I hadn't realised I'd needed. I missed them.

"We love you too, darling. Take care." With that, they disconnected the call.

Looking through my messages, I typed out a response to Conrad's message first.

HI CONRAD, I'M ALIVE AND OKAY.

Followed by the thumbs-up emoji for good measure.

Almost instantly, my phone rang. Conrad's name flashed on the screen.

I answered it. "You could have just sent a text."

"Too much effort. Calling was easier," he said.

"Why doesn't that surprise me?" I mumbled.

Of course, he was curious about the whole ordeal. So, for what felt like the millionth time, I recounted that night—what I saw and overheard and the encounters I'd had with Olivia beforehand.

"Interesting. I wonder what he had over him."

"He's not telling anyone," I muttered. "Do you think he had something to do with the accident?"

"Maybe. Who knows?" Conrad sighed.

"What I don't get is why she accused Zack in the first place," I said.

"Well, I think I know why. Zack and Mark got into a huge argument. Mark apparently made some comment about Zack's music career. Maybe she assumed the worst or jumped to conclusions."

That was news to me. Zack had never mentioned anything about an argument, but it did make sense of why she'd pointed the finger at him.

Conrad went on, "Still, she should've dealt with it another way. Now she's facing charges and the possibility of going to prison. My parents are really upset with her. They've made it clear she's not welcome at their house anymore."

That didn't surprise me. The Baltimore family had always valued their reputation. Olivia, with her public outburst and reckless actions, had tainted that.

And if the Baltimores had cut her off, everyone else in their social circle would follow.

Olivia had gone from a grieving widow to a social outcast overnight.

She'd lost everything.

Despite everything, I couldn't help but feel sympathy for her. Her thirst for revenge had backfired. Not only had she found herself in legal trouble, but she'd also effectively severed her ties with the privileged world she'd once thrived in. The life she'd known was gone.

We said our goodbyes and I ended the call, eager to get back to Lindsey's and Seb's messages. I typed the same message to each of them.

HI, I'M OKAY. SHOULD BE OUT OF HOSPITAL SOON.

Lindsey's response pinged back.

WE NEED TO CATCH UP BEFORE I'M BURIED UNDER EXAM PREP! I'M DYING TO HEAR ALL ABOUT WHAT HAPPENED—I NEED THE TEA!

She didn't beat around the bush—she went straight to the point.

I texted back:

COME OVER SATURDAY.

It was obvious everyone wanted the lowdown. It wasn't every day that someone they knew got shot. They had questions—including ones I didn't want to answer but would have to at some point.

Seb liked my message and replied:

OKAY. TAKE CARE.

That was it. No follow up questions. Just… detached.

The words stung more than my bullet wound.

I stared at the screen, my stomach sinking. The media had mentioned that I was Shane's girlfriend. *Seb knew.*

I should have told him about Shane. I should have been honest.

Our friendship, which had been bordering on something more, seemed as if it was crumbling before my eyes, and it was all my fault.

By evening, I was ready to be discharged from the hospital. The night shift doctor entered my room—paperwork, dressings, and a sealed medication bag in hand—to go over my discharge instructions.

One by one, he handed me the items. "Here's a letter for your doctor. Your antibiotics and pain relief are in this bag. Take one antibiotic twice a day with food. The pain relief is strong, so only take it as needed. I recommend pairing it with paracetamol—it works better that way." He handed me a small pack of dressings.

"Leave the one you have on for about five days before changing it. It's waterproof, so you can shower with it. Avoid lifting anything over five kilos to prevent aggravating the wound, and make sure to schedule a follow-up appointment with your doctor to monitor your healing. The stitches will dissolve on their own."

I nodded, absorbing the information.

"Do you have any questions?" he asked.

"No," I said.

Shane had come to drive me home in my BMW, which had been left at his place. The ride was quiet, each of us lost in our thoughts. When he parked in the underground car park of my apartment building, he turned to me as if searching for something to say. But the moment passed, and he climbed out and went to the elevator.

Once inside, a sense of ease swept through me. My apartment. My space. It was comforting to be in familiar surroundings.

I set my handbag on the kitchen counter and turned to Shane. "Thanks for driving me home."

"No worries." He trailed behind me, placing my car fob beside my handbag. "I was going to stick around. Stay over tonight."

I should have expected this.

"Umm… I need some space to think things through," I said, scared to tell him I wanted to break up. "I want to be alone right now."

His expression shifted. "Are you sure?"

"Yeah." I met his gaze. "With everything that's happened… it's a lot to process."

The weight of it all pressed down on me—what I'd overheard Olivia accuse Shane of, the truth I couldn't unhear, his lies, and the shooting. The person I had thought I was falling for wasn't the person standing in front of me.

Shane ran a hand over his jaw. "I'm so sorry about what happened." His reluctance to leave was written all over him, but he didn't fight me on it. He stepped closer and kissed me. "I love you."

I closed my eyes briefly. Then in the quietest voice I'd ever used with him, I said, "Please go."

Without another word, he left. The click of the door echoed through the apartment, leaving behind a hollow silence.

I let out a long sigh, the tension in my body slowly uncoiling.

That was it.

I was alone.

A quiet meow attracted my attention to the windowsill. Lucky sat perched there, his tail curled neatly around his paws, eyes fixed on the city lights beyond the glass. Usually, he would greet me at the door, but tonight he seemed more interested in the world outside.

"Hey, buddy," I murmured, walking over. "What are you looking at?" I ran my fingers through his soft fur.

He meowed.

"I guess it's just you and me, huh?"

19

Sleep remained elusive, just out of reach. Each time I closed my eyes, my mind rebelled, replaying the events of that night in loops. I tossed and turned, exhausted.

How had it come to this?

Who would have thought I, Jessie Florence, would find myself here again: unable to sleep, trapped in a mind that refused to switch off—a state I deeply despised.

With a weary sigh, I pushed back the covers and sat up. I picked up my phone and checked the time—11:53 P.M. Lucky, ever attuned to my movements, lifted his head from his spot at the foot of the bed, watching me.

I reached for a cigarette I had stashed in my nightstand and padded through the dark to the balcony off my room. The moment

I slid the door open, a breeze rushed in, sending a shiver down my spine. Outside, the park stretched out before me, eerily still under the moonlight, the trees casting skeletal shadows across the ground.

I sat in the hanging egg chair, tucking my legs beneath me as I lit my cigarette, inhaling deeply. Lucky, in stealth mode, jumped onto my lap. I stroked his fur absentmindedly as I exhaled, watching the smoke swirl into the night.

Would this ever fade? The memory of Olivia, the gun, the deafening bang—it haunted me in a way I hadn't anticipated, lingering in the corners of my mind like an unwelcome ghost.

And then, there was Zack.

The dream was at the edge of my mind as if Zack had truly been there. I missed him. More than words could ever express. Zack, who had loved music more than anything, who had never let greed dictate his choices. He wasn't like Shane.

A dull ache settled in my chest.

"Zack, why did you have to leave me behind?" I said as if he were standing right beside me. "It's not fair that I have to be here without you."

His absence was a gaping wound, one that refused to close no matter how much time passed. No one else could fill that space.

I took another slow drag of my cigarette, my thoughts drifting to Olivia.

The more I thought about the incident, the more I

understood her. As much as I wanted to be angry—wanted to hate her for what she had done—I just couldn't. She was facing her own struggles that, to the outside world, didn't make sense, but they were real to her. And maybe, just maybe, if I had been in her position, if I had lost Zack in the same way she had lost Mark, and someone had been blackmailing him… Would I have been any different?

Still, none of this would have happened if it weren't for Shane—if I hadn't stepped in to save his life and ended up taking the bullet. He had driven Olivia to the edge. It was his actions that had set this tragedy in motion.

I finished my cigarette, stubbing it out in the ashtray on the ground. The last of the smoke trailed into the night air while I went back inside with Lucky. The chill of the night lingered on my skin as I moved to the living room. Maybe some mindless TV would lull me into drowsiness.

I collapsed onto the couch and flicked through a few channels, stumbling upon a news report.

"… the targeted attack at a Glenelg residence last night…" echoed through the room.

My own nightmare was being dissected for public consumption. The reporter's voice was detached as she stood outside Shane's house. Just another story to them.

They called it a "targeted attack."

They mentioned the shooter—Olivia—as someone

"known to the resident." They reported that she was in police custody, awaiting psychiatric evaluation. It was surreal hearing it from an outsider's perspective, stripped of its rawness, its reality.

I switched off the TV and tossed the remote onto the coffee table, frustrated.

Why couldn't they move on?

I understood now why my parents hated the media. Newscasters weren't interested in the truth. They were interested in the spectacle, in spinning my pain into headlines for the public to dissect.

I vowed there and then to avoid watching any channel that featured a news segment.

Leaning back against the couch, I stared at the blank screen, the silence pressing in on me.

* * *

Almost a week had passed since I'd left the hospital, yet sleep still didn't come easily. Most nights, I tossed and turned, haunted by flashes of that night. Even when exhaustion finally claimed me, it never lasted long.

The thought of counselling had crossed my mind more than once, but I shoved it away every time. I wasn't like Olivia. She'd lost herself chasing vengeance, turning her pain into something unstable and dangerous. If I ever reached that kind of darkness—if grief ever pushed me that far—I'd seek help. I'd have to. But I wasn't there. Not yet. I didn't need someone analysing me because I couldn't sleep—I just needed time.

This morning was no different.

Pain pulled me from sleep, a deep, throbbing ache radiating from my shoulder. I groaned, realising I had rolled onto my injured side in my sleep. I shifted onto my back, wincing as the movement sent another sharp sting through me.

There was no going back to sleep now.

Kicking off the covers, I climbed out of bed and made my way to the kitchen, craving caffeine before I could even think about facing the day.

I brewed a strong cup of coffee, then I took my antibiotics and painkillers, swallowing them with a few sips of water. I leaned against the counter, waiting for the meds and the caffeine to kick in, before heading to the bathroom for a shower.

When I stepped out, I wrapped a towel around myself and caught my reflection in the mirror.

I hated what I saw.

Too thin.

My collarbones and cheekbones jutted out more than they should have, my skin pale, my eyes hollow. The weight I had lost after Zack's death still clung to me. Depression had stolen my appetite, and even after all these months, neither it nor the weight I'd lost had fully returned. Most days, I only ate once or twice.

I tore my gaze away, refusing to dwell on it.

I peeled off the bandage, muttering, "Ouch, ouch, ouch" as the adhesive tugged at my skin. The pain was sharp but bearable. I replaced it with a fresh dressing, pressing down carefully to secure it.

From the other room, my phone buzzed.

I went over and grabbed it off the bedside table—a message from Mum and Dad.

They'd sent photos from Perth—the two of them standing on the foreshore of the Swan River, along with a few from Fremantle and Rottnest Island. This time, the caption was slightly different from their usual, "Guess where we are?" Instead, it read: HOPE YOU GIRLS ARE LOOKING AFTER YOURSELVES. MISS YOU BOTH. STAY SAFE.

I responded with a heart emoji.

Later that day, I stepped out on the balcony and leaned against the railing, staring out at nothing. A strange feeling washed over me— an emptiness I couldn't quite explain. It wasn't sharp like grief, wasn't suffocating like panic. It was just... *there*, a dull ache spreading through me, making everything feel distant. Meaningless.

I had tried to outrun my past, to start over, to leave the pain behind. But instead, I had been dragged into someone else's nightmare—Shane's nightmare—and now it was mine too. The thought made my stomach twist.

I didn't want to be part of it.

I didn't want to feel like this.

I didn't want to *be seen* like this.

Yet here I was, looking at the walkway below, contemplating the unimaginable.

It would be easy. *So easy.* One step and it would all be over—the pain, the emptiness, the weight of everything I carried. A merciful release. A way to be free.

I climbed up on the glass parapet wall.

Do it.

… but I just couldn't.

I pulled out my phone, my fingers trembling. I needed someone. Someone who understood me. Someone closer than a friend. My sister.

I typed the message and hit Send.

I DON'T WANT TO EXIST.

Within seconds, my phone rang.

It was Alesha.

I answered.

"Are you okay? Where are you?" she said, her voice frantic, skipping any greeting.

"I'm standing on my balcony," I said.

"Jessie, don't do anything crazy." I could hear the fear in her voice. "Mum, Dad, and I love you. We need you here."

"I know," I replied.

"So, what's wrong?" she asked.

"I feel like I keep spiralling back into the past," I confessed. "This was supposed to be my new life, a fresh start. And here I am, caught in the middle of someone else's mess, splashed across the media. It's dragging me back mentally." I closed my eyes.

"Don't add to it with another headline," she said.

"No thanks to Shane," I muttered. "It's not fair."

"Nothing in life is fair," she said. "The only thing you can do is fight back and live on."

My phone vibrated in my hand. A text from Shane.

Hi Jessie, hope you're on the mend. I would love to see you. I miss you heaps. X

I miss you heaps—as if nothing had happened. As if my life hadn't just been turned upside down because of *him*.

Moments later, he called, and I ignored it. I was still on the phone with my sister. Speaking to her was comforting, her voice a lifeline pulling me back from the brink. I climbed down from the ledge when the buzz of the intercom echoed through the apartment. I wondered who it could be.

"I've got to go. Someone's at the door," I said.

"Okay, but call me if you need anything. I mean it, anytime," she said.

"I will. Thank you for everything." With that, I ended the

call. I went inside to the intercom and pressed the button. "Hello?"

"Hey, it's Lindsey!" came the cheerful reply. I remembered I had asked her to come over on Saturday. Here she was, a rainbow in my otherwise grey day.

"Come on up," I said, buzzing her in.

I took a deep breath, trying to steady myself. A few minutes later, there was a knock at the door. I opened it to find Lindsey standing there, a smile on her face and a bottle of wine in her hand as always. She looked vibrant, dressed in a stylish outfit, while I was in an oversized sweater and leggings, having forgotten about her visit.

"Hey, you," she said, stepping inside and wrapping me in a big hug. "How are you?"

"Better now that you're here," I admitted.

"I come bearing gifts," she said, holding up the bottle of wine and a bag of snacks. "I figured these would be good for this afternoon."

For a moment, I eyed the bottle. "Wine?"

As much as I liked to have a drink, I was still taking medication, and I wasn't entirely sure how wine would mix with it—or if it might slow down my recovery. But maybe one glass wouldn't hurt. The doctor hadn't said I couldn't, and the label on the box only warned against driving.

She grinned. "One glass won't kill you."

It didn't take much to convince me. "Okay."

We made our way to the living room, where Lindsey set the wine and snacks on the coffee table before making herself comfortable on the couch. As she uncorked the bottle, I fetched a couple of glasses from the kitchen.

"So, how are you really doing after the shooting?" Lindsey asked.

"I'm okay, all things considered," I lied.

The truth was far uglier, and admitting how close I'd come to a breaking point would only scare her, and I didn't want to do that. She'd probably hover over me in a way that would only draw attention to what I'd rather keep hidden.

"The wound is healing." I pulled away the edge of my sweater to give her a glimpse of the bandage, freshly changed that morning.

"I've heard bits and pieces from the media about what happened that night, but I know how they twist things. I want to hear *your* side of it," she said, pouring wine into our glasses.

"It's a mess, Lindsey." I wasn't sure where to begin, so I told her everything I knew about the ordeal—Shane's lies, Olivia and Mark, the blackmail, the revenge Olivia had been chasing, and how Shane refused to tell me anything beyond how he'd met them.

"And you got caught in the middle of it," Lindsey said, shaking her head in disbelief. "So strange that he doesn't want to tell you more."

"Let's face it, it's her word against his. And if no one

knows the truth, then he has a chance of clearing his name and making Olivia look crazy. Honestly, it's probably better he didn't tell me anything—I don't want to be dragged into it any more than I already am."

"You know, when I worked at the real estate agency, my boss and the other agents always wondered how Shane could afford such a fancy house at twenty," she said, a hint of suspicion in her tone. "He had such a massive deposit for it. We all assumed he came from a wealthy family who gave him the money."

"His parents aren't poor, but they're not the kind of wealthy that hands out a million-dollar house deposit. And he isn't close to them—there's no way they'd help him out."

Lindsey nodded, piecing things together. "It makes sense then. Mark would've been his express ticket to wealth. If Shane wanted the house paid off and that flashy lifestyle he always flaunted, blackmail would've been the quickest route. There's no way he could service a mortgage that size on his salary, even with the commissions." She took a sip of wine. "I never thought he'd be involved in something like this though. He always seemed like a decent guy."

"That's what I thought," I admitted. "But now? I feel like I don't know him at all. And the worst part is I keep thinking about what Olivia said. What if it was all true?"

"That's scary. So... I assume you two are over?" she asked.

I paused. "Yes and no… I don't know anymore." I took a long sip of the wine, savouring the bittersweetness.

"How come you didn't tell me you two were together?"

"I'm sorry for not saying something sooner. It happened so fast… maybe too fast. I wanted to wait before I said anything to anyone. I liked him, but I was afraid that if I talked about it, I'd jinx it. That I'd kill the excitement before it even had a chance to become something real." I sighed, memories of how things had begun with Shane rushing back. "But honestly? It's already dead. Shane made himself out to be someone he's *not*. I don't feel like I can trust him. I keep wondering, what else is he hiding."

"Sounds like he was hiding a lot from you, so who knows? That's not fair to you. You deserve better."

"I know, but I think I ruined 'better,'" I confessed.

"So, you do like Seb?" she asked, raising her eyebrows.

"Yeah, but I was with Shane at the time and, in a way, cheated on him by being in Seb's presence—even more so when he kissed me."

"Oh, that's right. You mentioned he did."

"Yeah… The worst part is Seb found out about Shane from the media and now hates me. He hasn't even bothered contacting me since I left the hospital. Not that I blame him. I wasn't honest with him."

"They did mention it on TV and in online articles that Shane was your partner. It feels strange that you two were together and kept it a secret. I guess we all have our reasons. Have you tried to contact Seb?" She took a sip of her wine.

"No, I don't want to annoy him. I assume he doesn't want to see me. I know I wouldn't if I felt someone played me. It'll be interesting next year when I'm on campus and run into him." I dreaded the thought.

Lindsey leaned back on the couch. "You know, Jessie, people make mistakes. But it's how you deal with them that really matters. Maybe you should try talking to Seb. Clear the air."

Considering her words, I said, "Maybe you're right. I just don't know if I can face him."

"Trust me, it's better than living with regret," she said. "He's a great guy. If he really likes you the way he said he does, he'll forgive you."

I hesitated. "Will he? I don't know. Maybe I should take a break from dating. I feel like I rushed into things with Shane while I still wasn't fully over Zack. I should be focusing on myself."

"Who is Zack? And what happened?" she asked.

I had let more slip than I intended. Maybe it was the wine mixing with the medication that blurred the line between what I meant to say and what tumbled out. I reached for a chip, more to occupy my hands than anything else. "A tragedy I hope to never relive in my life. Once was enough."

"Is that why you moved to Adelaide?" Lindsey probed gently.

I refilled my glass and stood. For a second, the words caught in my throat. Then, with a sigh, I let the truth spill out. "Something like that… I had to escape," I confessed, my voice barely above a whisper. "Adelaide was a city I'd never lived in. It was a fresh start. Sydney… After what happened, I just couldn't stay there."

Lindsey's expression shifted. "What happened?"

I closed my eyes. "Zack took his own life…"

Until that moment, I had bottled it up, reluctant to even acknowledge what he'd done, let alone voice it aloud. I hadn't even told my parents how he'd died. I just couldn't do it. But now, here I was, confronting the painful truth.

"Why? Why would he do that?"

"He was depressed," I said quietly.

Since his death, I'd tried to forget the darker moments that had loomed over us, focusing only on the good—the way people flip through photos and keep only the flattering ones or edit photos until they looked perfect. It was easier to cling to the golden moments than to admit how dark the unfiltered reality really was. That was my way of coping. My way of altering reality to drag myself out of the void that had consumed me and my perception on life.

But the unfiltered truth was that I'd watched Zack slowly spiral while I convinced myself it was a passing phase. Days before he took his life, I'd gone over to his place and found him in the entertainment area, sitting alone at the bar. Half a bottle of whiskey sat open on the counter.

There were moments like that—him alone in his own world, sometimes at the piano, sometimes staring into nothing. He had friends, but he didn't always want to be around them. And while he wasn't drunk-drunk that night, the heaviness in him was unmistakable. He was too quiet. Too still. Too unlike himself.

"Zack?" I'd asked softly as I walked in. "Are you… okay?"

He let out a shaky laugh. "Yeah. I mean… no. Not really."

I slid onto the stool beside him. "What's wrong?"

He dragged a hand down his face. "Life. Everything. I feel tired in every way imaginable."

I froze.

I'd seen him low before—withdrawn, distracted, hiding behind silence—but he had never opened up—not once. Every other time I'd asked if he was okay, he'd brushed it off with a grin or a shrug, burying whatever he carried so deep I could barely catch glimpses of it.

But that night… something had cracked.

He stared at his hands. His silence wasn't empty—it was *full*, packed with things he couldn't say out loud. I didn't need to hear his thoughts to know demons were clawing at him from the inside.

I reached out, gently touching his arm. "Zack… you can

talk to me. I'm always here for you. I always will be."

I'd wanted him to open up. I wanted him to let me in. And I could feel—down to my bones—that something was off. But instead of speaking, he lifted his hand and brushed his fingers along my cheek, slow and deliberate, as if grounding himself in the shape of me.

Then he leaned in and kissed me.

It wasn't our usual kiss.

It wasn't playful, passionate, or teasing.

It was raw. Quiet. Almost like a plea for closeness—for escape—for anything that made him feel less alone.

"You're so gorgeous," he murmured against my lips. "I love you so much."

"I love you too." I kissed him back, my hand sliding to the back of his neck. In that moment, all I wanted was him.

In the days that followed, Zack and I immersed ourselves in a world of art and music. One afternoon, we wandered through an art gallery, playfully photobombing each other's snapshots of paintings. Our laughter echoed through the halls, drawing a few amused glances from strangers as we went from one exhibit to the next.

And then there was the music festival—his favourite one.

I could still picture him there, dancing with abandon under the open sky, his face alight with pure joy. His favourite DJs graced the stage, playing tracks that had inspired him to be a music producer. Watching him in those moments, engrossed and free, was a memory etched in my heart.

He'd seemed genuinely excited. I remember thinking he'd bounced back, that whatever he had been dealing with was already behind him—that the happiness I saw meant he was okay.

But looking back… I realised how easily a smile could be a façade.

A part of me harboured a quiet guilt over Zack's death. It gnawed at me, feeding a growing sense of self-reproach.

I felt as if I had failed him, failed to be the partner he'd needed, the one who could have reached into his darkness and pulled him back into the light.

I hadn't realised how much I'd said until the room fell quiet again. Only then did it hit me—I had told Lindsey everything. All the parts I'd never spoken aloud. All the pieces I'd kept locked away for so long.

Lindsey's eyes brimmed with tears. "I'm so sorry. I shouldn't have asked. It was thoughtless of me."

I sat down next to her, touching her arm. "Hey, it's okay. Don't be upset."

Lindsey wiped a tear that had escaped down her cheek. "I just can't imagine. I don't know how I'd cope if anyone I was with did that. I don't think I could cope. You're much stronger than I am." She hugged me. "I'm sorry for what you've been through."

"It's not easy," I admitted.

In the days after his death, I'd thought about committing suicide too. On bad days, I still did. I'd thought about ending my life in many different ways so I could escape the misery and be with him again. I'd found myself in a dark space where I'd never been emotionally, and I couldn't escape it. I was an absolute mess for months.

Zack had been more than a partner; he was my soulmate, the love of my life, and his loss had left a void I was still trying to navigate. I felt robbed. Nothing could bring him back. Not a single action, thought, tear, or prayer. Nothing. This was a world without him. A world without what he could have offered, or achieved, or become.

"After Zack's death, I completely shut myself off from the world," I confessed. "I blamed myself. It got to the point where I couldn't sleep. I'd lost my appetite, barely ate anything. I lost so much weight..." That hadn't changed much. I was a shadow of my former self. "I fell into this deep depression."

Feeling the magnitude of my admission, I paused. "Moving to Adelaide was like... It was like dragging myself out of the darkness I was drowning in and finding hope again. For the first time in ages, I felt like doing something. I regained some motivation. Until recently."

I'd never told anyone this, not in such detail. I guess that was because I'd needed time to recover without an outpouring of sympathy. Admitting to that was a different story.

"You can't blame yourself for his death. It wasn't your fault," she said.

I looked down, my fingers tracing the fabric of the couch. "I know, but part of me still does. He never fully opened up about what he was going through. I wish he had."

"Maybe he didn't want to burden you with his problems," she suggested.

"Maybe." I took a deep breath. "But it left me wondering: Was it because his father kept joking that music was only a hobby and that he should get a real career like his brother? Or was it the comments from his friends, telling him his old man could get him a proper job tomorrow or making digs that he didn't need to work hard because he had money? He never talked about how those things made him feel, but I saw it. I saw his expression change every time. Even when he tried to hide it. Or was it something else?"

"But you can't carry responsibility for what he didn't tell you. You loved him. You showed up for him. That's more than most people ever get," Lindsey said.

"He left me a letter. In it, he said he loved me." My voice faltered as I recalled Zack's words, the love intermingled with pain. "But if he truly loved me, if I really brought him happiness, why would he leave me like that? Why would he choose to go? We'd known each other our whole lives. We were together for over five years. I thought I was his safe place. And yet he still…

killed himself."

The words broke something open inside me. I'd been holding everything in—every question, every ache, every what-if—for so long that when I finally spoke the truth out loud, the emotion surged up before I could stop it. My breath hitched, and tears spilled uncontrollably as I sat back on the couch.

"That's what hurts the most, Lindsey." I choked out, wiping at my face but failing miserably. "I would've rather he burdened me with everything—every dark thought, every fear, every ugly thing he was fighting—than lose him."

"I'm sure he didn't do it to hurt you. He probably thought there was no way out, that he had no other choice. When someone's suffering that much, they're not thinking straight." She moved closer, wrapping an arm around my shoulders. "People in that place... they don't think about who they're leaving behind. They only want to end their pain. It's not about you, Jess. It was never about you.

"You loved him," she whispered. "And he loved you. That part was real. But loving someone doesn't always mean they can see their way out of the dark. And you didn't fail him. You loved him the best way you could. Don't punish yourself for the things he didn't let you see."

"I hate that I still feel like this. I hate that part of me still wonders if I could've saved him."

"You couldn't have," Lindsey whispered.

I nodded, though the part of me that still hurt didn't fully believe it.

"Why don't we get out of here for a bit? Let's go to the beach while the sun's still out."

I was surprised by the suggestion—but relieved by it too.

"Come on," she coaxed with a smile. "The ocean will help clear your head. It does wonders for me when I'm stressed or upset."

The beach was a short walk from my apartment. Before we left, I grabbed a packet of cigarettes from the kitchen bench, one of a few I had around my place. Lindsey topped up our glasses, put the bottle into her handbag, and we headed out the door. We weren't supposed to be walking around with glasses of wine or drinking at the beach, but as long as we didn't make a scene, no one would notice or care.

By the time we reached the beach, the sun was setting and there were only a few people around. We kicked off our shoes, letting the cool sand sift between our toes as we headed closer to the shore. Lindsey set her handbag down near our shoes while I pulled out a cigarette and lit it. The two of us wandered towards the water.

Holding the wine glass in one hand and the cigarette in the other, I walked into the water without thinking it through. It was cold but not unpleasant.

I took another drag of my cigarette and kept going in

farther, until I was waist deep. My clothes clung to me, but I didn't care. I felt as if the ocean was absorbing the emotion and pain I couldn't carry anymore. It felt amazing.

Behind me, Lindsey laughed. "Jess… you're soaked!"

20

Opening up to Lindsey the day before had lifted a weight that had been pulling me down mentally, yet one nagging thought still clouded my mind: Seb.

Lindsey's words echoed in my head: *Try talking to him.*

Easier said than done.

I sat on the kitchen counter, my phone lying beside me like an accusing reminder of my indecision. I picked it up, my thumb hovering over the screen.

Call him? No.

Text? Maybe.

I typed:

HI SEB, CAN WE TALK? JESSIE.

I winced. It was pathetic. Desperate.

I sighed and deleted it.

"Chicken," I muttered, tossing the phone back onto the counter with a thud.

As if on cue, a message buzzed through. I gasped. Maybe it was him. Maybe, somehow, he had been thinking about me too.

I grabbed the phone, heart pounding.

Shane.

I groaned. *Not now*.

His messages had been pouring in all morning, just like yesterday.

HEY, HAVEN'T HEARD FROM YOU. EVERYTHING OK?

Another message read:

I LOVE YOU.

Followed by another:

CALL ME WHEN YOU GET A CHANCE?

Then…

JESSIE?

I stared at the screen. Shane wasn't apologising—because in his mind, he hadn't done anything wrong. To him, everything was fine—normal because it was his problem, not mine.

But it wasn't.

I swiped my thumb across the screen, hesitating. Maybe I should respond. Maybe I owed him that much. What was left to say? I'd already told him I needed space. Words seemed futile.

I placed my phone on the counter, letting its screen go dark.

Letting the silence stretch between us.

Letting it speak for me.

* * *

For the next couple of weeks, I drifted through my days like a ghost. I met up with Lindsey, went shopping, and visited different parts of Adelaide—anything to keep myself occupied and avoid Shane and Seb.

I told myself that giving it time, letting the dust settle, would make it easier to smooth things over later. But deep down, I knew the truth. I was avoiding, and worse—I was a coward for it.

Shane, however, refused to be ignored. His messages piled up, each one more insistent than the last. Some were casual, as if nothing had changed. Others grew frustrated, demanding answers. I ignored them, hoping he'd get the hint. He didn't.

One morning, the incessant ringing of my phone jolted me awake. I groggily reached for it, squinting at the screen—missed calls, unread messages. Shane. Again.

With a sigh, I switched off the phone and let it fall onto the bed beside me. I just wanted peace.

I drifted back to sleep and woke hours later, just in time

for brunch. Opting for something quick, I grabbed an English muffin and slathered it with strawberry jam—the sugar hit I felt I needed.

As I stood at the counter, Lucky wove around my ankles, letting out a meow. I smiled, breaking off a small piece of muffin for him, knowing too well that his own bowl of food was never quite satisfactory in his eyes. He always wanted a taste of whatever I had.

Leaning back, I took a bite of the muffin, savouring the taste until it was gone. Then as I reached for the kettle to make coffee, a sudden knock at the door startled me.

I froze.

I wasn't expecting anyone, nor had anyone buzzed me from the front. It had to be a mistake, someone at the wrong apartment. It had happened before.

Wiping my hands on a tea towel, I made my way to the door. I wished it had a peephole or something so I could see who was on the other side. I paused for a few seconds, then slowly pulled it open.

Shane.

He stood there, barely resembling the man I'd once known. His dishevelled appearance was a stark contrast to his usual style—his hair was a mess, his clothes wrinkled as if he hadn't bothered to change in days. Dark circles underscored his eyes. Had he even been to work? Had he slept at all?

And now he was here.

I gripped the edge of the door. "What are you doing here?"

His haggard look spoke of more than just exhaustion—it hinted at something deeper. He didn't answer, didn't wait for an invitation. Instead, he stepped past me into the apartment.

"How did you even get up here?" I let the door swing shut behind him.

Shane ran a hand through his unkempt hair. "I told the building manager I was worried about you, that you weren't answering my calls, so he let me in." His words did little to ease my discomfort.

I frowned. "He shouldn't have done that without contacting me first." The thought of someone being able to talk their way into my home without my permission made my skin crawl. That wasn't okay. That wasn't safe. "I'm going to have a word with him about this," I muttered more to myself than to Shane.

But Shane didn't seem to notice, or maybe he didn't care.

"I've been so worried," he said, moving closer.

I backed up, flattening myself against the wall, hoping he wouldn't try to kiss me.

"I've been stressing out," he continued. "With everything that's been happening with Olivia, with us…"

I caught a whiff of alcohol coming from him. "Have you been drinking?"

He brushed off my question, frustration flickering across his face. "My life's a mess," he muttered, slurring his words as he stumbled to the living room.

I followed him.

"I'm so upset you didn't answer any of my calls or texts," he continued, pacing in erratic strides. "You're the only one I can turn to."

His chaotic energy set me on edge.

"Olivia's been talking. She's told the police everything—and more." He ran both hands through his hair, his breathing uneven. "Now I'm under investigation. I'm going to lose everything—my job, my house, and the little money I have left after the renos... The fines, the lawyer fees. Jessie, I could end up in jail."

"Shane, you need to calm down," I said, watching him.

"Calm down?" His voice rose. "Calm down?" He let out a hollow laugh. "Greg suspended me until further notice because of all the media attention. He doesn't want the bad publicity for the agency."

His words hung in the air.

I could see the fear in his eyes—he knew that his carefully constructed life was crumbling. His arrogance, his bravado, all stripped away. What was left was something raw, vulnerable... afraid. And for a fleeting moment, I felt a pang of sympathy. But sympathy wasn't enough to rebuild trust.

"Panicking won't solve anything," I said, my voice steady. "What's done is done. You need to take responsibility, Shane. You created this mess, and now you're upset about the fallout."

"This is Olivia's fault," he shot back. "The woman is nuts. She trying to ruin my life."

"So you keep saying, but what about your involvement in all this?" I countered. "You blackmailed her husband to gain wealth. You lied to me about knowing them. And now you're playing victim?"

Shane crossed his arms. "So what if I did blackmail him? The money wouldn't have even made a dent in his account."

My jaw dropped.

"What?" he shouted as if I were the unreasonable one.

The reality of who he was and what he was capable of doing scared me. "You had something to do with the accident, didn't you?"

There it was again—silence.

He went to my fridge, grabbed a bottle of wine, then a glass from the cupboard, and poured himself a drink. "I'm not like you, Jessie. I didn't grow up with parents who are property developers sitting on hundreds of millions. I didn't get handed anything. I had to do it on my own. You don't even know how lucky you are."

"I see you've done your research." I rolled my eyes.

"Please," he scoffed before draining the glass of wine and placing it on the counter. "Everyone at school knew who your parents were. You bought a real estate portfolio worth more than most people will earn in their lifetimes. People talk. How could I not know?"

I clenched my fists, anger flaring through me. "So, is that why you're with me?"

"No, it's not—"

"Isn't it?" I cut him off, my voice laced with bitterness.

He opened his mouth, but the words never came.

I shook my head. "You know what? I don't want anything to do with this mess anymore or you."

Shane looked at me. "Jessie—"

But I was done listening. I held up a hand, stopping him mid-sentence. "You lied to me, Shane. You need to leave." The trust, the connection—whatever we had—was gone, buried under the weight of his lies and deceit.

"What? Why? You're overreacting," he slurred. "I love you. I want us to be together. Don't do this to us."

A sharp ache twisted in my chest. Not because I felt the same way, but because I didn't want to hurt someone who claimed to love me. Though it didn't matter what he said at this point or how it made me feel as it wasn't enough to change my mind. "It's over, Shane." I pointed towards the door. "Please, go."

He glared at me, jaw clenched as if daring me to take it back. For a second, I thought he might try one last plea, a last-ditch effort to salvage whatever was left between us. But instead, he stormed to the door, wrenched it open, and slammed it shut behind him. It set off a vibration I swore could have cracked the walls.

I made my way to the kitchen and sat on the stool at the counter. I stared blankly ahead, my vision blurring. The tears threatened to spill.

Don't cry.

I whispered it to myself, trying to hold back the tears.

Lucky leapt onto the counter beside me, his soft fur brushing against my arm. He nudged his head against mine, purring.

Part of me felt lighter—relieved even—as if by ending things with Shane, I had unshackled myself from the chains of his problems. Yet anxiety pulsed through me, a residual effect of seeing him so unravelled, so desperate.

The image of him standing in my doorway lingered. It was a version of Shane I barely recognised—forceful, invasive, crossing boundaries as if they didn't exist. He'd barged into my apartment uninvited, disregarding my request for space.

I kept glancing at the door, half expecting it to burst open. The thought of another encounter with Shane and his unpredictable behaviour made my heart race.

I needed to get out.

Grabbing my keys off the counter, I slid them into my pocket. "I'll be back soon," I murmured to Lucky.

He blinked at me, tail flicking lightly, as if to say, "I'll be here when you get back."

Stepping out into the hallway, I closed the door behind me and headed for the elevators. In minutes, I was outside of my apartment complex. My eyes instinctively scanned the area for any sign of Shane. The coast was clear, but it didn't stop the paranoia from creeping in.

I forced myself to walk.

The closer I ventured to the beach, the more the tightness in my chest loosened. It was the perfect spring afternoon—a cool breeze swept through my hair.

When I reached the sand, I slipped off my shoes and made my way to the shoreline. The cool water lapped at my feet as I surrendered to the tranquillity of it all before stepping farther in. The waves swirled around my ankles, then my calves.

A bark cut through the calm, jolting me back to reality.

I turned, greeted by a familiar sight in the distance.

Seb and Luna.

My heart skipped a beat before panic took hold. As much as I liked him—and as much as I wanted to apologise—I wasn't ready to face him. Not now. Not like this.

I quickly averted my gaze, pretending I hadn't noticed him. My pulse raced as I forced myself to act natural, though every fibre of my being screamed at me to get away.

Hesitating for only a second, I walked in the opposite

direction, quickening my pace to put more distance between us. The crash of the waves grew fainter as I hurried off the beach, my bare feet moving swiftly over the sand.

Don't look back.

The urge to glance back was strong, but I resisted. I couldn't let Seb see me like this—nervous, unprepared, and more vulnerable than I cared to admit.

By the time I reached my apartment complex, my nerves were frayed. I entered the foyer, the cold air hitting me, but it did little to calm my racing thoughts.

Instead of heading to the elevators, I paused at the reception desk, trying to gather myself. Shane's intrusion lingered, an unsettling residue I couldn't shake.

The desk was unattended, so I pressed the bell. The sound echoed in the empty lobby, and a moment later, the building manager emerged from the back office.

"Jessie," he greeted. "Can I help you with something?"

I took a deep breath. "Earlier today, you let someone up to my apartment. An ex of mine."

He frowned, concern flashing in his eyes. "Oh, I'm really sorry about that. He told me he was your boyfriend and seemed concerned because you weren't answering you phone or the intercom. After seeing the news… I assumed he was still your partner." He sighed. "Serves me right for believing reporters. That was my mistake."

It wasn't entirely his fault. He'd trusted the wrong person while Shane had used that to his advantage and pushed boundaries, even lied about the intercom too.

I nodded. "I understand, but you shouldn't have let him up there. Please, in the future, contact me before you send anyone up to my unit. And if Shane shows up again? Don't let him in. If he refuses to leave, call the police."

His expression turned serious. "Absolutely, I'll make sure of it. I should've been more careful. I promise it won't happen again."

"Thank you," I said as I went to the elevators. "I appreciate it."

21

A few days later.

I poured myself a glass of wine, then took out my laptop and settled onto the couch in the living room. I'd received a few deposit notifications from my bank over the month and wanted to review them, along with my stock investments.

Logging into my banking portal, I went to my investment account first. A few of the companies I had invested in had increased in value, one by a significant amount. *Not bad.*

Then I looked at my main account, skimming through the transactions without much thought—until something made me pause. I blinked, leaning in closer.

Dividends from a couple of my investments had landed, and rental income from my properties had been deposited by the real estate agencies managing them.

"Shit," I whispered, staring at the balance.

Though I'd always had a decent amount of money, this was the first time I'd seen such a gain from my investments. It felt… different. Empowering.

I took a sip of wine, letting the numbers sink in.

Maybe I should reinvest—buy another local rental property or shares in the companies that had performed well. There was enough money for both. I could also give some to charity since I'd planned to earlier on but hadn't decided on a cause until now. I wanted to donate to an organisation that provided support programs to people with depression—Zack had suffered in silence, and it felt right to honour that.

Opening a new tab, I navigated to the real estate website, scrolling through listings—apartments, units, houses—losing track of time as I skimmed through potential opportunities.

My phone rang, snapping me from my thoughts. I glanced at the screen. *Lindsey.* I hadn't spoken to her for a few days.

"Hello?" I answered.

"Jessie! Guess who's officially survived uni this year?" Lindsey's voice burst through the phone.

I laughed. "I'm going to take a wild guess and say you?"

"Got it in one!" she exclaimed. "I haven't got my results back yet, but honestly? I'm not even stressed. I know I've passed. And now, I'm in serious need of celebrating."

Lindsey always had a way of turning any occasion into an adventure or a party—or both.

"What do you have in mind?" I asked, already picturing her hatching some elaborate plan.

There was a brief pause. "Actually, I hadn't thought that far ahead. But I'm in the mood to celebrate."

"Seriously? Here I was thinking you had planned something wild because, let's face it, you always have ideas." I drained the last of the wine in my glass. It was the last bottle in the apartment. "Great. I'm out of wine," I muttered to myself, making a mental note to stop by the bottle-o next time I went to the shops.

"Vineyards," Lindsey suddenly said.

"Vineyards?" I asked.

"Vineyards," she repeated. "Have you ever been to one?"

"Yeah, I've been to a few around Sydney. My parents are big wine collectors. They love to visit vineyards, sampling different bottles, and then buying way more than they need. Sometimes in bulk—several cartons of a single wine. Though to be fair, that's usually for the parties they host."

"Your parents sound like they know how to have a good time," Lindsey teased. "You know what we should do?" She didn't wait for me to answer. "We should make a day of it. Visit a vineyard. I've been to the ones in McLaren Vale, but I've never made it up to the Barossa Valley."

"A trip to the Barossa sounds good."

"Let's do it," Lindsey replied. "It's going to be epic."

I opened a new browser tab on my laptop. "Okay, where do you want to go? Let's start planning this thing."

"There are so many places, but we have to hit Jacob's Creek."

"Are we inviting anyone?"

"Yeah, nah," Lindsay said. "John and the others you met at my birthday still have exams. We'll probably all head out clubbing next weekend when everyone's finished."

"Fair enough," I said.

I typed in "Jacob's Creek," bringing up their website, and scrolled through the offerings. "They've got a tours and tastings… Oh, and we can have lunch afterwards. How does that sound?"

"Lock it in."

"When do you want to go?" I asked. "Tomorrow, or is that too soon?"

"Too soon? Are you kidding me? I'd go today if we didn't have to book in advance."

I smirked, clicking through the website. "I'll book the tour and tasting now. It will be at eleven o'clock tomorrow." My fingers flew across the keyboard, securing our spot. A confirmation pinged in my inbox seconds later. "All done! And I've reserved us a table for lunch at their restaurant too. We're set."

"Great!" Lindsey sounded thrilled. "I'll come over around nine o'clock tomorrow morning so we can hit the road."

The next morning, Lindsey buzzed my apartment right on time, and I let her up. As soon as I opened the door, she practically bounced inside.

"Jessie, ready for the trip?" she chirped.

Lindsey looked effortlessly chic in a short black-and-white dress, which she'd paired with white sandals. Her hair was pulled back into a neat bun, and a touch of jewellery completed her look. In contrast, I had chosen a light, knee-length floral dress bursting with colour and ballet flats—ideal for the warm day ahead.

"Do you want to drive us there?" she asked as we headed out. "I want to have a few drinks."

"I guess so," I said, knowing I'd have to limit my drinks.

After grabbing my keys and handbag, we left the apartment and took the elevator down to the basement carpark, then hopped into my car.

"Flash car," she said, running her fingers over the leather interior.

I smiled, shaking my head as I started the engine. Pulling out of the garage, I stopped in the driveway to enter the vineyard's address into the GPS.

As I sped off, Lindsey hit me with the question I'd been dreading. "Have you contacted Seb yet?"

My grip on the steering wheel tightened. "I haven't," I admitted, keeping my focus on the road. "I actually saw him at the beach the other day, but I couldn't bring myself to confront him."

"Jessie, come on," she said. "You should reach out. I know it's hard, but avoiding him isn't going to make it any easier."

"I know, I know," I replied, frustrated mostly at myself. "It's just… every time I see him, I feel like such an idiot and panic. I don't even know how to start the conversation without sounding—" I cut myself off, searching for the right word. "Messy."

"You're overthinking it," she said. "Just be honest. He deserves to hear from you, and you deserve some peace of mind, knowing where you stand."

She was right, of course. I couldn't keep running from this—from him. But that didn't make it any easier to pick up the phone and make the call or to see him in person. The thought of confronting him scared me. I didn't want to disappoint him.

"Maybe," I murmured, though even I wasn't convinced.

"Promise me you'll think about it?"

As we entered the Barossa Valley, the terrain transformed into vibrant greens and earthy browns, stretching as far as the eye could see. Each vineyard had rows upon rows of grapevines combed into the landscape. Here and there, farmhouses and wineries emerged like jewels nestled on plantations, their charm magnified by the expanse of nature that surrounded them.

Lindsey rolled down her window. "God, it's gorgeous out here."

I couldn't disagree. There was something peaceful about this place. Maybe today was exactly what I needed.

We pulled into the parking lot of Jacob's Creek, finding a shaded spot beneath a towering gum tree. As I climbed out, I took in the picturesque surroundings that stretched out in every direction. Grabbing my phone, I snapped a few photos, wondering if there'd ever been a grape farmer who let their vines go wild like a hedge gone rogue. But I was sure harvesting that would be a nightmare.

"Are you coming?" Lindsey called, already a few steps ahead.

Tucking my phone into my handbag, I hurried after her. We'd arrived thirty minutes early, so we had some time to kill. We wandered around the entrance, soaking in the atmosphere as people arrived, some heading straight inside, others lingering like us, waiting for the wine-tasting tour.

Lindsey and I were in full tourist mode, snapping selfies near the entrance, in front of the vineyard's sign. As I turned to take another shot, a familiar pair of faces caught my eye. I froze, my phone nearly slipping from my grasp.

Mum. Dad.

They were walking straight towards us, their expressions a mirror of my own surprise. It was as if they'd materialised out of one of their "Guess where we are?" messages.

For a heartbeat, they stopped and none of us moved. We just stared at each other, caught in a moment too surreal to process. Then, all moving at once, we closed the distance.

"Mum? Dad?" I managed to say as I threw my arms around them, hugging them tightly. The feel of them, real and present after almost a year apart, was overwhelming. I hadn't realised how much I'd missed them until that moment.

The last update I'd had from them was from Coober Pedy—photos of opal mines, endless desert landscapes, and panoramic views from various lookout points. The wealth of colours of the arid desert filled each shot, unlike the lush vineyards we were standing in.

"How… When did you get here?" I asked, pulling back slightly to look at them.

"We got in late last night," Mum said. "We were planning to call you once we arrived in Adelaide so we could catch up, but it looks like we don't need to now."

"We had no idea you'd be here today," Dad said, sounding dazed.

"This is insane. What are the odds?" I was reeling from the unexpected reunion.

"It's a wonderful surprise, isn't it?" Mum replied.

I nodded, the reality of the moment sinking in. Of all the places in the world, of all the *days*, we had ended up here—at the same vineyard, at the same time. It felt like the universe had conspired to bring us together.

Then it hit me—I hadn't introduced Lindsey.

"Oh!" I turned, flashing her an apologetic smile. "Mum, Dad, this is Lindsey. She's a friend of mine."

Lindsey stepped forward, extending her hand. "Hi, it's so nice to meet you both!"

"Lovely to meet you too," Mum said, shaking her hand.

"We're here to celebrate Lindsey finishing her uni exams." Then with a sheepish grin, I added, "And, well… I ran out of wine."

Dad chuckled. "Sounds like a good enough reason to me. We stopped here because I want to expand our collection. I've been looking forward to tasting what they have on offer. We'll be going to McLaren Vale next." He glanced at his watch, then gestured towards the entrance. "The tour's about to start."

As I was about to follow them, something—or rather, someone—caught my eye in the distance. My stomach twisted.

No.

You have got to be joking.

Shane.

He was walking through the car park with his coworkers, heading straight for the same entrance. I recognised his coworkers from the awards night—his boss, Mitch, Kylie, and a few others. They were dressed casually but polished enough for a work outing. Kylie was wearing a dress while the guys were wearing black pants and button-down shirts.

What's he doing here?

I'd only seen him a few days ago—drunk, panicked, and spiralling about how he'd been suspended and was terrified of losing everything. The last thing I'd expected to see was him strolling into a vineyard like nothing had happened. Had he been reinstated? Lied to me? Or exaggerated the whole situation to manipulate me into feeling sorry for him?

I didn't know.

But of all the places, of all the *days*, did the universe really have to throw *this* at me?

It was one thing for my parents to show up unexpectedly. That had been a pleasant surprise. *This* was anything but.

Before I could react, Lindsey nudged me with her elbow, her expression hovering between amused and sympathetic. "Look who's here."

Panic flared in my chest. My fingers curled around her arm, gripping tightly as I pulled her in the direction my parents were heading. "Let's stick with my parents, okay? Ignore him."

"Aye, aye, captain," she replied under her breath. "The last thing I want to see are my former coworkers."

I kept my gaze forward, refusing to look back as we reached my parents. The entrance was only a few steps away. I could hear my mum and dad chatting about the wines they were excited to try, oblivious to the tension that had taken hold of me.

Dad turned towards me with an excited grin. "Ready for the tour?"

I plastered on a smile that I hoped looked convincing. "Let's do this."

We went inside.

Displays of the many types of wines from different years decorated the foyer. Dad took a few photos of the displays as we headed to the outdoor waiting area. A small crowd had already gathered, talking among themselves as they waited for the tour to begin. Lindsey and I joined them, standing close to my parents.

A man and a woman in vineyard-branded shirts approached our group.

"Welcome!" the man said. "I'm Rob, your guide for today's tour and tasting experience."

He waited a few minutes, scanning the area as if checking for stragglers. That's when I saw him again.

Shane.

He and his coworkers strolled into the waiting area, casually blending into the group. Mitch and his boss were chatting animatedly with Kylie, their laughter ringing out as if they didn't have a care in the world. Shane, however, was different. He was trailing behind them, barely listening, his attention fixed on me.

"Great," Lindsey muttered under her breath, having noticed them.

"This vineyard was established in 1847…" Rob began, leading us into the sprawling fields of vines. "Here is where the magic begins." Stopping in front of rows of grapevines, he explained the stages of growth from budburst through to harvesting and how to recognise the different types of grapes before going on to the winemaking process. "Once the grapes are picked, they're put through presses, breaking them down gently to extract the juice before they're transferred to the open fermentation tanks…"

My awareness of Shane sharpened.

I could *feel* him.

Even though I hadn't looked his way, his presence loomed like an unwanted shadow at my side. Lindsey and I had been careful to avoid making eye contact, to act as if he wasn't there. But Shane, being Shane, couldn't leave it alone.

He edged closer. "Jessie," he whispered.

The sound of my name on his lips sent a ripple of unease through me.

Lindsey stepped between us and shoved him to the side with a single, deliberate motion. "Shoo."

Shane stumbled back a step, caught off guard.

The brief exchange felt like a bomb going off, but somehow, no one else seemed to notice—except Dad. His gaze flicked to me.

"Is everything okay?" Dad mouthed.

I nodded.

Rob led us back to the main building, where the wine-tasting room awaited. The space was inviting, with wooden tables neatly arranged, each set with rows of wine glasses and order forms ready to be filled.

"Now, for the highlight of the tour," Rob announced with a grin. "You'll get to taste a selection of our finest wines."

"Oh, good," Dad said, rubbing his hands together. "This is what I've been waiting for."

We settled at a table to the left of the room. But as fate would have it, Shane and his coworkers chose the table right next to ours.

I kept my focus on the wines, ignoring how close Shane was. One by one, we were presented with different wines, their colours ranging from deep reds to sparkling golds. Rob shared insights into the flavours, the process, and the passion behind each bottle.

"This is incredible," I whispered to Lindsey.

"We have to buy a few bottles," she agreed. "This is too good to pass up."

We continued sampling our way through the selection, each wine offering something unique.

Dad couldn't resist. He ordered almost the entire range, adding to his already impressive collection back home.

Caught up in the moment, I filled out my own order form,

selecting a carton of my three favourites to be delivered to my apartment. A humorous thought struck me. "My neighbours are going to think I've developed a serious drinking problem when this turns up."

Lindsey laughed. "They might steal a bottle or two for themselves." She quickly followed suit, marking down her favourites. "I'm going to need a bigger wine rack."

As we stood to leave for lunch, I looked up—and locked eyes with Shane. I could see that he wasn't going to let this chance slip by.

"Jessie?" he called.

I couldn't ignore him this time. "Shane," I acknowledged in my most neutral tone, taking in his appearance.

He looked different from the last time I'd seen him—calm, composed, put together. Gone was the drunk, desperate man who had shown up at my apartment. The contrast was striking. Had he somehow managed to resolve his legal troubles in a few days? Or was he concealing his turmoil, presenting a polished facade while his world continued to crumble behind closed doors? Either way, the man standing before me wasn't the man I had once trusted. And the worst part? I could no longer tell which version of him was real.

I didn't ask Shane any questions, though they swirled in my mind. I kept my thoughts to myself as I didn't want to be involved in his problems or life. Instead, I turned on my heel, following my parents and Lindsey to the restaurant.

"We have a reservation for lunch," Mum said.

"So do we," I added.

Dad glanced at me, then at Mum. "Why don't we merge the reservations and have lunch together?" Without waiting for a response, he walked off to speak with the staff. A few minutes later, he returned. "They said they can get us seated at the same table but need to switch a few reservations around."

We were ushered to our table in a corner that had a view of the plantation. As we settled in, an all-too-familiar figure and his entourage entered the restaurant. They were led to the table right next to ours.

Out of all the available tables, *why that one?*

The odds felt almost laughable. I scanned the restaurant. It was busy, but surely they could have seated them elsewhere. Why had they given them the table next to ours? Was the universe playing some cruel joke?

Shane slid into a seat that put him directly in my line of sight. His posture was relaxed, but his gaze was anything but—it was locked onto me, unreadable. Was he *glaring* at me? Or was I imagining things?

Lindsey leaned in. "Is he stalking you?"

"Maybe. No…" I was lost for words. "I don't think so."

The waiter arrived, offering us menus. Each of us placed our order, choosing meals that caught our fancy, accompanied by a glass of wine.

From the corner of my eye, I noticed Shane still staring. A slight smirk tugged at the corners of his mouth. A nagging thought crossed my mind—had he planned this?

No. That was ridiculous. There was no way that he could have known we'd be here today. Lindsey would *never* have spoken to him, and I certainly hadn't. It had to be a coincidence.

Didn't it?

My father's voice broke through my thoughts. "Isn't that the guy you broke up with?"

I knew exactly who he was talking about, but I still followed his gaze.

"He looks like the guy who's been all over the news."

"Yeah, that's him," I confirmed.

Dad frowned, glancing back at Shane. "Why is he here?"

"I don't know," I replied. "Probably a work thing." It was the only logical explanation.

Dad didn't look convinced. "How does he still have a job after everything that's been floating around in the media? And how is he even free?"

I swallowed hard. I knew my father had been following the story closely. Anything that involved Mark was too close to home, too close to his company. Bad press was the last thing he needed before his retirement.

And now, here we were—sitting within earshot of the very

man who had started all of this.

Dad cleared his throat. "How have you been holding up since… you know?"

I knew exactly what he meant. Olivia. The shooting. All of it.

Considering his question, I took a deep breath. "I'm okay given everything that's happened… My shoulder has almost healed completely, but there's a scar," I admitted before steering the subject to something lighter. "I haven't shown you the apartment I bought yet."

I pulled out my phone and scrolled through the photos until I found the ones of my place. It was something I was proud of. I handed my phone to Dad.

He flipped through the images. "It's nice," he said, turning the phone so Mum could see.

"I've bought several other properties around Australia too," I added, the words slipping out before I could stop them. "I wanted to build an investment portfolio."

Dad glanced at me. "How?"

My heart skipped a beat. *Shit.*

I hadn't meant to say that. The money my parents had given me was enough to buy my own place, but not *several* properties. Neither of them nor Lindsey knew about the money Zack had left me. I hadn't been planning on telling them either. That inheritance had come at too high a cost.

I forced a laugh, trying to brush it off. "Oh, there are ways."

Mum nudged Dad. "See? Our daughter isn't bad with money after all," she teased before turning to me. "Your dad was worried you'd blow whatever money you had access to."

I raised an eyebrow. "Seriously?"

"Well, you hadn't decided on a career path, and well..." She hesitated before adding, "You do love shopping."

Lindsey, who had been listening quietly, shot me a look—curious, amused.

"Dad!" I protested, though I couldn't exactly argue. "I thought you knew me better than that. You always reminded us to be smart with money..." My voice trailed off as the truth settled over me.

He wasn't entirely wrong.

Up until Zack's death, I'd been drifting through life. Lacking direction. Filling in the void with shopping sprees, nights out, things that didn't really matter...

Then I lost him.

And everything changed.

My perspective. My priorities. Me.

I saw the world differently now.

That didn't mean I wouldn't enjoy the occasional shopping spree in future, but the difference was now I knew exactly what I wanted.

Dad smiled. "We're proud of you, Jess. You proved me wrong."

"I'm financially independent now," I added. "I don't need any inheritance."

Dad shook his head. "You might be financially independent, but you're still going to get your portion. We'll be splitting it between you and your sister."

I didn't argue. I knew better than to challenge Dad on things like this.

When the time came to wrap up lunch, we settled our bill and made our way to the carpark.

"Well, I guess I don't need your 'Guess where we are?' update this time," I joked.

"Don't count on skipping the update," Dad said with a wink. "We can't break the cycle now."

True to form, he pulled out his phone, capturing a selfie of the four of us. Lindsey and I each flashed a thumbs-up. I already anticipated my sister's reaction—no doubt she'd bombard me with questions the second she saw the photos.

As we prepared to part ways, Mum and Dad pulled me into a tight hug, the kind that made you feel like you were home no matter where you were.

"So, where are you heading next?" I asked, curious about their travel plans.

Mum started listing off places. "Adelaide, Hahndorf, then

Kangaroo Island—"

But Dad cut her off. "Don't ruin the surprise!"

"Anyway, we'll see you soon," Mum said.

"Stay safe," they said in unison.

"And remember, we're just a call away, no matter where we are," Dad added.

"I know," I said. "Take care and have a safe trip."

As they walked away, a familiar ache settled in my chest. It was a mix of happiness from seeing them and the immediate pang that followed their departure. It was clear in the way they looked back that they felt it too.

I pulled out my car fob, ready to leave, when I saw Shane approaching us, looking awkward and out of place.

"What are you doing here?" I blurted.

"I… I'm here with the team from work." He stumbled over his words. "We're having an earlier work Christmas party since we're all busy in December. A few of us are going on holidays."

Crossing my arms, I cut straight to it. "Thought you were suspended."

"I am," he admitted quickly. "I'm not allowed to sell, contact clients, or do anything public facing. They even removed my profile off the website. As for today, this was paid for months ago, and Greg said I could come along."

"So, how's the situation with Olivia?"

Shane shifted uncomfortably, glancing at the ground

before meeting my eyes again. "My lawyer's working on clearing my name," he said, but his voice lacked confidence. "I don't know what the outcome will be yet."

There it was again—that flicker of doubt beneath his polished surface.

"Right… So, what do you want from me?" The question came out colder than I intended, but I didn't take it back.

Shane blinked, visibly taken aback. For a second, he just stood there as if he hadn't expected me to be so blunt. He glanced at Lindsey standing beside me, then back at me. "I… I don't want things to be like this between us, Jess."

"Shane," I said, choosing my words carefully, "we both need to move on. There's no going back to whatever was between us. You need to figure out your own life. I can't be part of that anymore."

"This is ridiculous. Can you stop playing games with me?" His eyes locked onto mine, searching for something—anything— that would suggest I hadn't made up my mind.

"I'm not playing games," I said.

"Don't you see?" He circled around me like a hawk closing in on its prey. "This must be some sort of sign. What are the odds of us meeting here? It's like the universe is trying to tell us something. It *wants* us to be together."

"Shane, that's not how this works." Or was it? A part of me wanted to believe that everything happened for a reason, that there were no true coincidences. But this? *This* was nothing more than chance. *It had to be.* "Us running into each other? That's just bad luck. Not fate."

"I want us to be together," he said. "I love you."

His words should have meant something. They once had. But now? They only reminded me how far I'd moved on.

"Well, I don't know how I feel about you," I admitted. "One minute, you're this ideal guy, and the next, you're lying and keeping things from me, blackmailing people, and doing *whatever* it takes to get ahead. How do I know you're telling me the truth now?"

"I'm sorry," he said as if that was supposed to fix everything.

"Our relationship crashed and burned, Shane. You could've been honest with me, but you weren't. And now you expect me to forget that?"

"I can promise you I'll tell you the truth going forward," he said. "But whether you trust me or not? That's your decision, not mine."

I let out a bitter laugh. "Then I guess my decision is already made."

Lindsey's voice cut through the tension. "Ready to go?"

"Yeah." I nodded, eager to put an end to this conversation. "Let's get out of here."

As I approached the car door, I felt a sudden grip clamped

around my wrist. Too tight. Too forceful.

Shane yanked me back, pulling me towards him. His desperation was palpable, written in his grip and the wild look in his eyes.

"Jessie, please," he begged, his voice raw, almost frantic. And then—before I could shove him away—he kissed me.

It wasn't gentle. It wasn't wanted.

Panic flared in my chest. My entire body recoiled. Every instinct screamed at me to get away. I pulled my arm free, stumbling back, breath ragged and heart racing.

"Shane, *no*," I gasped, my voice shaking. "It's *over*."

He said something—I wasn't even sure what. The world around me blurred at the edges, my mind drowning in shock and disgust. The only thing that was clear was the urge to get away. Not only physically, but completely—out of his life, out of this mess.

A sudden *crack* split the air.

Shane staggered back, clutching his mouth, eyes wide with disbelief.

Lindsey.

She stood rigid, fist still clenched from the punch she'd thrown. Blood welled at the corner of Shane's lip. "What the *fuck* is wrong with you? You don't *force* someone to kiss you! Who the hell do you think you are?"

Shane blinked, stunned, as if he couldn't believe what had just happened.

"Jessie!" Lindsey said. "Come on, let's go."

I didn't need to be told again.

We jumped into the car, slamming the doors shut. My hands trembled as I gripped the wheel, my breath unsteady. As I pulled away from the vineyard, I caught one last glimpse of Shane in the rearview mirror.

He stood there, shoulders slumped, blood on his lip, looking lost. Hollow.

And for the first time since I'd met him, I didn't feel an ounce of sympathy.

Only relief.

Because I was finally free.

22

When I walked through my apartment door, Lucky trotted up to me, meowing. His tail was high in the air as he brushed against my leg, welcoming me home.

"Hey, buddy." I reached down to scratch behind his ears.

He purred, rubbing against me.

I wandered into the kitchen, tossing my handbag onto the stool by the counter. I sighed, the exhaustion of the day settling over me. My mind replayed the events at the vineyard—including the uncomfortable run-in with Shane—as I grabbed a tin of cat food from the fridge and filled Lucky's bowl.

I needed a shower. Something to reset.

In my room, I peeled off my clothes and jumped into the shower. Steam curled around me as the hot water pounded against my skin, washing away the stress. But no matter how long I stood there, I couldn't wash away how the kiss at the vineyard had left me feeling violated. The force of it. The way he had taken it. The way he had grabbed me, as if he had a right to.

A shudder ran down my spine, and I pressed my palms against the tiles, trying to steady myself.

Once I stepped out, I stood in front of the mirror, absently towelling off. My gaze landed on my shoulder. The scar—once raw and red—had healed. Now it was only a mark where Olivia's bullet had torn through my skin. I ran my fingers over it, wincing slightly at the memory it carried.

Shaking off the thoughts, I slipped into my pyjamas and padded back to my room. Lucky had already claimed his spot on the bed, curled up in a ball.

I grabbed my phone from the nightstand and climbed in beside him, resting my head against the pillow as I checked my notifications—two messages. One from my parents and another from Alesha.

My parents had sent a collection of photos from the vineyard—scenic shots of the vineyard, candid moments of us from the tour, and the group shot we'd taken before parting ways—but it was the caption beneath the photo that caught me off guard:

WHEN THE UNIVERSE BRINGS US TOGETHER ♥

Universe. That word had come up too many times today.

I stared at it. Like my parents, I'd always believed in signs, believed that chance encounters weren't always chance at all— that sometimes the universe nudged people together for a reason. And maybe it had, but not in the way Shane thought. Maybe this hadn't been fate trying to push us back together. Maybe it was the universe showing me, in no uncertain terms, that it was over. That I needed to close the door and never look back.

I liked their message and scrolled down to Alesha's response.

JACOB'S CREEK!? I'M SO JEALOUS.

I liked her message, and almost immediately, my phone rang. Alesha. Instead of texting back, she'd gone straight to calling me.

"Wasn't texting easier?" I answered.

"No," she replied. "I've had enough of texting. I wanted to hear someone's voice—your voice."

"Right," I said. "That's kind of strange in a psycho-killer way, but you're pregnant, so maybe that's—"

"Don't remind me."

"I assume you're still hiding from the world?"

"Maybe." She paused. "When are you coming home for Christmas and New Year?"

"I'm not sure yet."

"You *are* coming home, right?" she pressed.

"Of course," I said.

"You should come early."

Alesha wasn't the type to admit when she was lonely, so the fact that she was asking this way told me she really needed me.

"I'll think about it," I said.

23

Two weeks later.

December arrived, and with it came my long-awaited trip back to Sydney. I'd be spending over a month with my family before returning to Adelaide. But instead of booking a flight, I was going to drive.

Packing, as always, was a process. I tossed an assortment of summer essentials into my suitcase—flowy dresses, bikinis, tops, and shorts to survive the Sydney heat. I wanted options but tried not to go overboard. If I ran out of clothes, I could always go shopping.

Once my suitcase was nearly full, I did my usual mental checklist, pacing around the room as I ticked off items one by one. Toothbrush? Check. Toothpaste? Check. Makeup, hairbrush, sunscreen? Check, check, check.

I was notorious for forgetting things whenever I travelled. Usually, I'd be halfway to my destination before realising I'd left something behind—phone charger, razor, once even my entire makeup bag. Not this time. This time I was determined to get it right and save myself the hassle of having to buy stuff again.

Lucky sprang onto the bed and climbed into the open suitcase, making himself comfortable right on top of my folded clothes. He was reminding me not to leave him behind.

I laughed, scratching behind his ears. "Don't worry, I'm not forgetting you."

After coaxing him out of the suitcase, I finished packing and turned my attention to the fridge, clearing out anything that wouldn't survive a month of my absence. Milk, eggs, yoghurt, a forgotten bag of salad—it all went into the trash. The last thing I needed was to return to a biohazard in my kitchen.

Finally, I opened Lucky's pet carrier and scooped him up, placing him inside. He settled in without too much fuss, his green eyes peering at me through the mesh, watching my every move.

"Ready for a road trip, buddy?" I asked.

With everything packed and organised, I hauled my suitcase to the elevator and went down to the basement parking. Each step echoed off the concrete walls, the wheels of my suitcase clattering behind me. My BMW waited in its usual spot, gleaming faintly under the fluorescent lights. I popped open the boot and carefully loaded the luggage, pulling a mesh over it to stop it from shifting during the drive.

Then it was one last trip up to my apartment for my handbag and Lucky. A few minutes later, I was back at my car, placing his carrier in the backseat and securing it in place.

I threw my handbag in the front passenger's seat, slid behind the wheel, and took a deep breath. This was it—me, Lucky, and the open road. I punched my parents' address into the GPS to track my progress along the way.

Two days later, I pulled into my parents' driveway, somewhat exhausted. I gazed up at the grand entrance as I stepped out of the car, stretching after the long drive. The front door swung open, and Alesha came hurrying down the steps. She was wearing a short dress, looking much cheerier than the last time I'd seen her.

"Jessie!" she called, beaming as she reached me.

"Alesha!" I grinned, pulling her into a hug. "You look amazing."

She laughed. "Well, the pregnancy isn't showing yet, so I still feel like myself. But give it a few more weeks, and it'll things will be different."

"I can't believe you're actually going to be a mum."

"Tell me about it," she said, rolling her eyes. "I'm not even prepared, but I have started looking at buying my own place not far from here."

I looked past her towards the house. "Are Mum and Dad home yet?"

"They're not due back for another week," Alesha replied, glancing over her shoulder as if expecting them to suddenly appear. "They have a few more places they want to check out on their way back."

I nodded, knowing they weren't far away. The last photos they'd sent were from Canberra.

Alesha peered through the car window and gasped. "Oh my gosh, look at him! He's gotten so big!" She opened the door, reaching in to grab Lucky's carrier.

"Yeah, he's grown," I said. "And a little more spoiled, if you ask me."

I grabbed my suitcase from the boot and followed her up the steps into the house. We made our way upstairs to my old bedroom, which looked exactly as I'd left it—other than the bed and nightstands, it was empty.

Alesha set Lucky's carrier down and unlatched the door. He clung to her the second she scooped him out.

A sudden knock at the front door echoed through the house. Alesha and I exchanged a quick glance.

"Are you expecting someone?" I asked.

She shook her head. "Nope."

We headed downstairs, through the foyer to the front door. I pulled open the door and was taken aback to see Conrad standing there, his hands casually shoved into his pockets.

"Conrad?" I raised an eyebrow. "What are you doing here?"

"I thought I'd stop by and see how you were doing."

I tilted my head, arms crossed. "You're not stalking me, are you?" I teased.

He chuckled. "Hey, don't flatter yourself. I saw your car pulling into the driveway when I got back from my afternoon walk. We're neighbours, remember?"

"Fair point. Come in." I stepped aside to let him in. He brushed past me, and I caught a faint scent of cedarwood and something fresh—soap, maybe.

As we walked through the foyer, Conrad asked, "How are you holding up?"

"I'm okay," I said.

He nodded, watching me closely. "Yeah, the news still seems to be peddling updates on Olivia because she was a model and is somewhat famous. They're really digging into every detail. It's hard to avoid."

"It'll probably relaunch her career," I muttered, rolling my eyes.

"Let's go out to the patio," Alesha suggested.

"Okay, I'll join you in a moment," I said, already heading towards the stairs.

Up in my room, I went straight to my handbag and

unzipped it to pull out a pack of cigarettes. As I did, my gaze caught the mirror above my dresser. The familiar face staring back at me looked different—maybe a little more worn, a little more guarded. There was a time when my eyes had been brighter, my features softer, untouched by grief, regret, and all the mess in between.

With a sigh, I tucked the cigarettes into my pocket and made my way downstairs. I grabbed a bottle of wine from the cellar and three glasses from the kitchen before heading outside.

Alesha was lounging on one of the outdoor chairs, scrolling through her phone as they waited for me.

I poured us each a glass of wine—even Alesha, just to keep up appearances—and set the bottle on the table. Then I took a seat next to her, pulling out a cigarette and lighting it with a practiced flick. I took a drag, feeling the nicotine relaxing me.

Conrad cleared his throat, glancing at me. "So… was it true? About Shane, I mean. Was he really… your partner?"

I knew the question would come up at some point. I hesitated, taking another slow drag as I mulled over how to answer. A part of me wanted to shrug it off, to laugh and say it wasn't anything serious, but that wouldn't be the truth. And if anyone deserved the truth, it was Conrad.

After all, Shane had come into my life at a time when I was desperately trying to fill a void left by someone I loved.

"Yeah," I admitted finally, exhaling smoke. "I'm sorry I

didn't say anything sooner. I jumped into that relationship way too soon, thinking it would help me… I don't know, move on, I guess. Help me let go of the pain after losing Zack. But it didn't work. If anything, it made things worse. Shane turned out to be someone completely different from who I thought he was, and now my name is being dragged through the media."

Conrad didn't say anything right away. He just watched me, his expression unreadable, as though he was trying to piece something together. I couldn't tell whether he was judging me or simply taking it all in.

"It's okay," he said eventually. "We all make mistakes."

Alesha smirked. "Some mistakes are better looking than others, at least. Mine wasn't and didn't even stick around."

A humourless chuckle escaped me. "Fair point." Leave it to Alesha to find the comical side of it.

Conrad's gaze shifted to Alesha. "Wait… Your boyfriend left you?"

"Yeah. He left me for someone he'd been seeing behind my back. Guess I wasn't enough for him," she said.

"I'm really sorry to hear that," he said. "But it's his loss. Seriously. And every other guy's potential gain." He shot her a smile.

"Well, any guy would be getting a two-for-one deal now."

Conrad's brows pulled together. "Two-for-one?"

"Yeah… Surprise, I'm pregnant," she said, the words

tumbling out as if she'd been holding them in, building up the courage to finally share. I could tell she was bracing herself, rehearsing for the moment when she'd have to tell our parents. I could see she was daring the world to judge her.

Conrad's eyes widened, and he nearly choked on his wine. "Wait, what?" His eyes darted between us as if waiting for one of us to laugh and say it was all a joke. "You're really pregnant?"

"Yep. I sure am," she said.

"Wow. Alesha, I had no idea," Conrad murmured. "Congratulations."

"Thank you," she said. "It's a little scary, to be honest. Especially now that I'll be doing it alone. Liam didn't return my calls or message me back, so he doesn't even know. He just cut me off, like I was some inconvenience he could ignore."

Silence settled between the three of us, the gravity of her news settling in.

Alesha was going to be a mother. And me? I was going to be an auntie.

Conrad looked as though he was still processing it, then his expression shifted from disbelief to something darker—anger, maybe. "What a wanker!" His jaw tightened. "To just leave you like that. What kind of guy does that?"

"Apparently, the kind of guy I picked," she said. "I thought I knew him, but clearly I was wrong."

Conrad leaned forward. "So, what are you going to do? Do

you have a plan?"

She shrugged, looking hopeful and lost at the same time. "I've been thinking about buying a place nearby. Something close to Mum and Dad so I'll have family around when the baby comes. Honestly? I have no idea what I'm doing. I'm trying to take it one step at a time."

"How far along are you?" he asked.

"Almost five months," she replied. "My parents don't know yet, so I'd appreciate it if you didn't say anything to anyone."

24

A few days later, Alesha and I were knee-deep in glitter, tangled in strands of fairy lights, and surrounded by an explosion of Christmas decorations—poinsettia clips, delicate glass baubles, crystal snowflakes, and ornate butterflies and birds perched on metal clips. Boxes were scattered across the floor, their contents spilling out like festive treasure troves.

Every year, our parents insisted on going all-out for Christmas. Unlike most families who stick with one Christmas tree, ours had to have multiple, each grander than the last: a towering tree in the foyer, its branches dripping in lights and ornaments, the first thing you saw when you walked through the door; another in the living room, where we put our presents and unwrapped them on Christmas morning; and a third, smaller one in the entertainment room, near the bar where Dad would mix his cocktails.

For as long as I could remember, it had always been the same—red-and-gold glass baubles and velvet bows that were carefully packed away in January, only to be brought out and recycled each December. How boring!

This year, I wanted something different. Something fresh.

So, with a spark of inspiration and maybe a bit too much free time, I'd gone to the shops and loaded up on new ornaments. No more standard colour schemes. No more repetition. Instead, all three trees would have a nature-inspired theme, with decorations in crisp whites, greens, and oranges. I wanted them to look like the ones in shop displays.

Alesha watched me move around the tree, carefully placing ornaments and adjusting branches. "You've really outdone yourself this year, Jess," she said, holding up a glittering white star for the foyer tree. "I'm impressed."

I stepped back to admire my work. "It's like therapy. Something about arranging each ornament just right… making everything look perfect. I guess I needed a project to detox my mind."

"I think it's beautiful. You've got an eye for it."

We'd left the Christmas tree in the living room for last. It was getting late, and Lucky, who'd been dozing on the couch, suddenly sprang to life, batting at one of the glass baubles dangling from a low branch.

"Oh no, you don't." I swooped in just in time, carefully prying it from his paws and swapping it for a plastic ornament instead. He pounced on it, rolling it across the floor. "Little troublemaker."

The front door creaked open, and we heard suitcases rolling across the marble floors.

Alesha and I exchanged a glance before rushing towards the foyer. There they were—Mum and Dad, their luggage beside them, looking a little weary but happy to be home.

"Mum! Dad!" Alesha was the first to reach them, wrapping her arms around them both. "I missed you so much!"

"We missed you too," Mum said.

Dad pulled back. "Jessie, you're here too."

"Of course. Why wouldn't I be here?"

As Dad opened his mouth to say something, Lucky trotted over, tail up and curious about the newcomers. Dad looked down at him with a raised eyebrow.

"And who's this little guy? A black cat?" he asked. "Aren't they supposed to be bad luck?"

I rolled my eyes, scooping Lucky up as he tried to rub himself against Dad's leg. "Come on, Dad, that's just an old wives' tale. Lucky's not bad luck—he's the best thing to happen to me since I moved to Adelaide."

Mum stroked Lucky's head. "Welcome to the family,

Lucky."

Dad's gaze shifted past me to the Christmas tree. "Jessie, Alesha, this is… incredible. Did you two do this on your own?"

"It was all Jessie's idea. She went all out this year," Alesha said.

"I thought it was time to mix things up a bit. We're almost done too. I only need to put the finishing touches on the one in the living room."

"Great work," he said. "Now all that's left to do is finalise our annual New Year's Eve party. Our trip set us back, so we're skipping the Christmas party this year, but New Year's… That's still happening."

Of course it was. My parents had a reputation for hosting extravagant Christmas and New Year's Eve parties. Friends, family, neighbours, and business connections—they'd invite everyone, transforming our backyard with lighting, live music, and enough food and drinks to keep people celebrating well past midnight. It was a tradition, one I'd always loved—even if it meant the house would be buzzing with people from now until the new year.

Dad was already mentally running through his list. "I'll be making a few calls tomorrow to make sure everything's still on track—catering, decorations for the backyard—and confirm the band hasn't cancelled on us. It's a busy season, and I'd rather catch any issues early…"

25

Christmas was quieter this year—only the four of us. No cousins or aunts and uncles filling the house, no friends, no neighbours, no business connections wandering around with glasses of wine. I wasn't used to the stillness, the way the holiday felt more intimate. Growing up, Christmas had always been a big, boisterous event. But this year, it was just us, and while it felt different, I couldn't deny that there was something comforting about it too.

Before I knew it, New Year's Eve had arrived, and that familiar buzz of energy was back in full force. Early in the morning, event planners arrived, swarming the backyard. They set up round tables draped in white cloths, positioning them to look out over the Sydney River with an unobstructed view of where the fireworks would ignite the sky later that night. A dance floor was laid out, and a stage took shape along the edge of the yard, where a well-known Australian electronic trio was set to perform. Dad had spared no expense, as usual, and I couldn't help but feel a rush of excitement. This would be an unforgettable night.

Inside, the caterers had taken over the kitchen, turning it into a whirlwind of activity. Pots clanged, knives chopped, and the smells of fresh herbs and roasted vegetables filled the air. Platters of hors d'oeuvres were already lined up on the counter, waiting to be served, and every available surface was stacked with cartons of wine and champagne flutes.

Navigating around the chaos, I tried to get to the walk-in pantry for some cereal, only to find myself blocked by crates of glasses and stacks of plates. I managed to grab two bowls and poured some milk over cereal, balancing everything carefully as I headed up to my room where Alesha was waiting.

She was on the balcony. Her hair was in a messy bun, and an oversized sweatshirt was hanging off one shoulder as she leaned against the glass railing, taking in the view. Lucky was nowhere to be found—probably hiding in some quiet corner of the house, spooked by the sudden invasion of strangers.

"Breakfast is served," I announced, stepping onto the balcony and handing her a bowl.

"Fancy," she teased as she sat on a chair. "Is this the chef's special?"

"Don't push it," I shot back as I took a seat next to her. "It was either cereal or getting trampled in the kitchen."

We ate in comfortable silence, watching the backyard transformation unfold below us. The workers were setting up the final touches on the dance floor, testing the sound system as snippets of music floated up to us. The whole scene felt like something out of a movie.

After breakfast, we headed back inside to get ready. With hours to spare before the guests were due to arrive, there was no rush. We took our time, each of us lost in our own preparations. The theme for the night was "bling," and I was determined to embody it.

I straightened my hair until it fell in a sleek sheet. For makeup, I went bold—smoky eyes and deep-red lips that complemented my short, metallic dress. I wanted to look as fierce as someone who was done dwelling on the past.

From down the corridor, I heard Alesha singing along to a playlist in her room as she curled her hair and did her makeup. A little while later, she appeared in my doorway in her golden gown. It was floor-length with a high slit that shimmered as she twirled in front of my mirror.

I slipped on a pair of heels and gave myself one last look in the mirror. I felt… ready. Ready to close the door on the year that had been one of my worst and step into a new era of me.

"Look at us," Alesha said, a grin spreading across her face. "Silver and gold—matching but not matching. We're a theme."

"Leave it to us to accidentally coordinate." I laughed.

We headed downstairs and went out into the backyard. It was mid-afternoon. Everything was ready—the tables were set with gold cordless LED lamps, and lights had been strung up around the LED dance floor.

As we took it all in, our parents joined us. Dad was in a crisp suit and Mum in her metallic pink-sequined floor-length gown.

"Tonight's going to be awesome," I said.

One by one, guests arrived for the New Year's Eve party. The front entrance was guarded as usual, with security hired to keep out any would-be crashers. Around me, conversations and laughter echoed through the yard as people gathered, ready to welcome the new year in style. I was about to slip back inside and find Alesha when one of the security guards approached me.

"Miss Jessie, there's someone here to see you who isn't on the list," he said.

I frowned, glancing over his shoulder towards the entrance. I had no idea who it could be—probably some overconfident partygoer hoping to sneak in under the guise of "knowing the family." Curious but slightly wary, I motioned for him to lead the way. I saw Alesha as I headed inside. She'd overheard the conversation and tagged along.

As we reached the open double doors, another guard nodded to me and pointed down the driveway.

And there he was…

Seb.

The sight of him stopped me cold. I hadn't expected to see him again, especially not here and certainly not tonight. He looked… Well, he looked incredible. He was dressed in black pants and a midnight-blue button-down shirt, the top buttons casually undone. His sleeves were rolled up to his elbows. There was something about his appearance, like he'd made an effort, maybe even dressed up specifically to see me.

"Seb?" I managed to say. "What… What are you doing here?"

He took a few steps forward. "I came to see you. I hope you don't mind."

My heart pounded. The initial shock wore off just enough for me to find my voice. "I mean… no, I don't mind. I… I didn't expect to see you here."

It felt surreal.

The last time we'd spoken, his messages had been short and distant. I'd assumed he wanted nothing to do with me after everything that had happened. I'd forced myself to accept that, to push him to the back of my mind and move forward. I'd never expected him to show up at my parents' house of all places.

Seb glanced around, taking in the grand entrance. "This is your parents' place?" he asked, sounding impressed. "It's incredible. Makes me think I chose the wrong career." He shot me a grin, though there was something almost wistful in his tone.

I laughed a little too loudly, still processing the fact that he was standing here in front of me. "Trust me, Seb, it's not as glamorous as it looks. Property development isn't exactly a dream job. There's so much stress, so many risks involved. You wouldn't believe the number of times they've been on the brink of losing it all."

"I'll take your word for it," he said.

Then a thought struck me. My eyes narrowed as I crossed my arms. "Wait a second... How exactly did you get this address?"

Seb shifted. "Don't be mad, but... Lindsey gave it to me."

How did she know my parents' address?

It took me a moment to connect the dots—the hotel. When I checked in, I had written down the address on the form. That was how she knew.

"Of course she did." Leave it to her to meddle.

"Look," Seb continued, "I've been thinking about you since... well, since the pub crawl. Since that kiss." He paused. "When I found out you were with someone else, I was hurt at first. I thought... I had *assumed* you were single. But the truth is, I never asked. I just jumped to that conclusion, and that was stupid of me. I let my pride get in the way, and I'm sorry for that."

I blinked, stunned by his honesty. "Seb..."

He shook his head. "Lindsey told me... about Zack. And

about everything else you've been through. I get it now."

I felt a flare of irritation. "She had no right to tell you that."

"Maybe not," he said. "But I think she told me with good intentions. She thought I deserved to know, and maybe she was right. It's not easy to understand someone if you don't know what they're going through."

Behind me, Alesha cleared her throat, cutting through the moment. I'd almost forgotten she was there. She leaned in and whispered, "Who is this guy? You never mentioned him."

Seb glanced at her.

"Uh… yeah." My voice came out awkwardly as I scrambled for words. "Alesha, this is Seb. We met in Adelaide."

Alesha's eyes roamed over him, clearly sizing him up. "Well, he's even better looking than Shane."

I groaned, facepalming. "Oh, God, Alesha, not—"

"What?" she cut me off. "I'm serious, Jess. Where do you find these guys?"

I glared at her.

As if the universe hadn't dealt me enough surprises for one night, I saw another figure coming down the driveway. My stomach sank. Shane strode towards us in dark jeans and a white shirt. His hair was messier than usual. Oh, God… Another unexpected—and very much uninvited—guest.

One of the security guards stepped forward to intercept him, but Shane lifted a hand and shouted, "I'm here to see Jessie!"

Alesha looked bewildered. "What is he doing here?"

I shrugged. "Your guess is as good as mine." Then I muttered, mostly to myself, "Any other people or ghosts from my past want to show up tonight?"

She snorted. "If they do, you're going to need a whole team of therapists by midnight."

"Either that or Jerry Springer."

Steeling myself, I turned towards Shane as he approached and met his gaze with a look I hoped was pure indifference. "What are you doing here, Shane?" My voice was sharp, but I didn't care. His presence on the doorstep of my parents' home was the last thing I'd expected and, frankly, the last thing I wanted.

He stopped a few steps away, glancing around as if taking in the scene before focusing his attention back on me. "I came to see you."

"How did you know I was here?" I demanded.

He hesitated. "I assumed you'd be with your family around this time of the year."

I rolled my eyes. He'd carefully staged this intrusion into my life. "So, you decided to come here on New Year's Eve. Why? What do you want?"

Seb watched the exchange, as did the security guards hovering nearby, clearly interested in the drama but unsure if they should intervene. Alesha, too, was silent, though I saw the hint of amusement in her eyes. She was clearly enjoying the absurdity of it all.

Shane moved closer. "I want to be with you, Jessie. You're the one. I can't just… let you go." The words spilled out, a silent plea dangling between us.

I stared at him, speechless. I had no idea how he could still believe there was something left between us after everything that had happened. I'd made it clear at the winery that it was over, that I wanted nothing more to do with him. And yet, here he was, clinging to some romanticised version of us that only existed in his head.

From beside me, Alesha leaned in, her voice low. "Do you have some sort of spell cast on these guys or what?"

I shot her a look, barely holding back a groan. This wasn't the time.

Shane noticed Seb. His expression darkened as he looked him up and down. I could see the wheels turning in his mind, piecing things together. "You're not security. Who are you?"

"I'm Seb," he said.

Shane looked between us. "Are you with my girlfriend?" The accusation in Shane's voice was unmistakable, as though he was already convinced of the answer.

"Shane," I said, "I'm *not* your girlfriend anymore."

But he didn't even flinch. Ignoring me completely, Shane's focus stayed locked on Seb.

"You stole my girlfriend!" Shane's voice rose, and I felt the tension spike as he let his emotions get the best of him.

Seb, unfazed, stood his ground. "It doesn't sound like she's still with you."

The words weren't a jab—they were a statement of fact, one Shane didn't seem equipped to handle. And that truth cut deeper than any insult ever could.

In the silence that followed, I heard the muffled laughter, conversations, and music drifting from the party in the backyard. Our guests remained blissfully unaware of the scene unfolding on the front steps. It was surreal—two men facing off over me while, metres away, people were celebrating.

I took a deep breath. This was it—I had to put an end to Shane's delusions. "Shane, stop." My voice was firm, leaving no room for argument. "There's nothing between us anymore. I've told you that already. I don't know what you think you're doing here, but you need to leave. Now. Before I have security escort you off the property."

"So, that's it? After everything… you're just going to walk away? Like it didn't matter?" To him, this wasn't over. Not by a long shot.

"To *you*, it didn't," I snapped. "You lied to me. And you think this—showing up at my parents' house—changes any of that?"

The sudden roar of a V8 engine cut through the tension.

My gaze shifted towards the driveway, catching the sleek form of a white Porsche as it came to a brisk stop. Olivia emerged from the car. She was wearing a colourful dress, a contrast to the sombre black I'd become accustomed to seeing her in. It added a new layer of absurdity to the night's unfolding drama. Her presence, uninvited and unexpected, brought a surge of apprehension. It had been almost two months since I'd seen Olivia, since she'd put a bullet in my shoulder and nearly destroyed everything.

What was she doing here? Was she following me? Watching me? I couldn't help but wonder, the shadow of our last encounter looming large in my mind.

Olivia strode up the driveway, heels clicking against the pavement, her chin held high as if she had every right to be here. Her colourful ensemble might have marked the end of her year-long mourning, a possible attempt to re-enter the world as a new woman, but her intentions seemed far from celebratory.

"You're crazy to be with someone like Shane!" she blurted, her accusation slicing through the distance between us. "He's a manipulative liar who only cares about himself and money. A greedy con artist. A murderer. He's pure scum." Her voice rose with every descriptor she hurled, painting Shane in the darkest hues.

The truth was, I'd already come to those conclusions myself, but hearing them from her, out here in the driveway, was bizarre.

Beside me, Alesha shifted uncomfortably.

One of the security guards stepped forward, stopping her from getting any closer. "Ma'am, you can't park your car in the driveway. You'll need to move it to the street."

"I'll park wherever the hell I want," she snapped, waving him off with an irritated flick of her hand. She wasn't here to play by anyone's rules. "Get out of my way."

The second guard moved quickly, grabbing her arm before she could get any closer. "I'm going to have to ask you to leave. If you don't, we'll have no choice but to call the police."

"Take your hands off me!" she spat, struggling against his hold.

The security guards looked at me, waiting for instructions.

"Let her go," I said finally.

The last thing I wanted was a scene—or worse, another headline or two. Olivia was already unhinged enough without us giving her a reason to spiral further.

The guards exchanged a concerned glance but ultimately released her, stepping back to keep watch. Olivia straightened her dress, giving me a look that was half smug, half wild, as if she'd won some invisible battle.

"I'm not with Shane anymore," I said, desperate to put an end to whatever narrative she'd constructed in her mind.

She scanned the scene, confused as her eyes landed on Shane. "Then what is he doing here?"

Standing there, sandwiched between Shane's unexpected intrusion and Olivia's uninvited appearance, the insanity of the situation settled over me. The evening, meant for celebration, had somehow turned into a soap opera scene I'd never auditioned for.

"He came here uninvited," I explained, the words tasting bitter. "He has a knack for 'coincidentally' showing up wherever I am." The irony wasn't lost on me, and I could tell by the flash of anger in Shane's eyes that my words hit their mark.

"You're lucky I'm out on bail," Olivia spat at Shane.

"They let you out on bail? What is wrong with the Australian justice system? They've let out a nutter to roam free and commit more crimes," Shane scoffed. "Why are you even here, Olivia? Did you come to finish the job?"

A flicker of doubt sparked in my mind, Shane's words planting seeds of fear. I glanced at Olivia, half expecting her to pull a weapon out of that vibrant dress. The memory of her with a gun flashed through my mind, and despite my attempt to keep a poker face, my body tensed.

"Are you armed?" I asked.

One of the security guards moved in closer. The atmosphere was one wrong move away from total chaos.

"Oh, relax. I'm not planning to add to my charges while I'm out on bail." Olivia turned back to Shane, her eyes narrowing with raw hatred. "You think you're untouchable, but karma's coming for you. And when it does, you'll lose everything. And I'll have front-row seats."

"Shut up, Olivia," he snapped. "Front-row seats? More like a prison cell."

As they continued to hurl insults at each other, the confession eating away at me slipped out under my breath. "I regret intervening that night."

Silence fell as all eyes turned to me.

"What?" Shane spat. "This isn't my fault! It's *her* fault! Olivia's the one who started all of this!" He gestured wildly at her. "And you!" He pointed at Seb. Then without warning, he lunged towards Seb, fists clenched.

Seb stepped back, deflecting Shane with a single push. Shane stumbled and almost fell before regaining his footing, ready to charge at Seb again, like a wild bull that refused to quit.

Before he could make another move, I stepped between them. "Enough! This stops now, Shane. You need to leave. If you don't, I'll have security escort you off the property."

Shane stared at me. I thought he might defy me, might push this madness even further. But then, something in him seemed to break. His shoulders slumped, and the fight drained from his stance.

"Fine," he muttered, spitting the word as if it left a bad taste in his mouth. He cast one last bitter glance at me. "Have a nice life, Jessie."

With that, Shane stalked down the driveway, his figure

fading into the darkness, leaving behind nothing but the faint echo of his footsteps and the weight of everything unsaid.

The silence that settled after Shane's departure felt different—calmer but still tense, like the quiet after a storm. I took a deep breath. I'd finally reclaimed some control over this chaotic night.

Seb shifted his attention to Olivia. "You're that woman who shot Jessie, right?"

Olivia's eyes met mine, and there was a flicker of regret. "About that… I came here to apologise to Jessie—I'm sorry."

I didn't know how to respond. Logic told me that forgiveness was out of the question. She'd shot me, put me in the hospital, and changed the course of my life forever. But I also understood loss—perhaps better than anyone else here. I knew what it was like to have your world shattered, to be left picking up pieces that would never quite fit back together. I knew, deep down, that the bullet was never meant for me—it was Shane she'd been after.

In some twisted way, I could empathise with her grief and the desperation that had driven her to that breaking point.

Alesha, however, didn't share my leniency. She crossed her arms, her gaze slicing into Olivia. "You're sorry?" she said, her voice cold. "You shot my sister, Olivia. Sorry doesn't even begin to cover it."

"Alesha… let it go," I said.

"You're seriously going to let this slide?"

I looked at Olivia. "I forgive you."

"You forgive her?" Alesha repeated.

"She didn't mean to hurt me," I explained. "She was after Shane. And honestly… after everything he's done, I understand."

Alesha's mouth opened as if to argue, but she closed it again, shaking her head. "Fine," she said, grabbing my arm. "Let's go back inside. There's a party waiting for us."

She navigated me towards the door, but I hesitated, glancing over my shoulder at Olivia and Seb. They were both standing there—two people who'd shown up uninvited. They were impeccably dressed, and the thought of sending them away didn't sit right with me, especially since Seb had come all the way to Sydney to see me.

"Wait," I said, stopping in my tracks. "I know this is strange—trust me, it's strange for me too—but why don't you both join us? There's a party going on. Maybe we can all use a drink."

The security guards exchanged uneasy glances, their heads shaking slightly as if to warn me off this idea.

"Jess, are you sure?" Alesha asked. "She *shot* you."

"She didn't mean to hurt me," I replied, a weak attempt at humour slipping into my tone. "If she wanted to, she had plenty of chances tonight."

Alesha looked as though she was about to burst. "That's

not funny."

"It wasn't supposed to be," I said. "But it's true."

She exhaled sharply. "You're unbelievable sometimes, you know that?"

"It'll be fine," I whispered. "Let's... try to enjoy the night."

Alesha threw up her hands in exasperation. "Fine. Whatever."

I stepped aside, waving them in. Olivia made her way inside, but Seb looked concerned.

"Strange to welcome your shooter into your home," he muttered as he moved past me.

"Olivia isn't just anyone. She's a business partner to my parents. Her husband was involved with them too, before he passed," I explained.

"Your parents know how to pick really intense business partners," he remarked as we walked through the foyer into the living room to the backyard.

I felt the urge to tell him more. "Olivia's been through a lot since her husband's death. It kind of unhinged her."

He looked at Olivia, studying her as if seeing her for the first time, piecing together a version of her story that made her less of a villain and more of a tragedy.

As we entered the backyard, the energy shifted. The band was playing a lively tune, and guests clustered around tables and on the dance floor, completely unaware of the drama that had unfolded out front. A few heads turned as we joined the crowd, but most people were too engrossed in their own conversations to notice.

Dad weaved between the guests, making a beeline for me. "Jessie." He stopped in front of us. "What's Olivia doing here?"

"I invited her," I replied, bracing myself for the reaction I knew was coming.

"Are you sure about that?" he asked, lowering his voice so only I could hear. He sounded as concerned as everyone else looked.

Olivia had become a pariah in our circles—her actions in Adelaide had made her the subject of gossip and judgment. She hadn't been welcomed anywhere since.

"It was… an unfortunate accident," I tried to explain. "Olivia's been through enough. She deserves compassion, not total isolation." I didn't know if I fully believed that, but I felt it was the right thing to say.

Dad raised an eyebrow. "You have a strange way of handling things, you know that?"

"Trust me, I know. But sometimes… you just have to make peace with the chaos."

"All right," he said, glancing at Olivia, who stood off to the side, looking as out of place as a thundercloud on an otherwise sunny day. "But if she so much as sneezes wrong, I'm calling security faster than you can blink."

I chuckled softly. "Deal."

Dad lingered a moment longer, his eyes scanning the crowd, and I could tell he was already mentally preparing for the inevitable whispers and sidelong glances that Olivia's presence would provoke.

I took a deep breath, glancing at Seb, who was next to me, calmly observing the scene. "Oh, and Dad—this is Seb," I said, gesturing towards him. "He's... a friend."

Seb offered his hand. "Pleasure to meet you, sir."

Dad shook his hand, giving him a quick, appraising look. "Nice to meet you, Seb. Any friend of Jessie's is welcome here."

We moved away, grabbing glasses of champagne from a tray a waiter was carrying—one for myself, one for Seb, and one for Alesha. She looked as though she could use a diversion. But before she could even raise the glass, Conrad approached, his eyes zeroing in on Alesha's champagne flute.

"Expectant mothers shouldn't be drinking," he said, plucking the glass from her hand.

"I... I wasn't actually going to drink it," she stammered, caught off guard. "It was just... you know, for appearances."

"I know. But I'd still rather see you holding a glass of sparkling water," he replied.

And that's when it happened.

Olivia, without any hint of discretion, blurted, "Wait ...

You're pregnant?"

Her voice was loud enough to turn a few heads nearby, including those of my parents. My stomach dropped as I watched the realisation ripple through the space. All around us, people paused, their conversations faltering as the words sank in, but no one looked more surprised than our parents.

Mum's eyes darted from me to Alesha, her face a mask of surprise.

Alesha's face turned beet red, her eyes wide as she processed the unintended reveal. She looked at me, almost pleading for an escape route. There was no going back. The cat—or rather, the baby—was officially out of the bag.

Seb leaned in close to me, his voice low. "Your family gatherings are… eventful."

"This is nothing. You should see us on a *normal* night." I drained the champagne in one gulp.

Acknowledgements

To my mother—my biggest supporter, believer, and best friend. Thank you for always reminding me that I could do this, even when I doubted myself, and for the help that gave me the time to write this book.

And to every reader who takes a chance on a debut author—thank you. Stories only come alive when they're read, and your time is the greatest gift.

About The Author

Kate Halena was born in Sydney and, after travelling extensively throughout Australia, resides in Brisbane. With a background in Professional Writing, she now focuses on writing her own novels while also supporting authors through editorial work.

You can follow Kate at @KateHalena on Twitter, Instagram, Threads, and Pinterest, and @katehalena.bsky.social on Bluesky

www.katehalena.com